Other Books by AJ Adaire

Friend Series

Sunset Island - Book 1

The Interim (a novelette)

Awaiting My Assignment

Thanks for reading.

Anything Your Heart Desires

by

AJ Adaire

AJ Adaire

Desert Palm Press

Anything Your Heart Desires

Friends Series Book 3

Copyright © 2014 by AJ Adaire

ISBN-13: 978-1496060327
ISBN-10: 1496060326

    This is a work of fiction - names, characters, places, and incidents are the product of the author's imagination or are used fictitiously. Any resemblance to actual person living or dead, business, events, or locales is entirely coincidental. All rights reserved.

    No part of this publication may be reproduced, distributed, or transmitted in any form or by any means, including photocopying, recording, or other electronic or mechanical methods, without the prior written permission of the publisher, except in the case of brief quotations embodied in critical reviews and certain other noncommercial uses permitted by copyright law.

    For permission requests, write to the publisher, addressed "Attention: Permissions Coordinator," at the address below.

Desert Palm Press
1961 Main Street, Suite 220
Watsonville, California 95076
www.desertpalmpress.com

Editor: Sue Hilliker
Editor: R. Lee Fitzsimmons
Cover Design: ©AJ Adaire

Printed in the United States of America
First Edition - March 2014

Dedication

I tend to disappear into my books. When I'm writing, I hear—but don't always listen. I observe—and don't always see. Couple this absorption with time spent thinking about new stories, editing already written stories, responding to mail from readers, publicizing the books, remaining visible on Facebook, Twitter and other venues. I give interviews as well as doing interviews of other authors, and it all adds up to too much time absent from the most important relationship in my life. For this reason I dedicate this book to my partner of thirty years. I'm still glad it's you.

Acknowledgements

As always, thank you to my early readers who point out things I've missed. Thanks to Beth, a retired HS English teacher, who settled the infamous comma discussions.

Special appreciation is extended to ICL and PAS who read and then read again each version of the story. I am very grateful.

Last, but never least, thanks to my readers. I especially appreciate those readers who take time to leave reviews or send me notes. Leaving reviews helps others decide which books to read and tells authors what you liked about their story and what you didn't. I love to hear from those of you who write notes to me to say how much you've enjoyed my stories. Knowing you've gotten pleasure from my tales makes it all worthwhile. Thank you.

Anything Your Heart Desires

Table of Contents

Chapter 1 3
Chapter 2 9
Chapter 3 13
Chapter 4 23
Chapter 5 27
Chapter 6 41
Chapter 7 51
Chapter 8 55
Chapter 9 59
Chapter 10 71
Chapter 11 81
Chapter 12 91
Chapter 13 97
Chapter 14 103
Chapter 15 109
Chapter 16 115
Chapter 17 135
Chapter 18 143
Chapter 19 149
Chapter 20 153
Chapter 21 161
Chapter 22 165

Chapter 23	169
Chapter 24	173
Chapter 25	179
Chapter 26	183
Chapter 27	187
Chapter 28	193
Chapter 29	201
Chapter 30	209
Chapter 31	217
Epilogue	231
The End	233

Anything Your Heart Desires

Chapter 1

MEG SLID AN ARM across Jo Martin's stomach and snuggled closer. Jo could tell by the woman's regular breathing that she was, thankfully, still asleep. *Oh God, what have I done now? Shit, shit, shit! I should have stopped this before we had sex. Why didn't I?* Jo groaned inwardly and exhaled a long sigh. *I could have just pushed her away, or simply said 'no.' What the hell have I done? How could I be so stupid?* The events of the afternoon raced through her mind. She wanted to put her fingers to her forehead and massage away the headache that was forming between her eyebrows but refrained, fearful of waking the sleeping woman next to her.

Earlier in the day, after returning from Christmas vacation with her family at their cabin in the mountains near Edinborough, New York, Jo had not even unpacked her suitcase when Meg stopped by unannounced. Jo had opened the door for her friend, expecting their usual brief greeting. A split second later, their normally casual hug and kiss hello took on a totally new dimension. Meg, definitely the aggressor, wouldn't release Jo after their brief hug. Instead, she pulled Jo firmly against her, pinned her against the wall, and kissed her thoroughly.

"I missed you more than you'll ever know." Meg pulled Jo against her to kiss her again.

As Jo's mind wandered through the earlier events, she realized that she'd responded more out of loneliness and surprise than out of desire for her friend. With the deed done, it was too late now to undo her error. Guilt and regret gnawed at her for what she'd allowed to happen. In her heart, she knew she didn't want a relationship with Meg. Until the kiss in the hall earlier, she hadn't even really thought of

Meg as a potential sexual partner. They were friends, never more than that.

Jo was normally attracted to women who were smaller in stature and shorter than her own height of five-eight. Meg was an imposing figure of a woman, standing just a bit less than six feet tall with ice blue eyes and nearly white short-cropped hair. Her muscular, almost masculine build attested to her avid interest in weight lifting.

Meg had told Jo how much she'd missed her before kissing her. Unfortunately, Jo hadn't thought of Meg once during the time she vacationed with her family. She groaned mentally.

Why did I kiss her back? Hell, more to the point, why did I have sex with her? Well, the answer is obvious, really. When was the last time I had a date or sex with anyone other than my vibrator? Jo calculated the answer to the question. *Can it be true that I really haven't dated anyone in over two years? The last person I've even been attracted to was the Director of Nursing at the hospital, Mallory Barnes.* Jo and Mallory both worked shift work. Between their two crazy work schedules, they had rarely been able to get together with each other outside the hospital. Jo often brought prisoners in for medical treatment, and they had become friendly during a two-week period when Jo was guarding one of the prisoners. As time passed, their initial attraction turned into friendship, and Mallory and her new partner Amanda had both become Jo's friends. Mallory Barnes was much more her type than Meg. Short and petite, easy-going, dazzling smile, great giggle. Yes, definitely her type. Jo quickly shook away her regret because she would never interfere in an established relationship. Someone paired was definitely off limits. Besides, Jo liked Mallory's partner, too. Once Mallory and Amanda had established their relationship, Jo had quickly contented herself with a friendship with the couple. Jo had two rules she never broke—never get involved with anyone already in a relationship, and never, ever date a straight woman.

Come on. Stop digressing and get back to the issue at hand. How do I handle this? It's not that Meg is unattractive. She's certainly comely enough, even if she's not my type. Jo continued to mentally list Meg's good points. *She's intelligent, kind, interesting, and unattached. Unfortunately, there's just something missing in my feelings for this woman sleeping next to me, and I don't see the potential for my feelings to change.* Their lovemaking had been sweet, although Meg was definitely more into it than she was. *Why on earth didn't I stop Meg after the first kiss? I didn't want to hurt her feelings. Plain and simple, I'm an idiot. Now it'll be worse. She's going to wake up all huggy and kissy, and I'm going to want to do a disappearing act. Only I blew it this time. This is my house. She's here. That means I have to ask her to leave. No...too cold. I can spend the rest of the day with her and beg off early saying I'm too tired. She'll want to go back to bed with me and spend the night. Well, I can't treat her like she's some meaningless one-night stand. Surely I remember those days. Let me see, when was the last time? Oh yeah, three, no more like four years ago? Oh no, she's waking up.*

The tall woman stirred and turned toward Jo. "Hi," Meg said with a sleepy grin. "Are you okay?"

Jo smiled. "Yes, fine. You?"

"I'm good." Meg smiled weakly. Before Jo could extricate herself from the uncomfortable situation, Meg solved her dilemma. "Look, Jo, I think I'm more into you than you are into me."

Honesty is the best policy, but be kind. Jo nodded. "I'm sorry."

Meg shook her head. "No. I'm sorry if I made it hard for you to say no. It's okay, really. It's just that I've had the hots for you since we met, and I knew if I didn't make a move, you never would. I thought if we well, you know, did this, maybe you'd start to feel something for me."

"I do feel something for you, Meg. You are a lovely, kind, and loyal friend. I care for you very much, and I treasure your friendship. However, I think this may have been a mistake. I'm sorry."

Meg exhaled a long sigh. "Please don't think it was a mistake. I enjoyed myself, and I hope you did, too. I know you feel differently about it than I do. I'm glad we made love. Maybe it'll help me get you out of my system."

Concerned about the ramifications of what they'd done, Jo put her hand on Meg's arm. "I hope this won't ruin our friendship?"

"Why should it?"

"I don't know. Will you feel awkward?"

Meg shook her head. "Look, we're both single adults. We like each other. I'd hoped for more. Unfortunately, it's not going to happen. I'm still not sorry we did it, and I hope you won't be either. Now, before you give me the 'it's not you, it's me' speech, let's get up and go get something to eat."

Wow! She's a mind reader. I'm famished. Phew! Maybe this'll be okay after all. "Sounds good to me. I'm hungry. Are you on call tonight?"

Meg was a physician's assistant by day. She volunteered much of her spare time on the EMS squad. She rode in the ambulance with another paramedic when she was on call three nights a week and every other weekend. She truly was a good soul to donate so much of her time.

"No, I'm not on call. I left my glasses in the ambulance and I'd like to stop by and pick them up if I can. Want to go with me? We can stop by and get some pizza on the way home. I can drop you back here on my way to my house. I have an early shift tomorrow at the office."

"Yes, sounds good."

They rolled out of bed, turning their backs to each other as they quickly dressed.

Meg checked with Jo. "You want to eat first, or find out where the ambulance is?"

"Let's get your glasses first, before we eat. Even though I'm hungry, it's still a little early for dinner."

"I'll call and find out if they're at the EMS squad room or out on a call." Meg flipped open her phone and punched in the number of the regular driver. "They're at the hospital. They just picked up a gunshot victim and are taking him to the ER. We can catch up with them there."

Jo tucked in her T-shirt as she walked to the breadbox where she kept her off duty pistol and holster. She picked up her weapon, reached behind her back, and clipped the holster and Glock into the waistband of her jeans. Then she put on a shirt, which she left unbuttoned. It was her standard attire when not in uniform.

Meg and she made small talk on the way to the hospital. Maybe making love with Meg hadn't been such a terrible mistake after all. Meg actually did seem okay that sex would not be a regular component of their friendship. She'd also seemed to accept the fact that this experience definitely would not result in any kind of ongoing or committed relationship between them.

The two women entered the emergency room and spotted the EMS team across the room. The team members who had just delivered the patient were talking to one of the doctors on duty, explaining the emergency treatment they had provided to the patient on route. Meg gestured with her head to Jo that she would be heading in that direction to talk with her friends as soon as they were free. Jo looked around and saw Mallory standing behind the main desk.

"Hey, Mallory! Busy tonight?"

"No, it's been strangely quiet. That's our first serious case, a shooting. Some kind of domestic dispute between two friends over some woman, I think. Apparently she slept with both of them, and one took particular offense."

"I hate those domestic dispute calls. You never know what you'll run into. One time..."

Before Jo could finish her story, there was a crash at the door and in an instant, a flash of motion. A crazed man rushed in past the shocked EMTs. He grabbed the closest person, Meg, and held a gun to her head.

"Where is he? I want to know where that bastard Smitty is."

Jo could hear Meg's reply. "I'm a visitor here, I swear I don't know."

While his attention was focused elsewhere, sticking to the perimeter of the room, Jo started to slowly make her way across the ER, moving nearer to the upset man. As she edged closer, his attention started to shift in her direction. He stopped to focus on Mallory when she dropped the chart she was holding in an effort to distract his attention from Jo.

Worried for Mallory's safety, Jo quickly moved closer to the gunman. Jo's hand flashed behind her back and emerged from under the shirt with her pistol in hand. She shouted, "Police! I'm a police officer. Drop your weapon."

The scene unfolded in what seemed like frame-by-frame action. The gunman pushed Meg viciously aside. As she fell, she smacked her head on the edge of the stretcher. She dropped, unconscious before she hit the floor.

As Meg lay unmoving, the gunman's focus shifted to Mallory. The man raised his weapon to fire, apparently not sure who had called out, or where she was standing. Jo tried to distract the gunman and yelled at the top of her lungs. "Hey you! Over here! Drop your gun." As if in slow motion, he fired once wildly before he zeroed in on Jo, turned toward her and pulled the trigger at the exact same time she did. They both fell to the floor. He was dead. She was seriously injured and bleeding heavily.

The EMS team and the hospital staff sprang into action. The wild shot he'd squeezed off had hit Mallory. Fortunately it only skimmed her arm causing a slight flesh wound. The hospital staff and EMS team lifted both Meg and Jo onto stretchers and began a quick but thorough assessment of their condition.

The action was over in an instant. *Thank God Jo was here*, Mallory thought as she watched them wheel everyone away. Meg, who was still unconscious, was admitted for observation. Jo was rushed into surgery to repair the serious wound to her thigh. Mallory's arm treated and dressed.

Mallory normally would not be working this shift if she weren't trying to catch up. She'd soon be leaving her position as Director of Nursing. She and her partner, Amanda, and their two closest friends, Nic and Dana, would soon be starting their own business. Thanks to a large inheritance Amanda recently received when a former lover passed away unexpectedly, she was investing in a business for the four of them so they could be in charge of their own professional lives.

Amanda. I'd better give her a call before she hears this on the radio and worries. Mallory reached for the phone.

Eager awaiting Mallory's return home, Amanda answered her phone on the first ring. "Hi, Honey, coming home soon?"

"Hey, Babe. No, but I didn't want you to be concerned. There's been a shooting at the hospital. Don't worry. I'm okay, I only got a flesh wound."

"Flesh wound! What do you mean? You've been shot?"

"Yes, but I'm okay," Mallory emphasized. "Honest. I'm not sure about Meg and Jo, though. They were both injured. Jo killed the gunman. She was very brave and really impressive. If not for her, I might have been more seriously injured and no doubt more lives would have been lost. If she hadn't called out to him to get his attention, I might not be making this call to you."

"My God! Are you coming home now? Should I come get you?"

"No, the police are on their way here, and I'm sure I'll need to answer some questions. Also, I want to check on Meg and Jo's condition."

"Then I'll come there to you. I'm leaving right now."

"There's no need for you to come. Really, I'm okay."

When Amanda strongly protested, Mallory recognized a losing battle and quickly gave in. "All right. I'll be in the surgery waiting room, waiting to see how Jo's surgery went.

Chapter 2

AMANDA RUSHED IN AND checked Mallory out thoroughly before wrapping her in her arms. She whispered into her lover's neck as she held her tightly, "Are you really okay?"

"Yes," Mallory assured her, "I'm really fine. I will say that, if Jo hadn't distracted him by yelling at him, I'm sure it could have definitely been much worse. It could have been me on that operating table. This was close, Honey, and I'm still shaking."

Amanda grabbed Mallory's hands. "I'll be forever grateful to Jo for saving your life. We owe her. How are Meg and Jo doing?"

"Meg took a terrible hit to her head. She's still unconscious, last I heard."

"And Jo?" Amanda asked. "Have you heard anything about her condition?"

"Yes, she's still in surgery. She was shot in the thigh." Mallory arched her brow and shrugged. "If you have to be shot, the hospital is the best place for it to happen. If she'd been shot anywhere else, she might not have lived. I know she lost a lot of blood. Fortunately, because it happened here, she was in the operating room in a matter of minutes."

A tall, well-built man with neatly trimmed grey hair and a well-trained mustache rushed in.

"Hi, John," Mallory said. "Amanda, this is Captain John Strayer. He's Jo's boss."

Amanda and the police captain shook hands and exchanged greetings.

As they were chatting, the surgeon exited from the operating room. He recognized Mallory and the police chief and approached. "Has anyone contacted Jo's family yet?"

"No, not yet," the Chief replied. "I thought I'd wait until I had something definite to tell them."

"Well, you know, as her physician, I can't legally give you any information. I think you can safely tell them that she made it through surgery okay and I'm guardedly optimistic. Have them give me a call for the details. I'm transferring her to the ICU. Mallory, I assume I'll see you up there?"

"I'll take care of that right away. Thanks, Doc," the Chief promised.

"Take care, Mallory, Amanda," he said nodding in their direction.

"Come on, Amanda," Mallory said. We're going to the ICU. In so many words, he just gave me permission to read her chart. I'll find out what's going on."

The Chief pulled out his phone. "I'll catch up with you as soon as I can, Mallory. We'll need to ask you some questions about what happened."

Amanda waited in the ICU waiting room while Mallory entered the restricted area. Ten minutes later Mallory came out and sat down next to her lover. "She came through the surgery okay. Unfortunately, it may be a career ending injury. She lost a lot of blood and they suspect she'll have some numbness, at least initially. She had a lot of muscle and nerve damage. Some of the feeling will return but probably not all. They worry now about infection, and she'll need rehab to get functional use of her leg back."

"Mal, does she have any family here?"

Mallory shook her head. "I know she's close to her parents. I think they live in Pennsylvania. Why?"

"She saved your life. Maybe we should offer to take care of her while she recovers. I feel like we owe her something for that, don't you? Besides, she helped rescue me when I was hurt after my run-in with the deer."

"Well, we already have a chair." Mallory laughed, referring to the motorized reclining chair, with the seat that helped raise a person sitting in it to a standing position. They had bought it for Amanda after she'd injured her leg in her biking accident with the deer.

"Was she awake yet?"

"In and out. I expect that she'll have a lot of pain. They'll keep her pretty doped up for a couple of days."

"Can you sit with her or do you have to go back to your office?"

"I need to check in. I still haven't talked to the police, and I'm sure they're waiting to see me."

"Can you get me in there?" Amanda asked, referring to the ICU.

Mallory smiled, before she pulled Amanda to her for a quick hug. "Time will be limited, but I can get you in there. You're a fortunate woman, you know, to have a friend in high places."

Amanda raised her eyebrow. "And don't I know it."

* * *

A couple of hours later, Jo woke up. Amanda smiled at her. "How are you feeling?"

Jo gave a wan smile. "Kinda like I've been assaulted by a bullet."

"Well, we're all glad that guy wasn't a better shot."

"How are Mallory and Meg?"

"Mal only got nicked on the arm, thanks to you. I know Meg hadn't awakened yet, last I heard. That was a couple of hours ago. I can check on her for you, if you'd like."

"Yes, in a little while. Can you stay with me for a bit?"

"Sure. Can I get you anything?"

"How about some water?"

"I'll ask the nurse."

When the nurse finished checking on Jo, she again allowed Amanda in to visit with her.

"Has anyone called my parents?"

"I think your captain planned to call. Would you like me to follow up and call them?"

"Could you? I'd appreciate it. My mom will want to come, as will my dad. They just returned home from a trip to the cabin, so I know they'll be exhausted. I'm concerned about them turning around and making the trip here. Taking care of my dad is a full time job for mom. I know she'll want to take care of me. I really don't want her to. I think it's too much for her." Jo clicked the trigger to release a dose of pain meds.

"Well," Amanda said. "I have a solution. I'd like to invite your parents, and you when you're well enough, to stay with Mallory and me. Mallory and I can take care of you, and your mom and dad can visit until they feel comfortable that you're on the mend."

"Amanda. I couldn't possibly take advantage of you that way."

"When it's offered freely, how is it taking advantage? Please trust me when I say it's something we can do. Besides, Dana and Nic will help too, I'm sure."

"Well, I really appreciate it. Would you call my mom and tell her I'm going to be okay and tell her not to worry?"

"I'll take care of everything. Now, you rest. I'll call Dana and Nic first to update them before I call your mom. I'll be back later after I've talked to everyone. Try to get some rest."

"Thanks. My mom's number is on my phone." Jo relaxed, thankful and reassured by Amanda's promise that she would have the support of her friends for what she knew might be a difficult recovery.

Chapter 3

"MRS. MARTIN? THIS IS Amanda James. I am a friend of your daughter's. I just came from seeing Jo. I know her captain called you, and you're probably concerned. Jo wanted you to know that she's awake and worried about you and her father making the trip to see her."

"Hello, Amanda, and please call me Josette. Thank you for calling. We've been so worried. I just talked to her supervisor a couple of hours ago. He hadn't seen her yet. How is Joanna?"

Amanda smiled at the formal name hardly anyone used to refer to their friend and was surprised to hear Mrs. Martin had a strong French accent. Jo had never mentioned that her mother was French.

"Your daughter is doing okay. I have good news. They just informed us that, now that they have her stable, they plan to move her to the step-down unit soon. They'll keep a careful watch on her there, and assuming she continues to improve, they'll probably move her to a private room tomorrow or the day after. Jo wanted me to assure you that although she still has some discomfort from the surgery, she's getting the best of care and she doesn't want you to worry."

"Thank you for calling and giving me this information. I feel reassured. No doubt I'll feel better when I can see her. My husband, Ben, and I plan to drive there to be with her tomorrow. I have trouble seeing at night, so we have to wait until morning to leave."

"I would like to invite you and your husband to stay with my partner, Mallory, and me. We've already offered to take care of Jo, so if you will stay with us, we can all pitch in and help."

Mrs. Martin expressed her relief at hearing that her daughter was feeling well enough to make these arrangements. "My daughter has mentioned her friends before. I appreciate your offer, and I'm grateful. I feel better knowing that Jo has such good friends there to help watch over her. Thank you." They agreed that she and her husband would come as soon as they could get there.

"Please tell her that we're coming as soon as we can and that I love her. And thank you so much for your call."

Amanda returned to find Mallory next to Jo's bedside, talking softly with her. The nurse on duty said, "You can go in, but keep it quiet in there, please."

"Not a problem." Amanda slid her arm around Mallory's shoulder, and Mallory circled Amanda's waist with her arm. Amanda related the details of her conversation with Jo's mother.

"Now, don't worry about your parents. We'll take care of everything. You just worry about getting better."

Mallory squeezed Jo's hand. "Thank you for saving me."

Jo smiled. "Thank you both for being here for me." Relieved, Jo closed her eyes and drifted.

"We can't stay too long. Technically, we shouldn't be here. I'll check in with you again before we leave."

"Thanks."

Jo's parents arrived at the hospital the next afternoon. Mallory met them when she went to visit Jo to check on her condition. Mr. and Mrs. Martin's day had been long and tiring. They'd left home early that morning, driven to the hospital to see their daughter, and spent several hours there in the uncomfortable chairs in the waiting room and visiting their daughter. With Jo's encouragement, her parents reluctantly agreed to leave before the end of visiting hours. "Really, Mom and Dad, I'm fine. Please go get something to eat and get some rest."

Mallory drove them home at the end of her shift. Amanda had dinner ready shortly after they arrived. Nic and Dana, their neighbors and close friends, joined them for dinner.

"Ben, Josette, we'd like to offer you to stay next door with us in our second floor guest quarters. We've all talked and agree that it will be best to put Jo in the first floor guest bedroom at Mallory and Amanda's. The second floor in Nic's and my place will provide you with a private area of your own to stay in, and we think you'll be more comfortable there. We know you don't know any of us, but we are friends of Jo's and hope you'll feel comfortable staying with Nic and me."

Josette smiled at Dana and nodded. "Well, we know we've never met you all before. Jo talks about you all enough that we feel like we know you."

"Thank you for your kindness," Ben said. "If you don't mind, we'd like to get settled now and make it an early night. We've had a long day."

"Of course," Dana said. "I'll show you to our house."

Nic extended her hand palm up. "If you'll give me your car keys, I'll get your bags."

* * *

A week later, Mallory picked Jo up from the hospital for her trip home. She was still on antibiotics and being monitored carefully for infection. She had progressed sufficiently that the doctor felt she was well enough to be released to the care of her family and friends. He was reassured knowing that Mallory would be directly involved in Jo's care. The physical therapy Jo received during her hospitalization helped her become comfortable with the crutches she required to support and stabilize her when she walked. Getting in and out of the wheelchair was still something she required assistance to do. The trip home was uncomfortable despite Mallory's attempt to avoid any bumps. Jo sighed as she sat in the living room chair surrounded by family and friends. "I'm glad that's over."

Mallory brought Jo a drink of water, a few crackers, and her pain pill, a kindness for which she received a huge smile in thanks.

"I've made arrangements with the PT department to send someone out. Your insurance will cover the visits until you're comfortable enough to make the trip into rehab for your therapy."

"That's a relief. I know you tried to be careful. Still, the ride home was no walk in the park."

"I know, Sweetie. It should be less problematic now that we have you settled."

The day after her return to Amanda and Mallory's place, Jo and her mother had an opportunity to speak privately. They lapsed into French, Jo's mother's native language. "I'm glad that you have such good friends, Honey. I feel happier with you living here alone knowing that you have all of your friends to help you and support you."

"So, you like my friends?"

"Your Dad and I like your friends very much. You are lucky to have so many caring people around you."

"How is Dad holding up being around so many lesbians?" Jo winked at her mother.

"You know, I think it's been good for him. He was very quiet at first. Now it seems he's really hit it off with Nic and Dana, and he's impressed with Mallory and Amanda taking such good care of you. I know he's feeling comfortable. He's been telling jokes."

After staying in Nic and Dana's house for nearly a week, with some encouragement Jo's mother and father felt comfortable leaving their daughter in the care of her friends. They agreed to return home once promised that Jo would call them with a daily progress report.

"We don't know how we can ever thank you," Ben said to the group of women.

"It's truly been our pleasure." Nic took the bags from Jo's father.

They all hugged each other goodbye. Nic, Dana, Amanda, and Mallory left Jo and her parents alone for their goodbyes and waited outside. They all waved as Jo's parents left for home. The group quickly settled into a new routine with two fewer guests and one semi-invalid to care for.

Jo did everything she could to be useful. She peeled vegetables and helped to the best of her ability in preparing meals. Her physical therapist came every other day until Jo could comfortably make the trip to the rehab center. Mallory had never seen anyone work as hard or as diligently to improve and to regain her strength as Jo did. Mallory did all she could by giving Jo daily massages to help stimulate the nerves and to relieve some of the stiffness and pain Jo felt in her injured leg.

As Jo recovered, Amanda, Mallory, Dana, and Nic were deeply involved in plans for their new translation business. Even though she wasn't actually involved in any of the planning for the business, Jo listened to their discussions as they each reported their progress.

"I've rented us a small space for our offices and classroom about a half hour from our homes, closer to the city," Amanda reported. "Mallory and I are splitting the responsibility of overseeing the painting and furnishing of our new office space. I've already put up a website and made all the necessary arrangements for advertising which is scheduled to begin in eight weeks' time."

Nic reached for Dana's hand. "We're lining up other translators who can moonlight for us once we get established."

With everyone involved in jobs, and Jo involved in her rehab, time passed rapidly. Before they knew it, Jo had been on leave from work nearly two months. Mallory went with her for her check up with the surgeon. He didn't sugarcoat his prognosis for her recovery. "Jo, I know you've worked extremely hard to make the amazing progress you've achieved in such a short time. I'm sorry Jo. No matter how hard you work, you'll never regain sufficient strength in your leg to return to your job on the police force. Don't get me wrong, you'll continue to improve, although I believe you may always have a slight limp and your leg will definitely help you predict the weather." He smiled kindly as he delivered the bad news. "I'll sign the necessary paperwork to allow you to retire on disability from the force."

"Thanks, Doctor, it's not the outcome I'd hoped for, although it's what I expected you'd say. I appreciate that you saved my life and my leg."

Jo and Mallory left the doctor's office with Mallory pushing Jo's wheelchair. Normally, she used crutches. However, they'd found that it was much less tiring if they used the chair when she had to cover larger distances or when the terrain made using her crutches too difficult. A short way down the hallway, Mallory quickly pushed Jo into a vacant office and closed the door, pulling up a chair next to her friend. "Are you okay?"

Jo sniffed once and wiped her eyes with her sleeves. "Yes. I've been expecting this news. I've worked as hard as I could to regain full use of my leg. Unfortunately, I just can't seem to beat the odds on this one. The physical therapist told me that my limp would diminish over time as I strengthen the leg. She'd already cautioned me to not hold out hope that I'd ever regain totally normal function. She said I'd always favor my bad leg. So I've been anticipating the bad news."

Returning home to Mallory and Amanda's, they found that Meg was there for a visit. She had recovered her health, although she'd lost her memory of events for most of the week before the accident. Jo thought it was a blessing in a way. Their friendship seemed to be back to where they were before the fateful night of the shooting. They passed the time chatting together until dinnertime when the four of them talked about lighter subjects.

Two weeks later, Jo's captain came to visit her at Mallory and Amanda's house and brought the necessary paperwork for her to apply for a disability retirement. She was due to turn forty-three on her next birthday.

"If you were closer to full retirement, I could keep you on. I don't think I can manage it for another two and a half years. I'm really sorry."

"I know, Chief. I appreciate your keeping me on this long."

The captain left, and Amanda came into the living room to sit with Jo. "Have you given any thought about what you want to do with the rest of your life?"

Jo shook her head. "I have no clue. I could probably be a part time dispatcher, I guess. I can't do that full time because they have the same pension plan I have. It may be possible that I could work up to twenty hours a week at that job without having to join the pension fund. Between that and my pension, I think I can earn enough money to keep me afloat with virtually no risk to my life and limb like I used to have. And my experience on the force should provide good background for dispatch work."

"Is that something you'd enjoy?"

"I guess it would be okay. At least I'd still be involved in helping people in a bad situation. At least I'd feel useful." Jo ran her fingers through her hair. "Well, I've taken up space here long enough. I need to start thinking about moving back home. First thing I need to do is trade my car. With my left leg injured, I can't use a stick shift any more. I'll need an automatic."

"I think Mallory would be better suited to help with that. Let's see if she'd like to go new car shopping. This is exciting."

Jo, Mallory, and Amanda took Jo's car and went shopping for a new vehicle that afternoon. Jo had obviously given some thought to her needs regarding a new vehicle. "I think I want a small pickup truck. I'd like to be able to throw my bike in the back and not have to bother with a bike rack. My intention is to ride as much as I can as soon as the weather breaks. I think it'll help me strengthen my leg."

"Okay, let's look around. They went to several dealerships looking for the perfect vehicle. "I don't want a huge truck. They're too high for me to get into," Jo declared. "I need something small."

They drove through the local car dealership without seeing any pickups out front. "Hey, look at that," Amanda said pointing to a small pickup at the back of the lot. There was no sign on it listing its price.

Mallory looked in the direction Amanda was pointing. "I wonder what the story is on that one." Jo looked interested. "Let's go check it out."

Mallory navigated the lot and parked next to the little silver truck. The three women got out of Jo's car and with cupped hands peered inside the vehicle.

"This is neat," Jo said. "It's just the right size, seats four people, and has a small bed. Look, it looks like this little rack flips back to extend the bed. I think my bike will fit in there. Let's talk to a salesman and get some information about it."

As if on cue, a tall, lanky salesman approached the group of women and, after a warm greeting, he asked, "How can I help you?"

"Yes." Jo drew the salesman's attention. "We saw the truck parked here and are curious about this vehicle. Can you give us any information about it?"

"Sure. That's a 2006. I sold it as a new vehicle to an older man four years ago. He recently died, and his family just sold it back to us. We're getting ready to clean it up and put it out front for sale. It has really low mileage, only has eighteen thousand some odd miles on it."

"Next best thing to it was driven by a little old school teacher," Mallory joked causing everyone to chuckle.

"Exactly." replied the salesman adding a genuine smile. "I'm Dan." He shook hands with each woman in turn. "Which of you is interested?"

Jo raised her hand. "That would be me."

"Okay, let me show you some of the other features of the vehicle." He opened the door and allowed Jo to get in. "This is the turbo model. It has an electric driver's seat." He pointed to another car on the lot. "It's built on the same frame as that model over there, so it rides like a car, has all wheel drive and the added functionality of a truck."

"That's good, Jo," Mallory commented. "It'll be good in bad weather."

"Yeah, and the power seat will be perfect for me. I can push it back to get out and in and adjust it easily to drive." Turning to the salesman, she asked the price. It was within the ballpark of what she thought she could afford with her trade. "Can we take it for a ride?"

"Sure, let me get a tag. If you give me the keys to your car, I can have it appraised for you while you take this one for a spin."

While he was gone, the trio looked over the neat little truck. Mallory lowered the tailgate and flipped the bed extender back. "Look," she added, "the back seat folds forward, and that little door folds down making the back open to the bed so you can put longer items inside. That's pretty neat."

The salesman returned with a tag. Mallory and Amanda got in the back seat and Jo drove. She was barely out on the road when she decided she wanted the vehicle. It answered all her needs. Returning to the lot, they negotiated a price and Jo made the deal.

"I don't think you stole it, although you probably got a fair price. Perhaps had you not been drooling on the hood when we started dickering about price, we could have done a little better," Mallory teased.

Jo glanced at Mallory. "I would probably have paid full price if not for your intervention. It's exactly what I need. It has low mileage, and he gave us the extended warranty at a reasonable cost and threw in that nice bed cover that'll be good, especially for the bad weather. It'll be nice to be able to lock things in the bed. I'm a happy camper." A huge grin spread across her face.

On the way home, the women stopped so Jo could treat them to dinner. As they were eating, Jo announced, "I think it's time for me to go home, Ladies. I can get around on my own now and should be able to care for myself. I might need help with shopping for a few more weeks. Other than that, I think I can manage." Jo had graduated to using a cane for stability and for the past couple of weeks had been navigating fairly well.

"We'll help you as long as you need us," Amanda promised. When she got home, Amanda offered and Jo accepted that she call their cleaning service and arrange for Jo's house to have a thorough cleaning so Jo wouldn't have to worry about it. She could see if she could maintain it on her own and make her own decision about whether to keep them on or not.

"I hope I'll be able to do it myself. Surely, I'll have the time." A wisp of sadness insinuated itself into her voice. She quickly forced herself to brighten her tone. "Just think, no more alarm clocks for me."

Mallory and Amanda had talked with Dana and Nic about the job offer they were about to make Jo. In the time Jo had spent at Amanda and Mallory's house, Jo had become a member of their extended family.

"Jo, we have an offer to make you. Initially, we won't need you much. However, you know that we're planning on opening the business in the next couple of weeks. Mallory is going to be office manager. She's still working part time at the hospital for a while and won't be available to be at the desk for all the hours we'll be open. Even after she leaves the hospital, there'll be too many hours for us to cover. Especially after business increases and Nic gets busier, we'll need someone to help us out. We were wondering if you would be interested in working for us part time to start, with increasing hours as the business grows. From time to time, we'll need someone who knows the business anyway. As it becomes successful, Mallory and I will want to be able to take time off to get away together as will Nic and Dana. We'll need someone we can trust to help out."

Jo, appreciative of all that her friends had done for her, jumped at the opportunity to be able to help them in return. "Sure, I'll even do it for free. I owe you guys so much. How will I ever repay you?"

"We won't hear of it. We feel we owe you more for saving Mallory's life. We're extremely glad you'll be with us in our new venture."

Chapter 4

STACY ALEXANDER SAT AT her desk located in front of a large window in her apartment. Her second bedroom served as her guest room and office. The window overlooked the main street of her little town, located just outside New York City. Shops and restaurants lined both sides of the street. Her apartment was in a freestanding house above a little shop that sold shoes and leather purses. She loved opening the door and stepping into the landing leading to the stairwell of her second floor space. As she entered, she always inhaled deeply to absorb the aroma of the leather that seeped into the hallway. Coming from a similarly sized town in Virginia, she appreciated living outside of the frenzy and hectic pace common to big cities. She had chosen the little suburb for its small-town feel as well as its proximity to New York City. As an author, she enjoyed being near her publisher for meetings when necessary and away from the hustle and bustle the rest of the time.

The process of writing was enjoyable to her. Stacy loved solving the challenges each story presented and especially loved the research involved. Her first job, as a researcher for an international company that did surveys and market research, was a job she continued to do on a freelance basis between novels. The current project entailed doing the data analysis for some French surveys. Having taken the language in high school and college, her French was passable but still not what she considered fluent. She felt more confident writing than speaking the language. Once she completed her report, she would translate it herself and then have her translation checked for accuracy before submitting it. As she worked, Stacy glanced out the window every so often to watch the progress on the little shop across the street. Workmen had been in and out over the previous weeks, painting and bringing in furniture. The cable people had arrived early and worked all morning and seemed to have finished making their connections.

Working on the plot outline for her fourth mystery novel, Stacy was stuck for a motive. For most of the morning she'd sat staring out the window, just thinking. In her first book, the motive had been adultery, and in the second, a crime of passion and opportunity. The third had been robbery. *What other reasons might there be that would cause one person to take another's life?* She ruminated on the subject, seeking another motive. *Blackmail? Yes, that's it. Blackmail. So, what could her victim, a twenty-five year old young woman living in a townhouse in a small town, possibly have done that someone could be blackmailing her about at such a young age?* She searched her brain for something different, something that would spice up her storyline. Nothing came to mind immediately, so she decided to take a break for a cup of tea.

In the kitchen she waited for the water to boil. After the kettle whistled, she prepared the tea and meandered back to the office, cup in hand, and settled again. Leaning her chin on her palm, she glanced out the window. She noticed that the short auburn haired woman, who had been in and out of the shop across the street for the past few weeks, was waiting at the door. A tall, dark haired, slender man dressed in trousers and a long Chesterfield styled coat strode up the walkway and hugged the woman. When they both turned towards the street, Stacy was surprised to notice that the taller person was a woman, not a man as she'd first thought. Her hair, although short, was stylishly cut. It was a few minutes until the two women waiting at the door welcomed two other women, one short and blondish and the other a strawberry haired woman of medium height. After hugs, they paired off, the two shorter women together and the taller woman with the mid-sized woman. They joined hands and followed one another through the door. Once inside, the two couples paired off and kissed each other on the lips.

Lesbians! They're all lesbians. Stacy watched in fascination as the two couples kissed each other, then separated to hug each of the other women. She found it an erotic sight, and the tingle she felt between her legs when the women kissed, surprised her. *Wonder what business they're going to open?* Idly, she pondered the question. Then a thought dawned on her. *Blackmail. Yes, her murder victim could be blackmailed for being a lesbian. Hmm. That might be a good reason for extortion.*

What do I know about being a lesbian? Nothing. She smiled to herself. *Research. I'll need to do research.* She watched for a while, hoping the women would kiss again. They seemed to be over the greeting stage and were starting to organize the office.

Soon a sign painter showed up and began painting the name of the business on the window. *Oui, Madame* slowly began to appear letter by letter. *Hmm, wonder what type of business that is?* Her question was soon answered as the sign painter added *Translation Services and Language School* below the name of the business. Stacy muttered aloud, her eyebrow arched. "Now isn't that convenient?"

Stacy put the novel aside for the time being, finally motivated to finish up the report she was writing. She would finish it, translate the report as best she could, and ask the women at the new business to proof it for her.

Chapter 5

MOST DAYS, STACY NOTED that three women showed up at the new business across the street...the tall one, the dark blonde, and another woman she had not seen that first day. The seemingly unpaired woman had dark brown, nearly black hair, that she wore pulled back into a ponytail. She was about five-eight, muscular for a woman, and carried herself with an air of authority and a particularly erect posture, as if she maybe had military experience or training. She used a cane and had a noticeable limp, favoring her left leg.

Stacy noticed that the woman with the limp walked for ten minutes each hour, and when she sat at the reception desk just inside the door she seemed to be exercising her leg. "What's that all about?" She spoke aloud despite the fact she was alone.

The weekly paper showed up on Saturday morning. Stacy noticed that there was an advertisement in the business section offering a discount on both translation services and classes for *Oui, Madame*. There were two classes to choose from, conversational Italian and conversational Spanish. Stacy gathered up the document that she'd translated earlier and headed across the street.

With a beautiful smile that transformed her face from merely attractive to entrancing, the woman behind the counter greeted Stacy warmly. "Hello there! How can I help you?"

Stacy took a brief moment to study the attractive woman she'd been surreptitiously observing for the past several days from her office window. She was cuter up close, and a bit softer than she perceived her to be from a distance. Besides the fantastic smile, she had the most unusual eyes. At first Stacy thought they were blue. After studying them for a few seconds, she decided they were actually more grey than blue. The ring around the grey iris was a dark grey blue, nearly black. She had to stop herself from staring. "I'm sorry, I've never seen eyes the color of yours before. They're beautiful." Stacy watched the woman blush.

"Thank you," she replied. In an effort to ignore the fact that her face was bright red, Jo turned straight back to business. She asked again. "How may I help you?"

"Well, I translated this report into French myself. I have passable conversational skills. My written language tends to be too wordy. I saw the name of the shop and thought that someone here surely can speak French. I wondered if someone could check my translation for me. I just live over there," Stacy pointed to her apartment across from where they were standing.

"I'm so sorry. We're not officially open yet. The Grand Opening is this Saturday. And right now, I'm the only one here."

"Do you speak French?"

"Uh...well...my mom is French, and I grew up speaking it. However, I'm not certified, nor am I hired here as a translator. I only help the owners out with reception and answering the phone. I expect Nic to be in any time now. If you want to leave the work, I'll have Nic or Dana translate it for you. Turn around will definitely be less than our normal twenty-four hours." She looked to her left then to her right and whispered, "You happen to be our first customer."

"Oh, I see." Stacy replied using the same hushed tone. "I wanted to get this in the mail this afternoon. It's really already translated. I just wanted a second opinion to be sure it was accurately done."

"If that's all you want, I can look it over for you at no charge, though I will warn you again that I'm not a certified interpreter. On a positive note, I've spoken the language all my life."

"That's good enough for this purpose." Stacy raised a finger in a gesture designed to delay a response. "I'll only accept your offer if you'll let me buy you dinner in exchange." A warm smile accompanied the invitation.

Jo hesitated for a moment before she stuck out her hand. "I'm Jo."

"Stacy. Stacy Alexander." She grasped Jo's hand. "So is it a deal?"

"I don't know how my bosses would feel about me doing this." Jo again cautioned the customer. "Are you sure that it's okay that I'm not certified?"

Stacy's nod and warm smile reassured Jo. "I can promise you that there are no state secrets contained in the document. I'm pretty comfortable with what I have already written. I just want someone to double-check my grammar and structure. I'll feel more comfortable submitting it if you can promise me that I won't appear to be an idiot in a foreign language."

"Okay." Jo winked and grabbed a pen from the counter. "I'm sure I can manage to do that. Just remember, you can never say I didn't warn you. Oh, and the dinner offer is not a requirement of the deal. I'll be happy to help out a neighbor."

"Thank you. I really appreciate it."

Hand extended, Jo said, "Let's see what you have. If it seems like something more than I feel I can handle, you'll have to wait for Nic. Agreed?"

Nodding again, Stacy handed the two-page report over to Jo who began a comparison from the English to the French. Half way down the second page, she pointed to a line. "This sentence here—I wouldn't word it this way. Technically it's correct. I just think it sounds stilted. I'd write it this way." Jo underlined the sentence and rewrote the phrase in the margin, then read it aloud to the woman.

"Oh, I see what you mean. You speak beautiful French. Good suggestion."

Nic came in through the back door. Having overheard the last part of the exchange, she entered the office from the back room and hung her coat on the rack. Smiling at the two women standing at the desk, she asked, "What's up?"

Jo heaved a sigh of relief. "Oh, good. Nic, this is Stacy. Stacy Alexander, Nic Bianchi. Nic is better qualified to help you than I am." Turning towards Nic, Jo explained, "Stacy knows that we aren't officially open yet. I told her we'd help her out as a favor because she's our neighbor."

It had never really occurred to Nic, nor had Jo mentioned, that she spoke French. It made sense, however, since Jo's mother, Josette, spoke English with a French accent. When with the group, Jo and her mother had always spoken English to each other because Mallory and Amanda didn't speak the language. Only Nic and Dana had spoken French with Josette.

Jo flipped the last page of the report over. "I'm almost finished. Nic, would you be willing to read it when I'm done, just to double-check me?"

"Sure. Let me see." Nic started on the first page while Jo finished the second. As she concluded reading the report, she turned to Jo. "That was a good suggestion you made. That sentence reads much more naturally now than it did originally." She then turned to Stacy. "You translated this yourself?

"Yes."

"You did a good job of it. What you had was grammatically correct. It's just that Jo's suggestion was a more colloquial way to say it."

Stacy nodded. "Thank you, Nic. Can I include you in my offer for dinner in exchange for checking my work for me?"

Nic laughed. "It would have been less expensive for you to pay us to translate it for you."

"Maybe." Stacy shrugged. "This way I get my document translated and get to know two of my neighbors." She turned and pointed to her office window. "I live up there in the second floor apartment. Anyway," she grinned, "I never said I was treating anyone to steak. It might end up just being pizza."

"Well, we're in luck then." Nic handed the papers back to Stacy. We're meeting the rest of the crew, Mallory, Amanda, and Dana, tonight at six at Antonio's for dinner. You can buy Jo dinner some other time. Tonight we'll go Dutch. However, you're welcome to join us if you'd like."

Stacy looked at Jo for confirmation. "Is that okay with you?"

Jo had taken the opportunity to study Stacy while she was talking to Nic. She detected just a slight accent, definitely southern, but not the Deep South. She liked the woman's petite frame and the fact that she was not stick thin. The girl had some curves and was a little taller than Mallory and Amanda's height, maybe four inches shorter than her own five eight. *Nice...just the right size.* Her naturally curly, soft looking, honey brown hair was sun streaked and worn in a short style. She had huge pale green eyes and a dimple in her left cheek when she smiled. *Yes, dinner could be a pleasant experience. Still, the big question had yet to be answered. Was she a lesbian?* Jo didn't get any overt vibes. *She did ask me out for dinner. Then again, maybe she's just the friendly type.*

"Yes, pizza for dinner works for me," Jo replied. "And if you don't want Dana, Mallory, and Amanda handing us our heads on a plate, we'd better get a move on."

"I'll get the car," Nic offered.

"I can make it," Jo said, instantly defensive.

"I know you can. It would help if you'd lock up here while I get the car. I just meant it would save us time."

Jo put a hand on Nic's arm. "Okay. Sorry I snapped. You know I'm trying my best to pull my own weight."

Stacy stepped outside while Jo turned off the lights, set the alarm, and locked the door. While they waited in front of the store, Stacy glanced down the street looking for Nic to return. "Nic is very nice and has a soothing way about her."

"Nic is a great friend. She and the others have been extremely kind to me since I got injured."

Stacy nodded her head in the direction of Jo's leg. "What happened? I see you walking back and forth a lot, exercising the leg."

"I got shot. There was an incident a couple of months ago at the hospital. Some lunatic shot up the ER."

"Oh, I read about that. Several women were injured. Which one are you? Oh wait a minute, Joanne Martini, right?"

"Close," Jo laughed. "Martin, like in Dean."

"Oh, sorry. I was close though." Stacy shrugged and smiled showing her dimple. "You're a hero. You saved some lives that day."

Jo nodded and responded seriously. "Yes, I did. I also took a life that day."

Nic pulled up and stopped. The two women got into her car and passed the time with friendly chatter. The ride to the restaurant took only a few minutes. Dana, Mallory, and Amanda were waiting for them when they arrived.

Nic noticed that the table was short one chair and asked the waiter to bring another. "Sure, Nicky. Right away."

Nic slid into the seat next to Dana. "Hi, Honey. I can't seem to break him of the habit of calling me Nicky."

"I kind of like it." Dana squeezed her partner's hand.

"Don't start, now," Nic said flashing a smile for her partner.

Introductions were made all around, and there was a quick discussion about what kind of pizzas to order. The friends chatted about the expedient issues of the day until the pies were served. Stacy watched the interaction between the two sets of partners, while Jo watched her watching them. Jo had a sinking feeling that Stacy might be straight.

All eyes turned to Jo when Amanda, assuming Stacy was Jo's date, asked her how she met Stacy. "She just walked in off the street. Actually, she's our neighbor. She lives in the apartment on the corner across the street. I helped her out today."

Nic turned to her partners. "Did you know that Jo is fluent in French?"

Amanda's brow furrowed. "No, I didn't. Had I thought about it, I might have figured she'd have some knowledge of it since her mother was born in France. But the two of them spoke only English when she visited us." Amanda turned to address Jo. "How come you never mentioned it to us when we offered you the job?"

Like a tennis match, all heads turned back to Jo. "You were all so kind to me, I felt like I would be taking advantage by mentioning it. Besides, I'm not certified. I'm just a native speaker, although I did minor in it in college. I always wished my mother was Spanish instead of French. It certainly would have been a more useful language to speak in my line of work as a policewoman. Due to the larger population of Hispanics in the area I patrolled, I've arrested many more Hispanics than Frenchmen. Besides, 'you stop' in Spanish sounds like more of a command than 'you stop' in French. I mean can you imagine yelling 'vous arrêtez' at a fleeing suspect?"

When the laughter died down, Dana brought the conversation back to the original topic. "You know, Jo, the certification is just a matter of a few tests. If you're interested, we can make arrangements. Until then, would you like to offer a class and tutoring in French? We can offer a 'Conversations in French' class along with our Spanish and Italian classes."

Jo's face registered surprise at the offer. "Really? Yeah, that would be fun."

Stacy joined in. "I'll sign up to be your first student. That conversation class sounds like it would be something I'd enjoy."

Interested in learning more about the woman, Amanda said. "So, tell us a little about yourself."

"Okay, I'm from Virginia...been here for about three years now. I've written three detective books. My main character is Veronica Price."

"Hey! I've read that series," Jo exclaimed. "Will you autograph my copies?"

"Sure, I'd be happy to."

Amanda removed the last slice of pizza from the tray and turned to Stacy. "I've read those books, too. I love that lead character. She should be a lesbian. Although, you wouldn't sell as many books if she were."

"Really?" Puzzled by that statement, Stacy asked, "Why would you say that?"

That confirmed Jo's suspicions. *Straight. Damn.*

Amanda responded. "Pure numbers. Think about it. It's estimated that gay people are approximately ten percent of the population. For the sake of argument, let's say half are lesbians. So, even if all of them were avid readers of detective stories, which of course they're not, your books still would only have the potential to appeal to less than five percent of the population. Since so many independent bookstores have closed access to lesbian literature has been further restricted."

Mallory offered her two cents. "At least it's better now that electronic books are available. It's easier to get books from lesbian authors now than it used to be. Also, if you're still closeted, you can use your e-reader and read a lesbian novel without having to hide it inside another book or in a plain brown wrapper."

Five of the women at the table laughed.

Stacy looked at them incredulously. "I never even thought about that. I've so much to learn."

"What do you mean?" Jo asked.

Stacy confessed to having watched the group open the business and to searching for a motive for her victim's murder. "So, that's how I got the idea that my victim would be being blackmailed for being a lesbian."

"Really? How common do you think that is?" Jo asked.

Dana raised an eyebrow. "I have a friend in Maine, Stephanie. She's an Investment Advisor. She was actually blackmailed by an ex-lover trying to wring money out of her."

"Still, I don't think that's something that happens every day." Jo leaned forward and looked from Amanda to Stacy. "Don't they tell you authors to write what you know?"

Ignoring Jo's question, Stacy asked, "Authors? Amanda, are you an author, too?"

"Yes, I am." Amanda looked pointedly at Jo. "And what are the odds of that, Jo? It's certainly possible that her victim could be being blackmailed. And as for writing what you know, half the books in the world would never be written if someone hadn't researched their information before they wrote about it."

"Maybe she's right," Stacy admitted. "I don't know anything about the lesbian lifestyle."

Jo exhaled sharply making a 'pffft' sound with her lips as she rolled her eyes.

"What did I say?" Stacy looked from one woman to another, both eyebrows raised, her concern evident.

Their exchange was interrupted as the waiter delivered another pizza. Conversation stopped as everyone eagerly grabbed another slice.

Stacy turned to Jo. "What did I say that was wrong?"

"It's not wrong exactly. It's just that straight people think of my life as a 'lifestyle'. I think of my life as a life. Do you live a heterosexual lifestyle? Or do you just live your life as a woman who happens to be heterosexual?"

"I'm sorry, I didn't mean to offend. Maybe I should change my motive," she said, a sad expression clouding her face.

Amanda jumped in. "Don't be silly. It's a great motive. You just need to do your research, that's all."

"Is there a place, a place you go to meet, or a magazine or newspaper that I could post an advertisement for someone to help me learn what it's like to be a lesbian. You know, things that I might need to know for my novel."

"Well, you're off to a good start. You've made friends with us," Amanda said, a kind expression on her face. "And since we're all lesbians, you'll learn about our lives from us. But, the four of us," Amanda pointed to her partner, Nic, and Dana, "are all about to be married. Jo is the only single one of the bunch, so she'd be the best resource for your book." Seeing Jo's reaction to her suggestion only spurred Amanda on. "You don't need to post an ad, just hire Jo." Jo looked on in horror. "Maybe Jo would allow you to shadow her for four to six weeks and answer all your questions in exchange for your helping her at home. She'd be a great tutor in the ways of the single lesbian."

Jo was shaking her head as she faced a losing battle. Obviously, from their expressions, she was the only one of the five friends who thought the idea sucked.

When the meal ended with the only evidence of the pizza's existence the crumbs in the empty trays, they all stood and gathered their belongings. Nic handed Jo the keys to her car. "Why don't you drive Stacy home? I'll see you at work tomorrow and collect my keys. I'll catch a ride home with Dana."

The ride back to drop Stacy off was silent until Stacy broke the ice with her first question. "Why are you so opposed to helping me?"

"I just don't think it's a good idea." Jo shrugged her shoulders. "I mean, what will you gain other than the knowledge of one single lesbian's life? It would be like me following you around and making conclusions about heterosexual women based on that brief glimpse into your day-to-day life." She snorted. "Anyway, lately my life consists of going to work and limping around the block. I haven't been out on a date in...well, virtually forever." She opted not to consider or reveal her embarrassing tryst with Meg. "You'll surely get a skewed viewpoint."

"But I like you and I trust that you'd be honest with me. You and your friends just seem like regular people who happen to be lesbians. That's something I'd like to convey in my book."

Jo was silent, first considering and then liking the response.

"Besides, Amanda said that you could use some help at home. What did she mean by that?"

"I just moved back to my house after living with Amanda and Mallory while I recovered. They took care of me until I got back on my feet." Jo smiled then hunched one shoulder. "I still need help with things like shopping. Cooking is a bit difficult, too. Standing for any length of time is still hard for me, although I think I'm getting a little better every day."

"Okay, let me help you. Move in with me for six weeks. You'll be right across the street from work. I'll cook, shop, and do whatever else you need. In exchange, you'll teach me about being a lesbian."

"This is a ridiculous premise. You'll still have no clue even if I lived with you twice that time. It's not about external things. It's internal. It's identity. Then there's sex. Until you have sex with another woman, you'll never understand completely. Don't get me wrong. It's not only about which gender you want to have sex with. It's also about being comfortable in your skin. This whole idea just makes no sense."

"All right, how's this? I'll pay your rent on your place. You move in with me. I'll make your dinner, buy your food, take you shopping, and help you in any other way I can. In return, I want you to do your best to answer all my questions honestly and to educate me to the ways of your world. You're right. This experience will be incomplete for me, due to my own limitations, not yours. I'll never know completely what it's like to be a lesbian because our deal does not include my having sex with a woman. Still, this arrangement should suffice to give me enough information to write my novel and not have you, and others like you, read my book and roll their eyes as they're doing it."

Jo shook her head. She had no doubt that it was a crazy idea. However, knowing her own limitations, Jo also recognized that being home alone for the past few days had been tough. *What the hell. I don't have anything to lose. If I hate it I can always leave.* "This makes no sense to me, but it's your dime. I'm willing to give it a try. When do we start?"

Not wanting to give Jo an opportunity to reconsider, Stacy said, "Right now. Let's go to your house and get your stuff before you change your mind."

Jo laughed. "You have to be the most determined woman I've ever met. Okay, let's go."

Two hours later, Stacy carried two suitcases of Jo's belongings up the stairs into her apartment. "Can you manage the stairs?"

"Yeah. I just have to go slow, using my good leg. The therapist taught me up with the good leg and down with the bad. She said it's like people. Good people go up to heaven and bad people go down to hell. Get it?" When Stacy nodded, Jo added, "It's tedious but doable. The cane and the handrail will help."

Stacy showed Jo to her office. There was a day bed in there that she used for guests. She lifted the suitcases to the bed. "I'll give you some privacy. We'll have to share the bath. I'll clean out a drawer in there for you so you'll have a place for your toiletries. You get the top left drawer of the vanity." Pausing at the doorway, Stacy gave a quick smile. "Come out to the living room when you've unpacked."

As Jo unpacked, her mind raced. *How the hell did I let myself get hooked into this? It's ridiculous. It was that damned dimple, and that cute 'almost accent' she has. I just couldn't say no. I'll probably bore her to death in the next six weeks. An added bonus is that I'll be right across the street from work.* Truth was, if Jo were to admit it she was having a hard time being home alone. It would also make her less dependent on her friends. If she put the pain and suffering aside, she'd enjoyed living with Amanda and Mallory and being around Dana and Nic while she recovered. Now, if home alone, she found that she could easily become depressed. Despite the counseling she'd received after the shooting, when she had time to think, she still had flashes of slow motion memories. She recalled Meg's head snap back as it hit the stretcher and saw Mallory turn and grab her arm. She thought about the guy she'd shot and the look on his face as he died. Being around other people helped her to restrict her recollections to her dreams rather than allowing them to invade all of her waking hours. After stowing her gear, Jo made her way to the living room.

"Did you get everything put away? Want a cup of coffee?" Stacy asked.

"Yes, and no. All my gear is stowed. If you have decaf tea, I'll take a cup of that instead of coffee,"

Stacy left for the kitchen and returned shortly with tea in hand.

"I can't believe we're doing this. We should probably both be committed. We don't know anything about each other, and in less than eight hours after meeting each other, we're living together." Jo laughed. "It's even worse than that old lesbian joke."

"What lesbian joke?"

"Oh, yeah. Well, lesson one. There is a belief that lesbians pair up almost immediately after they meet. So the joke is, 'What does a lesbian bring on the second date?' Jo waited, smiling as she watched Stacy's brow furrow as her mind searched for a response. "Give up?"

"Yes. What does a lesbian bring on a second date?"

Jo giggled. "A U-Haul. Get it?"

"I guess. That's funny?"

"See, I told you this wouldn't work," Jo said, shaking her head.

"Don't give up so fast. Besides, I probably know more about you than you know about me. There was a lot of information about you in the newspaper when you saved your friends. I know you have a degree in criminology, that you have an exemplary record on the police force..."

"Had. I had an exemplary record." Jo slapped her leg. "I had to retire."

"Retire? You're too young to retire."

"Yeah, I know. I'm still washed up at forty-two. My leg will never be right. I might be able to get it to improve. Unfortunately, I'll never be a cop again."

Stacy took a sip of her tea. "It seems that when one door closes another opens. Look, it appears that you'll be working with your friends. They seem like a great group of women."

"They are. I owe them a great deal."

"Is Amanda the leader of the pack?"

Jo smiled. "I think she is right now because the business was her idea. But each one is strong in her own way."

"Tell me about each of them."

Jo stirred her tea, took a sip, and began. "Well, Amanda is an author, as you already know. She and Mallory just got together a few months ago, around the same time Nic and Dana started their relationship. Mallory, the Director of Nursing at the hospital, decided to resign her full time supervisory position to return to part time nursing when the four of them decided to open the business. Nic and Dana met when they were both working for a company as translators on a job in Rome."

"How did Mallory and Amanda meet?"

"Amanda moved back here from California when her previous relationship ended. She and Dana have been friends for years, so Dana offered Amanda her place to live in while she was working in Italy. Mallory is Dana's neighbor. That's how they met. I met Mallory at the hospital when I was working there."

"The night you got shot?"

Jo shook her head. "No, I was off duty that night, and I'd already known Mallory for well over a year when that happened. After I got shot, I lived with Amanda and Mallory and they took care of me. I just moved home a few days ago."

"You all seem to get along so well together. I envy you your closeness." Stacy looked away. "I've been lonely since I moved up here."

"I'm sorry. Now that you've met all of us, you won't be lonely any more. I can promise that. Those women are the best friends anyone could ever ask for. I guarantee you'll never find better."

"I'm sure that's true. I felt welcomed by, and comfortable with, all of them." Stacy smiled, thinking about the dinner. "I think they all worry about you."

Jo adjusted her position and rubbed her leg to ease the stiffness. "Now that they're all paired, I'm sort of a fifth wheel. I'm sure they'd like me to join them in coupled bliss. Since I'm not even dating anyone, chances of that are pretty much zip. I know they love me and just want what they think is best for me."

"I agree. It's obvious they all love you." Stacy drank the last of her tea.

"I love them, too. I'm very blessed by their friendship."

After a few more minutes of conversation about Jo's friends, the conversation reached a natural stopping point, so Stacy suggested, "What do you say we call it a night and turn in early? What time do you have to be at work tomorrow?"

"I don't have to go in tomorrow. Nic is covering the office with Mallory. I'll only help them out a couple of days a week right now until the business gets more established."

"Good. Then when you get up tomorrow, we'll talk some more." Stacy picked up Jo's cup and took it to the kitchen along with her own. When she came back to the living room, Jo was already on her feet ready to head for her room.

"Jo, thanks for doing this. I know you think it's a dumb idea. Who knows? Maybe you're right. Until I got this idea, I'd been staring at my computer screen for longer than I'd like to admit. I'm now excited again about my story. I do want to do my best for the character and, without your help, I'm afraid I'd make a mess of things."

I could listen to her read the want ads. That hint of a southern accent and that low sultry voice is delicious, like warm honey. Jo forced her attention back to what Stacy was saying instead of how it sounded to her. "You know, I have to be careful around you. Your accent lulls me into a state of uh...I don't know the word to use that exactly explains the feeling, euphoria I guess. Listening to you makes me no longer in control of my brain. If I'm not careful, I'll be agreeing to things I don't want to do." She grinned. "You should patent that speech pattern of yours." Before she turned again towards her room, Jo shrugged. In an untypical moment of naked openness, Jo admitted, "Don't be too grateful. I probably need to be here more than you need me to be here. I've been having a hard time, and I'm glad for the company." Jo surprised herself by revealing so much to a virtual stranger. *Maybe it's easier to be so forthcoming because we are strangers.*

"Don't go, then. Stay and talk to me some more."

Jo gave the offer some serious consideration. "No, not tonight, I'm beat. We'll talk more tomorrow. Good night, Stacy." Jo turned and limped down the hallway.

Chapter 6

THE NEXT MORNING, STACY had breakfast ready to cook when Jo came stiffly into the kitchen from the hallway. "Good morning, Jo. Tea or coffee?"

"Good morning." Jo took a seat at the counter. "At least we're both cheerful people in the morning. That's a plus. I'll have tea," Jo said, starting to stand. "You don't need to wait on me. I can get it myself."

"I know you can. Please, let me. So what's on your agenda today?"

"Sometime this morning, I need to meet with Amanda to find out what I have to do to become certified. That's certified, not certifiable," Jo clarified adding a wink.

"And what about the rest of your day?"

"I'm not sure. Truth is, not having a job has been kinda tough for me. I'm not really used to it yet. I don't know what to do with myself at times. I'm not used to sitting around."

Stacy returned to the counter with tea for Jo. "What are your options?"

"I don't know for sure. I might be able to get a part time position in my old station as a dispatcher. I'll need to check if I can work for them. There might be an issue with my pension plan."

"What about your job across the street?" Stacy pulled up a chair and joined Jo.

Jo shrugged. "I only work a couple of days a week for the women across the street. As business picks up, the hours there will increase and take up some of my time. For now, that's enough, because I need to do the exercises for my leg. I've been trying to walk as much as possible. It's tough, though. I tire so easily. My muscles knot up and spasm, and I just can't go any farther. I've been pushing as hard as I can. By this spring, I hope to have my leg strong enough that I can ride my bike."

"And are you ready to tell me what you started to tell me last night?"

Jo exhaled a tight breath. "You mean why I need to be here more than you need me to be?"

"Yes." Stacy replied quietly.

Jo looked at Stacy who seemed genuinely interested and so far had not asked any unreasonable questions of her. "Well, I've been feeling at odds, I guess. In an instant I went from being an active, independent woman to being someone who hates to be alone, who's dependent on friends and on a stranger for companionship and support. I can't ride my bike, hike, go fishing, camping, or do any of the other things I like to do. I'm no longer a cop." Jo fought the tears that threatened. "I feel like I've lost everything. My identity, you know, who I am."

"Well, you're still a lesbian. Right?"

Jo smiled. "Yes, but that was never all of who I was. First, I was a human being. Then I was a daughter and a family member. I was all of those other things before I was a lesbian."

"So, you haven't lost everything then, have you?"

Jo was impressed by the way Stacy had directed her down a path to a foregone conclusion. "No, I guess not."

"Jo, you'll get better than you are now. You'll adapt. You'll learn that you're capable of much more than you think you are. Eventually, you'll find your way. Give yourself some time."

"Well, time is something I seem to have an abundance of these days."

"And that makes me a lucky woman because you have time to spend with me." Stacy treated Jo to a broad grin and a flash of dimple. "What time do you have to meet Amanda?"

"I think I'll hobble my way over there in a little while and wait for her to come in."

With breakfast concluded, Jo thanked Stacy before returning to her room to finish dressing. She put on her shoes and socks and added a sweater over her shirt. Stacy was still sitting there nursing a second cup of tea when Jo returned to the kitchen. "You know, I realized last night that you seem to know more about me than I know about you. I actually felt a little strange being here."

"You can't tell me that you've never met someone and gone home with them before." Stacy arched a brow.

"You mean like in a one night stand?" Jo chuckled. "Yeah, haven't we all? But it never lasted six weeks."

Stacy joined Jo in laughter. "I can guarantee we'll know each other well when our time is up."

"What are you going to do with your day today? Do you plan to do some writing? I can give you some time alone so your office is available to you."

"I have a few errands to run while you're over there meeting with Amanda and giving your friends a hard time for pushing you into this arrangement."

Jo looked up in amazement.

"Are you surprised that I knew that's what you'd do? It's what I'd do if I were you."

Jo shrugged. She felt her cheeks burn. *This gal's no fool.*

"Just keep in mind that they love you and just want what's best for you. They know you're hurting. I think they latched onto this idea, this offer, so you'd have purpose for at least a little while."

"Yeah, I guess you're right. I'll go easy." Jo grinned. She liked Stacy much more than she ever thought she would and was actually starting to enjoy sharing things with her. Although they'd only known each other for less than twenty-four hours, she felt a sense of ease and camaraderie with Stacy and harbored a desire that they might become friends. She'd already trusted Stacy with confidences she hadn't shared before, even with her close friends across the street. Sharing her feelings with Stacy just seemed right and effortless. She hoped that Stacy would eventually learn that they had more in common than she'd imagined. More than anything else, she wanted Stacy to understand that one's choice in sexual partners didn't completely define who you were as a person. She hoped she'd come to understand it was just one facet of the total package.

Jo made her way across the street leaving Stacy to make a few phone calls before she went downstairs to get into her car. First stop was the drug store where she picked up a companion chair. Then she stopped at the sporting goods store. By the time she arrived home and lugged her purchases up the stairs, the doorbell rang. She ran down the steps to let Jo back in. "I've got to give you a key," she said over her shoulder as they climbed the stairs.

"What's all this?" Jo asked looking over the objects piled in the living room.

Gesturing like the model revealing a prize behind the selected curtain, Stacy replied, "This is a companion chair. And since you're my companion for the next six weeks, I thought we could use it to take our walks."

"What walks?"

"I see you walk every hour or so when you're at the office. I thought maybe we could walk and talk at the same time. You can walk behind the chair 'til you're tired. Then you can sit and I can push you home, or you can rest until you can go farther. At least you'll get a change of scenery instead of covering the same six or eight squares of cement in front of there, where you work." Stacy gestured in the general direction of the shop across the street.

"I worked hard to get out of a wheelchair. I don't want to go back in one."

"It's a companion chair. It's not the same thing."

"Maybe not to you."

"I understand what you're saying. I'm just asking you to humor me and try it out. It'll give us an ability to go to places together at a greater distance than you can walk, in addition to letting you walk farther when you exercise." Seeing the doubt still evident on Jo's face, Stacy worked hard to make her case. "Say we want to go somewhere together, like a museum or something. With the chair, we can get you anywhere we want to go. Don't think of it as a step backward. You get into a car when it's too far to walk. Try to think of the chair as another type of vehicle instead of a symbol of your inability to make it as far as you'd like. And remember, six weeks from now, if you don't think you need it, I'll take it back to the drug store I rented it from."

"And what about that?" Jo pointed to the box in the center of the room.

Stacy focused on the large box Jo was pointing to. "Hmm. That. Well, it's something I'm not sure exactly how you set up. I think we'll be able to figure it out. You told me that you'd lost your ability to bike. The salesman assured me that this is a device that you can connect to your bike somehow, that allows you to ride indoors. It'll help strengthen your leg so that eventually, maybe by the time the weather is warmer, you'll have developed enough muscle strength to ride again."

Jo was overwhelmed by the kindness and thoughtfulness Stacy was showing her. Stacy's purchases demonstrated that she listened to every word Jo shared with her. Jo blinked several times to clear the moisture threatening to spill from her eyes and changed the topic. "Do you ride?"

"No, not anymore, not since I moved to New York. I used to love to ride when I was younger."

"You still look like a kid. How old are you, anyway?"

The dimple appeared in Stacy's cheek. "I'm older than you think. Thirty-eight. I was born on Halloween."

"What made you stop riding?"

"When I first arrived here, I rented a room in the city...no room for a bike there. Then, when I moved in here, I didn't know anybody. I found it hard to make friends because I work so totally alone and do not encounter many people in the course of my work. I met a few people when I lived in the city. Sadly, unless I go into town, I don't see them very often. God forbid they come here. In their defense, none of them have cars. So it's easier for me to go there than it is for them to come here."

"Do you get lonely with just your writing for company?"

"Sure. I have a few good friends from back home still. I keep in touch with them through email and video chat. I phone my parents and my sister regularly." Stacy leaned forward and exhaled. "I admit that it's lonely sometimes. When I first saw the group arrive across the way, women my own age setting up shop, I was excited to think that I'd be able to make some new friends."

"You couldn't find better."

Stacy stood up. "Come on, let's have lunch, and then take a walk."

"It's cold out there. Isn't a sweet southern girl like you afraid you'll freeze to death?"

"It gets cold in Virginia. I'm not as delicate as you think." Stacy's dimple flashed.

"We'll see about that."

They made peanut butter and jelly sandwiches, arguing the merits of bread with crust versus no crust and slicing the bread on the diagonal versus making a longitudinal cut. The good-natured teasing and banter left them both smiling by the time they sat down to eat. They cleaned up the kitchen and bundled up for their walk.

Stacy rolled the chair down the stairs. "Believe me, it's a lot easier taking this down than it is carrying it up."

"Maybe we can leave it across the street." Jo added a quick smile. "That way we, meaning you, don't have to carry it up and down all the time."

Their animated dialogue continued as they started their walk with Jo pushing the chair.

Across the street in the office, Nic looked out the window and waved to the walkers. A smile slowly spread across her face before she turned and returned to the desk to dial Dana's number to share the news with her lover that Stacy had managed to get Jo to use a wheelchair. It was something none of them had been able to accomplish despite their concerted efforts.

As Stacy and Jo started to walk, Stacy asked. "So, how did you know you were gay?"

"How did you know you were straight?" Jo rapidly retorted.

Stacy regrouped. "Okay, *when* did you know you were gay?"

Jo thought back to her first time she had kissed a girl. "I was fifteen, I guess. I had this friend, Beth. She was the cutest thing I'd ever seen. She was small and bubbly. We went to camp together and I ended up sharing a tent with her. She was a little older than I was and knew more about what sex had to offer. The night she kissed me, I thought my heart would pound out of my chest. I'd kissed a couple of boys and all I remember of the experience is that the first guy smelled and tasted of potato chips. The second one pushed his tongue in my mouth and I gagged!" She laughed at the memory. "But when Beth kissed me, as they say, the earth moved."

Jo looked back at the distance they had covered. They were chatting and walking slowly, and she hadn't paid attention to the amount of ground they had covered. She also felt reassured by the chair. Knowing that she could sit down if she had to and she wouldn't have to wait for someone to come rescue her gave her confidence to go farther.

"Tired?"

"No, I'm still okay. This is good. Thanks for walking with me. It gives me a sense of security that I'll make it back without having to call in the cavalry."

"So what happened with Beth?"

Jo raised her eyebrows. "You want details?"

"If you'll tell them, sure."

"Remember, I'm going to expect the same in return."

Stacy stopped walking and faced Jo. "When did that become part of our agreement? I thought you were supposed to educate me."

"Well, I'm kind of thinking I'll show you mine if you'll show me yours—figuratively speaking of course."

"Of course." Stacy pursed her lips then let them spread into a slow smile. "Okay, that's fair, I guess."

"So she kissed me, and I had a million thoughts and emotions run through my head. My first thought was 'Wow!' That was followed almost immediately by, 'What will my parents say?' The way she made me feel when she slid her hand under my pajama top and touched my breast...well, I decided I'd worry about all the rest later. I focused on what she was doing to my body and how it made me feel. I had my first orgasm that night and never looked back."

"What happened to Beth?"

"Camp ended and that was that."

"Did you tell your parents?"

Jo pursed her lips in thought, recalling the struggle. "Not then. All I knew was that I was different. You know, different in a way that I had better keep secret. It was hard at first, because I was terrified that if I told my family or my friends what I had figured out about myself they'd stop loving me. It's a heavy burden for a kid to have to carry. I was always afraid that someone would figure it out back then. I had an advantage in a way. I was always athletic. I was good at and interested in all kind of sports. I did a lot with my teammates. I went places in a group with them, and there were several of us who didn't date, we just always hung out together."

"So you didn't have a girlfriend?"

"Not until college. Then, figuring out I wanted to be a cop added an additional layer of concern. I was afraid that being a lesbian could prohibit me from getting a job. I was so worried about it that I finally confided my secret to my mother. Her name is Josette."

"Was she was okay with it? What'd your mother say?"

"I don't doubt that she'd have wished a different life for me. But when I told her, after we cried together, she hugged me and told me to be strong and to be true to who I was."

"Your mom, Josette, she sounds nice. Did you tell your dad?"

"No, my mom told him. His name is Ben. I'd say he was less than thrilled. To his credit, he let me know that he still loved me. He was okay as long as we didn't talk about it. It's like what he didn't see himself wasn't true or could at least be denied. When I got shot I recovered at Amanda and Mallory's place while my parents stayed with Nic and Dana. Living with all of us made it difficult for Dad to ignore the facts and to put it out of his mind. Luckily, as Dad came to know my friends, it was pretty interesting to watch him relax and realize they are just people who care for each other. When Mom and Dad left, my father hugged each of them goodbye and told every one of them that he loved them." Jo shrugged. "He told me, too. Of course, I already knew it. Still it was a huge step for him. We were all sobbing by the time we watched them drive away."

Fascinated by Jo's story, so different from her own reality, Stacy prompted Jo to continue. "So, you've never taken a girlfriend home?"

"No. I've had a couple of relationships although I haven't been seriously involved enough with anyone to bring them home with me. It's hard being a cop's partner. There's shift work for one. Additionally, cops see some ugly things. We're not easy to love. I think I probably haven't had a real date in two years or more. Although I will admit to having had a couple of one night stands here and there, and a few short term relationships. I rarely do that though because I don't really enjoy sex without some sort of emotional involvement. To me, sex without involvement—it's like wearing shoes without socks. It's functional, but more comfortable if you have both."

"Now there's an analogy for you." When Stacy chuckled, Jo grinned. "So would you say you'd never feel like settling down?"

"No, just the opposite. I'd love to be in a relationship like my friends have. I just haven't met the right person yet, I guess. I know that I keep hoping that I will, one day. I'd say I have a lot of love saved up for someone special. I've been saving it up all my life."

Stacy reached out and gave Jo's hand a squeeze. "I hope you find what, or should I say who, you are looking for."

"What about you?" Jo asked, "Anybody serious in your life?"

"No, my life is much like yours." Stacy pulled up the hood on her coat and adjusted her collar tighter. "I've been on my own for the past three years. I've had a couple of relationships that didn't last. In my line of work, I just don't meet many people. So unless someone writes 'for a good time, see Stacy, 454 Main Street' on a bathroom wall somewhere, it probably isn't going to happen. Of course, it would help if I went out to places where other people congregate once in a while, maybe join a gym, and get out in public more. It's just not worth the hassle to me."

"What do you mean?"

Stacy puzzled over how to answer the question. "In the past, it seems that things start off fine. Then, as soon as a guy gets what he wants, things seem to change. I don't know, maybe it's me who changes."

Jo hesitated wondering if her next question was too personal. She and Stacy seemed able to broach any subject head on so she asked without embarrassment. "Tell me if I'm overstepping by asking you this. Do you miss sex?"

"Not really that much. I guess I'm just not a very sexual person. I like the touching and the kissing. The rest I can take or leave. What about you? Do you miss sex?"

Jo stopped. "I think I need to rest a bit. There's a bench over there where you can sit. Let's sit down." They walked over and sat down facing each other, Jo in the companion chair and Stacy on the bench. Stacy helped Jo prop her leg up on the bench.

Jo pursed her lips. When she felt ready she said, "When I look at Amanda and Mallory, and Dana and Nic, I envy them. Not their sex lives specifically although God, Dana, and Nic seem to be in perpetual heat for each other. I envy the relationships those two couples have individually, as well as their friendship with each other. They're building something together. I know I'm their friend and that they love me. Sometimes I feel the void of being the only single one when I'm with them."

Stacy tipped her head in agreement. "I can understand that. Both couples seem to have wonderful relationships." After a few seconds when they were quiet, Stacy asked, "Nobody steady for you, then?"

Jo shook her head. "I was married to my job. I worked shift work. It's hard to make and sometimes even keep friends when you do that, let alone establish a relationship of any significance. And like I said, to me sex without commitment isn't what I want."

"Do most lesbians feel that way?"

Jo tossed back a quick response, answering Stacy's question with one of her own. "Do most heterosexual women feel the same way you do about sex?"

"No, probably not. I know some of my friends feel very differently. They're always talking about wanting to have sex with their guy."

"The same can be said for my team as well." Jo smiled. "It's why you can't refer to the lesbian lifestyle. People are people, Stacy. Everyone is different. For most of us, I think it's safe to say we all, gay or straight, want someone special in our lives. Don't you think?"

"Yeah, you're probably right. Hey! I'm freezing. Ready to go home?"

Just for a moment, Jo wished. "Yes, let's go home."

"Have you walked far enough today? May I give you a ride back?"

Jo turned to look back at the shop, amazed at how far they'd come. "I think I'd appreciate that."

Stacy pushed Jo back to *Oui, Madame*. They decided to put the chair in the alcove behind the desk in the outer office of the shop.

Nic smiled at Stacy. "I see you gave my friend a workout today. How far did she go?"

"Don't talk about me like I'm not here," Jo said as she made her way around the desk. "I went to the bench a block and a half down. I was so tired out, Stacy had to push me back."

"Good for you, Jo. I'm very impressed."

"Yeah, I'm a little impressed myself," Jo admitted with a grin. "Because we were chattering away, I wasn't paying attention to how far we'd gone or how much pain I had. It helped knowing I had a ride home when I got tired. Tomorrow I'll go farther." She grinned at Stacy. "Assuming I can get a lift home when I'm done."

"That's a promise."

When the two women headed across the street, Amanda came out of the back office and stood behind Nic who was seated at the desk. She leaned her forearm on Nic's shoulder and they watched together as the two women made their way to Stacy's apartment.

"How long do you think it'll take the two of them to realize they're good for each other?"

"I don't know if anything more than a friendship will develop. Stacy's straight."

"So was Dana once. You two worked it out. Maybe they will too. I like Stacy a lot. Besides, she's good for Jo. Jo needs someone to help her find her way and I think Stacy could do it. She's very good with her. Jo is calmer, more relaxed, when she's with her."

Turning to face Amanda, Nic cautioned. "We can't interfere more than we already have. It's up to them now."

"Yes, you're right. It is." Amanda said a small prayer that her friend would find happiness. Giving Nic's shoulder a squeeze, Amanda returned to the back office to finish her work.

Chapter 7

JO AND STACY RETURNED to the apartment after their walk. They made tea, and with cups in hand they went into the living room. "So, let's see what's in the box." Jo pointed to the large brown box sitting like an elephant in the middle of the room.

Stacy got out her box cutter and slit open the top of the cardboard container, reached in, and pulled out the directions before lifting the trainer out of the box. She looked over the instructions before handing the directions to Jo. "Does this make sense to you?"

Jo studied the directions then slid from the sofa to the floor and scooted over to the device. "Well, I think the instructions are more complex than necessary. It looks like you just secure the bike in here after you replace this piece with the supplied part, and then you're good to go."

"Let's go get your bike and bring it back to try it."

"Before we do that, let's first look it up on the Internet and see if we can learn any additional information about this thing."

"Good idea! You're not only cute you're smart, too. I'm surprised you're not beating women off with a stick."

Jo laughed and just shook her head. "Yep, that's me, the total package." Jo tried to get up. "Uh oh."

Concerned, Stacy approached Jo. "What's the matter?"

"I think I might need a bit of help getting up. The sofa slides if I push against it. Can you get me a kitchen chair?"

"Nonsense. I'll help you." Before Jo could protest, Stacy was behind her and had quickly slid her arms around Jo's torso. "Okay, on three."

Jo pushed up with her good leg as Stacy lifted. Jo could feel the softness of Stacy's breasts pressed against her back, and she felt herself respond. She hurriedly stepped away. "Thanks."

Stacy turned away, her face flushed. She looked down to assure herself that her erect nipples were not showing beneath her T-shirt. "No problem." She quickly headed off down the hallway towards her computer while Jo followed at a slower pace.

"Look," Jo said, pointing to the picture on the screen of the same trainer Stacy had purchased. "In his review of the product, this guy indicates that the instructions are screwy. He says to ignore the thing about the extra wheel. You just clip the bike in with the supplied pin. Most wheels will accept it. They all seem to suggest smoother tires are quieter. I'll use my racing bike instead of my mountain bike so I don't drive you crazy."

"Let's go get your bike."

"Now?"

Stacy stood up. "Why not?"

"We can take my truck. I won't need to install a rack on your car to hold the bike that way."

They made their way to Jo's house. Jo turned off the pickup. "Come on in for a bit. I want to get a couple of books for you to read. Then we'll get my bike."

While Jo went to her bedroom to look for two books by her favorite author of lesbian romances, Stacy looked at the pictures on Jo's mantle. Stacy studied a family photo of Jo and a beautiful woman who looked like an older, slightly heavier version of Jo, and a distinguished looking man standing near another woman who appeared slightly older than Jo. Stacy assumed she might be Jo's sister. On the opposite end of the mantle was a picture of Jo in uniform, hat tucked under her arm. She looked to be much younger, maybe in her twenties, with short hair and a broad smile. She was pointing to her badge.

Jo emerged from her bedroom, two books in hand.

"You have an attractive family, Jo. You look like your mom. I love your hair short like it was in this picture."

"Thanks." Jo seemed a bit embarrassed as she handed the books to Stacy. "These are two books by one of my favorite lesbian authors. If I had to choose, I guess I'd have to say I like this one the best." She pointed to the first. "This one is about second chances. You may find it interesting because both of the characters talk about their individual realizations that they're attracted to women. In fact, one of the characters is in her thirties and just figuring out that she's gay."

"That late in life?" Stacy took the books Jo offered.

"You might be surprised. It's a lot more common than you'd suspect. Add that topic to your list of questions for us to discuss. Let's get back to discussing the book. The dialogue between the two main characters is fun to read." She pointed to the second book. "This one is about betrayal of the worst kind and forgiveness. After reading these two books, I shouldn't have to answer any questions about what lesbians do in bed."

"Oh. Um...uh, thanks."

Seeing Stacy's apparent embarrassment, Jo put her arm around her and gave her a friendly squeeze. "Trust me here, we'll both be less embarrassed this way. Now, let's go get my bike."

With some effort they managed to get the bike up the stairs and into Stacy's apartment where they set up the bike and trainer in Stacy's office. "You try it first," Jo said. "I can't afford to break my good leg!"

"Geez, thanks a lot," Stacy said, giving Jo a playful smack on the arm. "Okay, I'll sacrifice my health and safety for the cause." With a quick smile, she got on the bike and began to pedal. "I'm glad my bedroom is at the other end of the apartment just in case the spirit moves you to exercise in the middle of the night. It's not as loud as a vacuum cleaner, but it's certainly noisier than the microwave. Luckily, I have no neighbors who will be disturbed by it. Come on, your turn."

In response to Stacy's offer to help to steady her as she climbed up on the bike, Jo responded, "Thanks. I think I can manage."

Jo grimaced as she made one complete rotation of the pedals. Stacy watched as the determined woman started to pedal. After less than a minute, she had to stop. Beads of perspiration dripped from her forehead more from the pain than from the exertion.

Stacy helped to steady Jo as she dismounted.

"Pathetic. I used to be able to ride for hours. Now I can't manage a minute."

"You'll improve. Here, let's keep track. That way you'll document your progress." Stacy pulled a tablet from the stack on her desk and handed it to Jo. "Now, ice or heat?"

"Well, heat feels better, although ice is probably better for me. It helps with the swelling."

"Lie down here and I'll get you some ice."

Stacy returned a few minutes later with a plastic bag filled with ice wrapped in a towel.

"Thanks." Jo accepted the ice Stacy offered and applied it to her leg. "It seems all I do is thank you. You've done so much to make me comfortable here. Certainly, I'll pay you for what you've spent for the chair and trainer."

"Nope. They are all part of the package." Stacy pulled out her desk chair and sat down. "After spending last night and most of the day today with you, I'm convinced that because of our deal I'll end up with the information I need for my book and maybe a good friend to boot."

Jo returned Stacy's smile "Yes, I'm sure that at least the latter is a given."

Chapter 8

THE FOLLOWING MORNING JO entered the kitchen where she found Stacy with her head buried in the novel she'd given her. "I love this book. I can see why you like it."

Jo leaned over her shoulder. "Let me see where you are. Hmm."

"Hmm, what?"

"Just hmm." Jo checked the temperature of the kettle. Pleased to find the water was still hot enough, she poured some into her cup and added a tea bag. "Got any questions for me this morning?"

Stacy didn't answer Jo's question, so tea in hand, she slid onto the stool at the counter opposite Stacy and sipped the warm liquid as she watched Stacy read. She repeated her question.

"Huh? Oh, let me just finish this chapter."

Jo reached over, took two tissues from the box at the end of the counter, and prepared to hand them to Stacy. She didn't have to wait long.

"Oh, no," she said looking up with tears brimming in her eyes. A large tear ran down her right cheek as she grabbed the tissues Jo offered. Stacy sniffed a few times and blotted her eyes. "Oh, that's not fair! They were so happy and perfect for each other."

"Not to worry, it's a romance. They all have a happy ending. The main character will eventually be happy, trust me." Jo promised.

"Don't you sometimes wish life could imitate art? Wouldn't it be great if we could all be guaranteed a happy ending?"

Jo propped her chin on her hand and studied Stacy. "What would be your happy ending if you were writing your story?"

"Interesting question. Wish I had an interesting answer for you."

"Okay, would you want, wealth, fame, children? What would make you happy? Let's say you were given three wishes. What would you wish for?"

Stacy closed the book and pushed it aside. She smiled. "No, not wealth or fame. They are fleeting. These are wishes just for me?"

Jo nodded.

"I guess I'd start with health. Without good health, not much else matters, does it?"

"Humph! You're preaching to the choir with that one," Jo grinned ruefully, and patted her injured leg.

"I guess I'd ask for happiness or at least contentment for my second wish."

"And the last one?"

Stacy sighed. "The last is the hardest, isn't it?" She ran her hand over her chin and around the back of her neck. "Can I wish for three more wishes?" Her voice was bright as she gave Jo a warm smile.

Jo laughed, as she shook her head, denying the request. "Sorry. Come on, play fair."

"Gee, I guess I would wish for true love. But I don't want any of that Romeo and Juliet kind of love. Nor do I want a lover who cheats. I want a romance that gives me joy. A reciprocal joy, because I like to give as well as to receive. For example, it made me happy to give you the trainer and to help you walk farther by having the chair available to you. Showing kindness to you made me feel good. Sometimes it would be nice to be in a relationship where I'd be on the receiving end. You know, give and take. I'd feel good both ways." Stacy waited for a reaction.

"Three good choices, for sure."

"What about you, Jo? What would you wish for?"

"Would you believe me if I said that I'd wish for the exact same things?"

"Why not?"

Jo shrugged. "I wouldn't want you to think I was dodging the question. But I do think your answer was perfect."

Stacy pointed to the book she was reading. "Can we talk about the book?"

Jo shook her head, denying the request. "Not until you finish it. You have a surprise or two coming. I wouldn't want to spoil it for you."

Stacy looked disappointed although she didn't argue her point. "Okay. So what's on the agenda for today? Do you have to work?"

"Yes. Today is the official opening of the store. I'll go help out for as long as they need me. I also would like to walk. If you're available, could you come with me? When you came with me, I went farther because we were chatting and I wasn't paying attention to my discomfort. We can go on your timeline. By the way, I already did a minute and thirty-five seconds on the bike."

Stacy was already deep into her reading.

"Oh Stacy? Did you hear me?"

"What?" Stacy reluctantly dragged her eyes up from the book she was reading. "No, sorry, I didn't."

Jo repeated what she'd said.

"Thirty-five seconds longer. Impressive."

Jo rolled her eyes. "Yeah, right. Not in my book." She checked Stacy for signs of insincerity. Finding none, she responded. "You're serious?"

"Sure, why wouldn't I be?" Stacy closed the book, holding her place with her finger. "I've watched you out the window for days. Every step you take causes you to wince. Still, you've walked a few feet more every day. I know how determined you are, and I respect that in you. I know you'll set your goals and will attain them. It's one of the many things I admire about you."

"How can you admire me? You don't even know me. We only met, what was it, um...two days ago?"

Stacy confirmed Jo's statement with a nod. "Yes, two days. Still, I think you'd be surprised what I know. I know you're honorable."

Jo met Stacy's eyes. "You think so? Based upon what?"

"Well, I know you think this whole idea is a stupid boondoggle. Still, once you agreed to it, you've certainly kept your end of the bargain. I also think that you are generally of good spirit. I mean, since you weren't wild about this whole idea of helping me do this in the first place, you could've been surly or only met your obligation to me with incomplete answers. Instead, I think you've been exceptionally forthcoming. You have loyal and caring friends, so I would assume you're a loyal and caring friend in return, although it's only an assumption. I can also say this because you put your life at risk to save the lives of your friends Meg and Mallory."

"Okay, enough. I stand corrected."

Stacy grinned, revealing her dimple. "Hey! Do you think I'd be welcome over there if I hang out with you today?" She gestured in the general direction of the shop across the street.

"Well, since this whole thing about me living here with you and you following me through my life was their idea, it would seem you'd have to be welcome. Don't you agree?"

"Gee, I'd hoped for a little more enthusiastic response on your part concerning my presence."

"Hey, I was only pulling your leg," Jo said contritely.

"I know, and I was tugging yours right back." Stacy marked her location in the book and put it aside. "I can be ready whenever you want to go."

Chapter 9

STACY AND JO WALKED across the street together. The store was just opening as they arrived. Already there were several local people waiting to check out the place. As they entered, the others greeted the visitors while Amanda came over to Stacy and Jo and hugged them both.

After a brief conversation, Jo noticed Nic waving to her to come over. She excused herself leaving Stacy to continue her conversation with Amanda.

"Stacy, so nice of you to join us."

"Thank you. I'm excited for all of you." Stacy glanced over at Jo. "I'm excited about my project, too. I hope to gather enough information in the next month and a half to be able to write the motive part of my story. Think you'd be willing to read and critique it for me?"

"Sure, I'd be happy to. Maybe we can help each other out. I'm almost finished the book I've been working on." Amanda glanced around. "It's a lesbian romance. Do you think you'd be comfortable doing a read through for me?"

"Jo just gave me a couple of her favorite author's books to read in that genre. I'm enjoying the first one of them now, so I'm sure I'd be equally comfortable reading yours."

Amanda plucked a business card from the container on the desk, flipped it over, and wrote on the back of it. "Here's my cell number. Call me when you're ready, and we'll set up a time to meet."

Stacy heard some laughter. Glancing around, she saw that Nic and Jo were speaking French to an older woman standing in front of the sign up sheet for the conversational French class.

Amanda took the opportunity to ask, "I know it's only been a couple of days, but I'm curious. How are you and Jo doing with your research project?"

"I'm very pleased with the arrangement so far. I'm honestly surprised at how open she is with me."

Amanda's face registered surprise. "Really? Our Jo? Open? I don't know anyone who would use that particular word to describe her."

Stacy smiled and told Amanda about buying the companion chair and trainer. "Jo has been using it and is progressing already. She works so hard. I've told her how proud I am of her."

"You seem to be capable of getting her to do things none of the rest of us would be able to do."

Stacy shrugged one shoulder. "She is very determined."

"Yes," Amanda said with a kind smile. "Determined can be one word that can definitely be used to describe Jo." Her eyes scanned the room coming to rest on Jo. Stacy's eyes followed the same path, finding the same target. "However, that same determination can also become stubbornness with very little apparent effort on her part. When that happens, and it will, don't push and try to force her. Coaxing works much better."

Sensing she was being watched, Jo looked up. When Jo's eyes met Stacy's, she flashed her a quick smile before she turned her attention back to her conversation.

"She's very attractive, especially when she grins that killer smile."

Amanda's eyes snapped back to Stacy's face to capture her expression. She didn't comment beyond a simple, "Yes, she is."

The opportunity for any further private discussion about Jo ended when Dana joined them. After greeting both women, Dana reported that the classes were growing. "I'm amazed at the number of people who have signed up already. We've had requests for tutoring as well, thanks to the coupon we offered. We'll need to focus on increasing demand for our translation services next."

"If you don't mind a suggestion," Stacy offered, "I just did a marketing survey a few months ago for this company I work for occasionally. Responses showed that a discount targeted to small or mid-sized companies via direct mailing was the most effective advertising tool. Of course direct contact can be very effective as well. That came in second in the survey."

"Thanks for the suggestions, Stacy. Dana, we should share this suggestion with the others."

"Absolutely." Dana nodded. "I'll make some calls to a couple of contacts I still have at some of the companies I used to freelance for. I agree with you that a personal touch never hurts."

Mallory beckoned to Amanda to join the conversation she was having with a woman and her son. Amanda excused herself, leaving Dana and Stacy alone.

Stacy followed Dana's gaze as she watched Nic, then her eyes returned to study Dana's expression, noting how it had softened as Dana focused on her lover. "Oh, sorry." Dana smiled. "I guess I'm still at that 'I can't believe she's mine' stage in our relationship. Although I feel like I've known her forever, it actually hasn't been that long."

Having concluded their business, a number of people departed, allowing Dana and Stacy a private moment.

"Really? How long has it been? Stacy asked.

"About six months. This being in love business is very new for me. I was alone for a long time before I met Nic. I think I'd probably given up hope of ever meeting 'Mr. Right,' and then Nic came into my life."

Stacy registered surprise. "*Mister* Right?"

"Oh, Jo didn't tell you? Get Nic to tell you about the first time she met Dana and Mallory. It's a funny story. To answer your question, yes, Mister Right. Historically, I've always dated men. I guess you'd have to classify me as a fallen or failed heterosexual at this point."

Respectful of the business environment, Stacy glanced around to be sure no one could overhear the conversation they were having. "So you don't identify as a lesbian despite being in love with a woman?"

"I'm still working on that," Dana replied, giving Stacy a quick smile. "I mean, obviously I guess I am. It's just that I've always perceived myself as straight before Nic. I still can't seem to wrap my mind around the fact that I'm not exactly who I thought I was. I suppose my brain hasn't progressed as quickly as my heart did."

"And you're not ever troubled by that?" Stacy watched as Dana carefully considered her question.

Dana's eyes quickly flicked back to her lover. "No, not at all. I know without a doubt that she is the one I'm meant to be with, so labels don't mean a thing to me."

"You're very lucky that you found the right person for you."

"I know," Dana replied softly. "I'm thankful every day."

* * *

Jo walked up behind Stacy. "I need to take a walk," Jo said softly into Stacy's ear. "Will you come with me?" Stacy nodded. "Dana, it's a good turnout for our first event, don't you think?"

Dana agreed. "Yes, actually much better than I'd even hoped for."

"I'm sorry. I need to stretch my leg. Can I steal Stacy away to go with me?"

"Sure, no problem. Stacy, I'm sure we'll talk again soon. I look forward to it."

"Me, too. Thanks, Dana."

Jo got the chair. Together, she and Stacy started down the street with Jo pushing the companion chair and Stacy walking next to her. They made small talk about the open house until they arrived at the bench. "Want to sit here awhile or go a little farther?"

"Let's shoot for the bench down there," Jo said, pointing to the bench on the next block. Jo's limp was more pronounced as they neared the next bench. "I think I'd better sit down before you have to pick me up again." Giving Stacy a quick grin, Jo sat in the chair, and Stacy pushed her the final fifty feet to their destination.

Stacy helped her raise the leg to rest it on the bench. Jo started to rub her thigh. Stacy said, "Here, let me." She gently began to stroke the knotted muscle. Jo closed her eyes as the tightness in her leg eased.

After a few minutes, Jo placed her hand on Stacy's to stop her. "Thanks. I'm good."

"I had an interesting conversation with Dana just now."

Jo smiled. "Really? Want to tell me about it?"

"Yes, actually, it puzzled me a bit. Dana told me that Nic is her first relationship with a woman, and that she's still not sure she's a lesbian. How can that be?"

"Sometimes it's hard for us to accept who we are. I think Dana surprised herself by falling in love with Nic. Apparently Dana had never really considered a relationship with another woman a possibility before Nic. A lot of us struggle with accepting that we're gay or lesbian. Some seem to accept it easily. There are others who struggle with it all their lives, even going so far as to try to get cured."

Stacy flinched, denying a concept she couldn't wrap her mind around. "Cured?"

"I'm sure you've heard the expression 'pray the gay away.' Sadly, there are actually gay people who are quite homophobic and even some who are self-loathing. Look at the suicide rate, especially for gay teens compared to heterosexual teens. It's much higher. Society teaches us that we're wrong, perverted, and deviant. Churches, not all, but many of them, disapprove of people like us. Until very recently, and still in the majority of the states, the government discriminates against us by not allowing us to marry. The tax code treats us extremely unfairly. Parents and friends disown us when we tell them about our same sex lover or preference. Why wouldn't it be a hard label to apply to oneself?"

Stacy shook her head as she processed all Jo revealed. "Hmm. I never thought about it that way before. It makes me feel sad." Stacy nonchalantly placed her hand on Jo's calf, an action that garnered Jo's attention instantly despite Stacy's apparent lack of awareness of the intimacy of her action. "Jo, you told me how your parents reacted when you told them you were gay. What about the others in your group?"

"I don't think anyone's parents would leap to their feet and do a happy dance," Jo said wryly. "You should ask Nic. Her mom came for Christmas, met Dana, and Nic came out to her mom. I wasn't there, so I don't know the details of what was said. She'd be a good person to talk to since her experience is recent. I think both Dana and Amanda's parents are gone. Amanda's family rejected her. They were still estranged from her when they died. Her brother hasn't spoken to her for years, ever since she came out."

Stacy's hand had wandered higher on Jo's leg. She was idly playing with the seam about mid-thigh on the leg of Jo's jeans and still completely oblivious to the effect it was having on Jo. "Tell me more about what your family said."

"I was one of the lucky ones. I was close to my dad and had an exceptionally open and honest relationship with my mom. I was always a tomboy. I filled the role of the son my father never had." Jo shrugged. "When I came home from college, I eventually told my mom about my tent sharing experience and the fact that I was a lesbian. I shared that I was concerned that my sexuality would impact my ability to be a cop. Mom's brother, who died in Vietnam, was gay, so she was already accepting. She warned me about what difficulties I might face and reassured me that she would always love me."

"I'm glad she was supportive. What about your sister?"

With a gesture of her hand, Jo indicated the impact was minimal. "By then my sister was already in college, so it had virtually no impact on her life. I think her comment was something like, 'Well, it sure took you long enough to figure it out.' I don't think I've ever really discussed it with my dad. He hugged me just as tightly after I told my mom as he did the day before I told her. The two of them never keep secrets, so I figured he knew. When I asked my mom about it on my next visit, she said that Dad still loved me. Then she advised me to not bring it up right away. In all honesty, he and I have never really talked about it. He seems to still love me as long as my sexuality is an invisible part of my life. Since I've never gotten serious about anyone long term, it's never been an issue. Like I told you, he's learned to be accepting of my friends and their relationships. It's probably different when it's your own kid. Lucky for him, it's not been a problem because I'm single."

There was a silence when Jo finished talking. Eventually Jo inquired, "What are you thinking about?"

"Nothing really." Then, as if remembering how forthcoming Jo was being with her, Stacy reconsidered. "No, that's not entirely true. I was wondering how my parents would react if I ever confessed something as important as that to them. I wonder if it's easier to tell your parents when you're younger, like you did, or to have to tell them later in life like Nic?"

"I don't think it's easy at any age. I have a friend who has never mentioned it to her parents although she has brought her lover of twelve years home every year for Christmas."

"Really? And they've never addressed the elephant in the room?"

Jo laughed. "Nope. Then I have two other friends, Peggy and Sue, who have been together since college. After ten years of living together as a couple, Peg finally got up enough courage to tell her sister she was a lesbian."

Jo paused for effect, causing Stacy to ask, "What happened?"

Chuckling, Jo revealed, "Her sister asked if Sue knew."

"Oh, no! Obviously more explanation was needed there."

"Yes, I'd say so. What do you say we head back?" Jo stood up and took the handles of the chair. "I think I can walk at least part of the way."

They made it nearly all the way back. When Jo started to limp, Stacy made her sit in the chair and pushed her the rest of the way to *Oui, Madame*. There seemed to be a lull in the festivities at the shop. All the visitors were gone, and the four friends were discussing the results of their grand opening so far.

"We got quite a few takers for our classes, enough for all three conversational classes, and several requests for tutoring. One request for a French tutor. Interested, Jo?"

"Sure. That would be great!" Jo rubbed her arms, working warmth back into them after her walk.

Amanda sighed. "I'm already tired, and we have another couple of hours to go. Anybody have enough energy to cook, or should we consider some alternative for dinner?"

Stacy made a suggestion. "Would you like to come over to my place? We could order Chinese. The place down the street has good food."

Everyone agreed that was a wonderful suggestion. They all met at Stacy's place at the end of the day. Dana was first in after Stacy opened the door. When she entered the landing and smelled the leather aroma, she turned to Nic and commented, "Umm, smell that! It makes me want to don chaps and a cowboy hat."

"If that's all you're planning to wear, I'll see if I can rustle some up," Nic replied with an obviously interested grin.

Stacy hurried up the stairs. She was glad no one would see her blushing. She heard Amanda say quietly, "Knock it off, you two. You'll embarrass our hostess."

Everyone removed their coats and handed them to Stacy who asked Jo to show everyone the apartment. "I'll stow these and then I'll find the menu."

With the group gathered in the kitchen after the tour, they huddled around the counter discussing what they wanted to eat. Once the menu was decided, Jo called and placed the order while Stacy set the table. Nic and Dana volunteered to go get the food. Stacy retrieved their jackets.

"We'll be back soon," Nic said, zipping her coat.

"You don't have to leave for like twenty minutes yet. The guy said the food won't be ready for half an hour," Jo countered.

"That's okay, we have to stop back across the street. Uh, I have to um, pick up my glasses," Nic said over her shoulder as Dana hurried her down the stairs.

When the door closed, everyone began to laugh except Stacy. "Did I miss something?"

"Not really." Amanda replied. "It's just that Nic is so honest, she's completely incapable of prevarication."

"Well then, what did she lie about?" Stacy looked from one face to another waiting for an explanation. Looking for an answer, she finally settled on Jo.

"Well, the amusing thing is that Nic doesn't wear glasses."

The peals of laughter started again. This time Stacy joined in the laughter.

Mallory sighed. "Hope everyone likes lukewarm Chinese food."

Amanda grinned mischievously. "Let's give them twenty five minutes, then call them and tell them to get a move on. If they are going to keep sneaking off for a quickie, they're going to have to learn to be quicker about it."

Forty-five minutes later, Nic and Dana showed up with the food. Mallory took the bags from them, then casually asked, "Did you get your 'um, uh, *glasses,*' Nic?"

Nic quickly looked to Dana for help. Dana went to her lover and put an arm around her waist. "You guys suck! They're just jealous, Honey. Pay them no mind."

Everyone laughed good naturedly at the teasing. Eventually even Nic joined in the laughter at her expense. Dinner conversation was lively with everyone taking turns telling of events of the day to illustrate how happy they were with the successful results of their open house.

Amanda gained everyone's attention. "Stacy made a good suggestion to Dana and me today. Since the coupon worked so well for the local community, she suggested we target small and mid-sized companies and offer to do their translating for them in exchange for a discount. Thanks, Stacy, it was a great suggestion."

Stacy acknowledged the compliment with a smile and a nod.

Amanda tipped her head, eyes twinkling. "I've been thinking about that idea ever since Stacy suggested it. Suppose we offer them a small discount of say five or ten percent below their current costs. To lessen the impact on our bottom line, in exchange for the discount we can offer them a contract for a specified amount of time, say maybe five percent for six months and ten percent for a year. Hopefully, they'll be so satisfied with our services that they'll keep us on at the end of their contract." Amanda looked around surveying reactions to the suggestion. "Let's see how they make out first. We have to balance getting enough work to keep us busy with not so much that we're swamped. We want to keep our turnaround time quick." When everyone nodded, Amanda said, "Good. Then we're all agreed on our plan?"

"Enough business. How about a change of subject?" Mallory glanced around the table at each of her friends. "Has anybody heard any good jokes lately?" When nobody responded, Mallory volunteered "No? Well, I'd love to credit whoever told the joke first, but it was emailed to me the other day with no reference to who authored the joke. I heard it a long time ago. I think it bears retelling. It's pretty funny." Encouraged by the chorus of 'let's hear it,' and 'tell it,'

Mallory proceeded. "All right, here goes. An old cowboy outfitted with a cowboy shirt, hat, jeans, spurs, and chaps, the whole nine yards, goes into a bar and orders a drink. As he sits there drinking his whiskey, a young woman sits down next to him. After she orders her drink, she turns to the cowboy, looks him up and down and says, 'Are you a real cowboy?' He tips his hat back and says, 'Well, I've spent my whole life on the ranch, herding cows, breaking horses, and mending fences, so I reckon I am.' He looks her up and down and says, 'What about you?'

She replies, 'I've never been on a ranch. I am a lesbian. I spend my whole day thinking about women. I get up in the morning thinking of women. While I work, when I eat, shower, or watch TV, I think about women. It doesn't matter what I do, everything makes me think of women.' They sit quietly for a while, and when she finishes up her drink, she leaves him sitting there. The cowboy orders another drink as a couple comes in and sits down next to him. They look him up and down and ask, 'Are you a real cowboy?' The cowboy looks them dead in the eyes and responds, 'I always thought I was, but I just found out that I'm a lesbian!'"

A burst of laughter from everyone at the table served to reward Mallory's efforts.

"Who wants coffee or tea?" Stacy asked after the laughter died down. Orders were placed for their beverages of choice. While Stacy got out the cups and made the drinks, Nic and Dana helped clear the table and stack the dishes. Jo came into the kitchen with the last of the remnants from dinner.

Jo slipped an arm around Nic's waist. "Hey, Nic, Stacy and I were talking today about coming out to our parents. I told her you came out to your mom over Christmas when she was here. Would you mind telling Stacy about it?"

Draping an arm idly across Jo's shoulder, Nic smiled in recollection. "Well, after she was here a few days, she was totally smitten with Dana, of course. Isn't everyone? The fact that Dana speaks Italian surely didn't hurt. Anyway, I didn't have to tell her. She told me. She cornered me in the kitchen one morning. 'Nicolina,' she said, 'I hate being without your father, so I know being alone is no good. Vivere da soli è molto triste. I have prayed you wouldn't know the same loneliness. I'm happy you have found Dana.' Then she hugged me and that was it. I do suspect that Mallory's mother may have had a hand in there somewhere, although she denies it. Then again, there's always that wink she gave me both times I asked her." Nic gave Jo's shoulder a squeeze. "I'm a lucky woman, don't you think?"

With the kitchen sorted, the three rejoined the group. The coffee and tea was poured and they drank their beverages, conversation waned as everyone was tired. "Stacy," Dana said, standing up to carry her cup to the kitchen. "I hate to break up the party. I've got some work I have to finish up before tomorrow morning. It was nice of you to invite us all over. Thank you."

The rest of the group agreed that it was time for them to go as well. Within five minutes, everyone had hugged and kissed both Stacy and Jo good-bye and disappeared down the stairs. Stacy locked up and joined Jo back upstairs. Jo was standing at the kitchen sink washing down two ibuprofen tablets with a large glass of water.

"Got a lot of pain in your leg?"

Jo shrugged. "Just a bit," she admitted. "I've been on it all day, and just now I think I sat too long."

"Will rubbing it help? I can massage it. Didn't you say that Mallory used to massage it for you?"

Jo was torn. On one hand, she recalled her reaction, or perhaps her response would be a better term to use, to the slow relaxing kneading Stacy had done as they sat resting during their walk. Another issue was her scar. Of her friends, only Mallory had seen the ugly wound the bullet and the surgery had left. Still, she knew that she'd have a much better night's sleep if her muscles were relaxed before she turned in for the night. "Yeah, I did. But she's a nurse."

"If it'll help, I could wear white." The dimple flashed and did its job, eliciting a chuckle from Jo.

"Okay, thanks. I'd appreciate it. The massage, I mean, not the other," Jo said blushing.

"Come on, your room."

Jo preceded Stacy down the hallway. Stacy made a short detour into the bathroom. When Stacy joined Jo in the bedroom, she had a bottle of lotion in her hand. Jo stood in the center of the room motionless.

"So, take your jeans off," Stacy demanded.

"Why? That's not necessary. You can massage me like you did this afternoon through my jeans."

"No way. I about rubbed all the skin off my hands. Drop 'em."

There is that annoying dimple again. Jo envisioned placing her lips there and teasing the depression with her tongue.

"Have you forgotten how to work a snap and zipper?" Stacy gestured in their direction. Impatient for Jo to remove her jeans so they could begin.

Resorting to a different tactic, Jo said, "For a straight girl, you seem pretty eager to get my pants off of me."

Stacy tipped her head slightly to the side and smirked. "No, that's not going to work, either. Come on, be a big girl, and take your medicine. Look, I'm modest, but you're being ridiculous."

"I'm not modest. It's just, ah what the hell." She unzipped her pants and stepped out of them, quickly searching Stacy's face for her reaction. Instead of the look of revulsion she expected, all she found there was concern and caring.

"I'm glad we're doing this tonight. Tomorrow, if I have to massage your leg on our walk, I'll know better where to touch you. Here, put this towel on the bed and get in."

Stacy's matter of fact attitude and kindness encouraged Jo to comply with her instructions.

"Move over a bit." Stacy sat on the edge of the bed, squeezed some lotion into her palm, and waited for it to warm in her hand. As she began the massage, her touch was gentle. "Show me where it's most tender and where it hurts the most."

Jo pointed to the most sensitive area. "This is still pretty tender here. My whole thigh seems to knot up." She pointed. "Especially here."

"Okay, I've got it. Just relax as best you can, and I'll see if I can make you feel better." Stacy began to massage, gently rubbing her fingers up Jo's thigh until she felt a knot, which she would knead until it relaxed. Stacy was pleased to notice that once every knotted muscle had been ministered to, the frown line between Jo's brows relaxed and her eyes closed. She added additional lotion to her palm and started on the other thigh.

Jo's eyelids snapped open. "What are you doing?"

"Working on your good leg? You probably don't realize that you abuse this one when you favor the other one. Please don't give me a hard time. Can't you just accept a gift gracefully and say thank you?"

A look of sadness flashed across Jo's face. "No. That's generally pretty hard for me to do." Jo lightened the tension with a grin. "But for you I'll make an exception because that feels so good."

Stacy finished massaging Jo's thigh. "Want your calves done?"

"No. Although I appreciate the offer, you must be tired by now. I think I'll be able to get a few good hours tonight, thanks to you."

Stacy stood up. Before she turned to leave, she brushed Jo's hair back from her forehead and then cupped her cheek with her palm. "I'm thankful you allowed me to give that to you. Now, sleep well." For some inexplicable reason, she didn't want to leave Jo. She forced herself to pull her hand away and went down the hall to her own room.

Chapter 10

JO OPENED HER EYES but didn't move. Stacy was at the computer. Jo took the opportunity to study her. *Cute. Her eyes and that damned dimple are her best features.* She went through the rest—nice body, petite but not skinny, full breasts, wavy honey brown hair cut short and nicely styled. Stacy had a way of running her fingers through her hair that made Jo want to replicate the action with her own fingers. She imagined the feel, the touch of what she was sure were soft and silky strands, magically falling back into place as they did for Stacy. She knew that if Stacy turned around, there would be a flash of pale green eyes, much lighter than her own, a pure shade similar in color to that collectable depression glass.

If I had a checklist of every physical characteristic that appeals to me, Stacy would achieve a perfect score. Jo knew she was not only attracted by Stacy's physical attributes. She found Stacy's personality appealing, as well. A good sense of humor, an inquisitive and intelligent mind, quick wit, and an easy-going manner all added to her charm. She wasn't a pushover, though. Jo recalled that Stacy had stood her ground and had gotten her way last night about the massage without being aggressive or demanding. Stacy also had her using a companion chair, something that Mallory had encouraged previously, but Jo had steadfastly and stubbornly resisted. *How had that happened? Remember rule number two,* she reminded herself, *no straight women.* Jo shifted in bed. Turning on her side, she propped her head on her hand.

Jo's movement caused Stacy to turn around. "Good morning, sleepyhead. I was worried I'd wake you. I've been here for forty five minutes and you haven't budged, so I guess I didn't disturb you."

"I admit that I slept like the dead last night. I got up to use the bathroom around five, figuring that would be it. But my leg still felt okay, so I climbed back into bed and, amazingly, I fell back asleep."

Stacy stood up and grabbed the lotion on her way over to Jo's bed. She grabbed the sheet and said, "May I?"

"What?"

"We had good success with the massage last night. Let's see if we can achieve the same benefits for some or all of the day today. Please tell me that you aren't going to be a pain in my neck and argue with me every time I offer to do this for you." Stacy gave a little tug to the sheet.

"Wait, I don't have anything on but my briefs."

"So what? It's nothing I haven't seen before." A brief scan of the room showed a pile of Jo's clothes neatly folded on the rocking chair at the foot of the bed. She grabbed the shirt from the top of the pile. "Here, we can use this to rescue your modesty. Now, turn over, face down. This morning I want to work on your calves, too."

If Stacy had not achieved such great results last night, Jo might have resisted more enthusiastically. She hadn't felt this good since before the shooting, so she shut up and did as she was directed.

She felt the sheet get pulled back followed immediately by the T-shirt being spread to cover her. A few seconds later, Stacy's caring fingers began their magic. She followed the same routine as she had the night before, doing a survey of the area with her sensitive fingers, locating the tender spots before working specifically to loosen the knots she found.

Stacy finished with Jo's calves and began working on the injured thigh. "This is much less knotted today. There's definitely some improvement."

"Yes, I agree. Even before you started to massage it, my leg felt much better than it normally does in the mornings. It's amazing how much better it feels now."

Stacy sat on the edge of the bed. She expected a fuss when she began to massage Jo's shoulders. "Your shoulders are tight from using the cane."

"Umm, that's nice. Where did you learn to do massage like this?"

"When I was in high school, a little boy in my neighborhood had CP. The family asked for volunteers to help massage him and exercise his joints. I volunteered, and the massage therapist trained a few of us. It was a great experience for me. I learned a lot about patience and fortitude in the face of adversity from that little boy. I've never met anyone before or since with such an upbeat attitude as he had when, in reality, he had very little to be so positive about.

"What happened to him?"

"He graduated from college and works with the CP foundation. I get a Christmas card from him every year with just three words on it, thank you and his name."

Finished with the massage, Stacy started a light scratching that alternated between her fingertips and her nails, covering the entirety of Jo's back. Jo actually moaned in pleasure.

"That feels wonderful. I can't remember the last time anyone scratched my back. I probably shouldn't admit this, but it's been my experience in the past that whenever I'm naked with someone, they're generally more interested in my other side."

Stacy pinched Jo's behind.

"Ouch! What was that for?"

"General principle." Stacy stood up." Now come on and get dressed. I'll get breakfast ready. Is cereal with fruit okay, or would you prefer a bagel?"

"Cereal and tea works for me. Do I have time to run through the shower?"

"Sure, no problem. I'll see you in the kitchen."

"Stacy?"

"Yes?"

"Thank you."

"You are most welcome. Now, get a move on, I'm hungry."

Less than twenty minutes later, Jo presented herself for breakfast. Although she still favored the bad leg, her stride was more secure and steady. "I can't thank you enough for the massage. What can I do for you in return? I'll buy you lunch, give you my first born—anything your heart desires."

"Well, although lunch is a tempting offer, you'll be bankrupt if you buy me lunch every time I rub your leg for you. Although the offer of your first-born is tempting, I think I'll hold you to the 'anything my heart desires' promise. Someday when you least expect it, I'll call in that marker."

"Okay, that's a fair deal. I give you my word I'll do anything you ask, whenever you ask it."

The two women readied their breakfast. Jo poured cereal into a bowl for each of them while Stacy sliced the bananas and added them. By the time she was finished, Jo had the milk in hand ready to pour.

Stacy touched Jo's shoulder. "Please, wait 'til I pour the tea. I hate my cereal to get soggy."

Once everything was ready, the two women sat across from each other at the counter and began to eat. "So," Jo asked, "no questions this morning?"

"Actually, I have a number of them. Ready?"

"Really?"

"Yes. I was trying to look this up on the Internet this morning. I'm kind of puzzled. I hope I won't be offensive in asking this."

"Offensive, to me?"

"No, just generally offensive." Stacy smiled, revealing her dimple.

Jo placed her chin on her palm and fixed her eyes on Stacy, bracing for the worst. "I'm ready. Shoot."

"Uh, I'm curious. I mean, if I met any one of your friends individually, I don't think that I would think to myself, 'Yup, she's a lesbian.' I mean, they all wear makeup, dress beautifully, and seem very feminine. Even Nic, who I originally mistook for a man from the back at a distance, is really quite feminine in an androgynous sort of way. When I was growing up, in my mind, the word lesbian always conjured up a woman who dressed in men's clothing, flannel shirts, had a crew cut, and assumed the demeanor of a man. Then, when Ellen came out on television, I realized that stereotype wasn't true. I mean Ellen wasn't like that. She was a bit tomboyish, yet still feminine. Now she's doing makeup commercials and is even softer appearing. But your friends just seem like..." Stacy hesitated searching for a way to phrase her thought. "I don't know, like regular women I guess."

"And you know why? That's what they are. They're regular women who happen to be lesbians. Don't get hung up on labels. There are many of them—butch, femme, lipstick lesbian, blue jean lesbian, androgynous, and soft butch. The list goes on and on."

"What's the difference between a femme and a lipstick lesbian?"

Jo inhaled a deep breath, expelling it slowly. "Well, femme used to refer to a woman who was more feminine and who preferred to sleep with women who portrayed a more masculine demeanor, probably what would be referred to as butch. Lipstick lesbian is, I guess, a more current term originally coined to refer to a feminine woman who preferred to sleep with another feminine women. Today, I think those two terms have intermingled and are pretty much used interchangeably." Jo chuckled. "You're really testing me here. I don't usually keep up on all the terminology. I'm not really into labels, myself." She shrugged. "Over the past years I've met some pretty masculine looking women who, when I've gotten to know them, are actually more femme than I'd expect from their appearance. Despite appearances, some actually think of themselves as femmes."

Stacy absorbed the information "So, it's not important to you if a woman is more feminine or masculine? How would you classify yourself and the others?"

"Wow! Tough questions this morning. Let me finish my cereal." Jo ate the last few spoonsful of her cereal and took a sip of her tea. "There, that's better. Ok, let's see. My tastes and our group..." Jo exhaled. "Personally, I'm not particularly attracted to butch women. Mostly I seem to be drawn to women shorter than me and maybe a bit softer. As to how I'd classify my friends. Gee, I never thought about it. What would you think?"

Stacy thought a moment. "Hmm, I'm not sure. Dana is definitely very feminine. At first glance, Nic is more androgynous looking, although, as you get to know her, she's really much softer than I assumed she'd be when I first met her. Mallory is feminine but more umm, I think I'd say athletic, like you. You and she give a stronger presentation than say Dana or Amanda, although neither of you is masculine looking or acting."

Jo chuckled. "Good descriptions of each. Again, they were descriptions, not labels. That's a good thing, I think. I don't really like labels, because those we apply may not be how someone actually is or, more importantly, how someone really self identifies. I've never thought to myself that I'm looking for a soft butch or a femme or a sporty dyke, or a whatever. I seem to like a specific type of woman, much like you'd probably be attracted to a particular type of man.

"I don't seem to be meeting any men I find I'm interested in becoming involved with at this point in time." She displayed her dimple for Jo's enjoyment. "Anyway, you never answered my question."

Jo arched an eyebrow. "You mean about the type of woman I'm attracted to?"

Stacy nodded.

Jo thought back to her encounter with Meg and how, although she liked Meg personally, she wasn't attracted to her physically mostly because of her height and maybe she came off less feminine than what she preferred. "Well, I don't really have a type per se. I seem to be attracted to women who are shorter than I am and who have curves. I'm generally not drawn to thin, bony women. Hair and eye color are not that important. They don't have to be beautiful. I tend to be attracted more by their personality. My first girlfriend was really rather plain. She had a beautiful smile and a sexy mouth." She smiled at the memory and then frowned when she recalled how it ended.

Stacy looked into her teacup, finding it empty. "More tea?"

"Please."

As Stacy filled the kettle, she asked, "Have you had a lot of girlfriends?"

Jo smiled playfully. "Define a lot."

"Um, more than five and less than ten."

"Define girlfriend," Jo grinned.

"Humph! Let's limit it to women with whom you had what you would consider a relationship of more than one night in duration."

They both laughed.

Jo sobered and turned serious. "I won't deny that I've had more than one or two one night stands in my time. Most were when I was younger. That's not really my style. Like I told you, I tend to find sex more pleasurable with someone I care about. The other can sometimes meet the need. Not for sex specifically, just that need for physical closeness. You know, the need to be held and touched that sometimes, I don't know, that just helps stave off loneliness I guess. As a policewoman, upon occasion, I've felt the need to connect with someone to help erase something distasteful I've seen. For me, sex is as much emotional as physical. It's not the actual sex act itself, it's more the physical need to touch and be touched, to connect that I want. Unfortunately, it's not what you get in a quick grab and tussle, is it?"

There was a lull. Jo marveled at what she'd just revealed to Stacy. Their conversations seemed to always come to a level of shared intimacies. "I know I haven't exactly answered your question about how many meaningful relationships I've had. I promise I will. Before I do that, will you answer a question for me? Have you ever felt that way?"

"You mean lonely? The need to connect?"

"Yes, I'm curious if it's a universal need or just a product of my being a cop."

"Sure, I've felt it." Stacy hesitated as she organized her feelings into a coherent sentence. "I think to be loved, cherished, comforted, and paired is basic human need we all have. I'm not sure, maybe it's because I've just never dated the right guy. I've always felt like a sexual relationship with a man is a negotiation, more like a barter than a true sharing. I give him sex, and he gives me physical affection in exchange." Stacy smiled ruefully. "So far, that's never been exactly what I need. Unfortunately, they seem to only want to give affection to the parts they like to play with." She cupped her breasts, and with a giggle she said, "Like here and the other obvious place."

"Yes, I understand your feelings. I guess things are more alike for us than might be apparent on the surface. We seem to want the same things."

The kettle whistled and Stacy filled their cups with hot water.

Jo smiled. "And to answer your question, two."

Stacy frowned. "Two what?"

"Two meaningful relationships of more than one night duration."

"Will you tell me about them?" Stacy, tea in hand, returned to the counter and slid Jo's cup towards her.

"More research?

"No." Stacy shook her head in denial. Softly she said, "No. I'd just like to know, for me."

Jo nodded, taking in a deep breath then exhaled it forcefully. "Okay, I fell in love in college. Mary. We went into the Academy together. I thought we'd be together forever."

"What happened?"

"Carlotta happened. Mary left me for someone else who didn't believe in the sanctity of a relationship. I swore to myself I would never do that to another human being. Then and there I created the first of the two rules I live by. Rule number one, be true to the person you love, and never become involved with someone who is already in a relationship." Jo took a long sip of her tea.

"My second relationship was with a woman named Jessica. I met Jess through some friends. I thought she was exactly what the doctor ordered. She was perfect." Jo's eyes traveled over Stacy's body. "Built much like you, she had a perky personality, made me laugh, and in bed we were amazing."

"She sounds perfect. Were you together a long time?"

"Yes, I thought Jessie was pretty perfect myself for the first six months. Then she slept with Marlon. She told me that what we had was nice. Unfortunately, she wanted to have kids and the acceptance of her family and friends. Neither of which I could offer her. Hence rule number two—never, never, never get involved with a straight woman."

"Why? Because one woman dumped you? I can see and understand rule number one. This one doesn't make sense to me."

Stacy ran her fingers through her hair, a habit Jo had come to enjoy. "I mean, Jessie could just as easily have left you for another woman, no?"

"I suppose. It seemed she really struggled with accepting herself as a lesbian. She got a lot of criticism from her friends for being involved with me. It's just easier if all that's over with and someone has settled in and accepted that she'll never want to sleep with another man."

"Or woman for that matter." Stacy sought Jo's eyes. "Correct me if I'm wrong, Jo. I imagine there are some lesbians who have never slept with a man. Still, there have to be a number of them who started out their lives thinking they were heterosexual. What would someone have to do to prove to you that she's a lesbian? Would she have slept with only women for a set amount of time, or never have slept with a man before? No wonder you don't have a girlfriend, you're limiting an already limited pool of people to a small percentage of the base."

"Yes, that may be true. However, I feel that it's worked for me so far." Jo stood, preparing to wash her cup.

"Has it? Really?" Stacy stood and joined Jo at the sink. "Jo, I appreciate that you're so honest with me and talk to me like a friend. I'm going to do the same with you because in just this short amount of time we've shared together, I've grown to really like you a lot. You're a wonderful person. However, please allow me this observation. You resist too much. You resisted your friends' efforts to help you when you refused a wheelchair. You resisted me when I wanted to do a massage for you. You resist being open to a whole subgroup of women who might have something to offer you because of an emotional insult you suffered in the past. You seem to want to consistently deny yourself what you need most. Why?"

"For someone who hardly knows me, you've jumped to some amazing conclusions."

"Have I?" Then more quietly, "Have I really, Jo?"

Jo was silent for a while, letting Stacy's words sink in. "Okay. I'll concede that I can be stubborn sometimes. But..."

Stacy turned and wrapped Jo in her arms, hugging her close. At first, Jo just stood there. After a moment's hesitation, she eventually accepted the embrace and offered her own in return.

"Yes. There you are, stubborn but lovable." Stacy gave Jo a squeeze before she released her from the hug and resumed her seat across from Jo at the counter.

Chapter 11

STACY AND JO FOLLOWED a similar pattern as their time together passed. Long talks during the day, massages at least morning and night, walks, and biking on the trainer daily. Jo's leg was feeling much better, and she had cut back substantially on her pain meds.

"What's on your agenda for today, Stacy?" Jo asked as they shared breakfast.

"I have a couple of hours of work to do. I'm tallying the results I've gotten back from a survey I'm taking. You can help if you have nothing better to do."

"I need to stop in across the street to find out about the class they want me to teach...you know, like how many people, what their levels are, what they want me to teach. Then I'll need to come up with some games and activities for my class." Jo paused to take the last bite of her bagel. "I think I'll start with vocabulary building exercises and then work on some games so people can practice the words they've learned. I figure that'll depend on the ability level of the people in the class and what needs they have. I've never taught before. I think I'm starting to be nervous."

"You'll do fine. I'll help any way I can," Stacy promised.

"Thanks." Jo stood up. "Feel like a walk?"

"You mean now? Sure. I think, if I have time after our walk this morning, I'd like to read some more of that book you gave me."

"Okay, how about this. First, we walk. I'll go see Nic while you read your book, then I'll come back and help you out with your survey."

"That works. When you go to the office, will you say hello to Nic for me? I've come to like her very much. She's easy to talk to, and I feel that she always gives an open and honest answer or opinion in response to whatever she's asked."

"I agree. She's very easy to like." Jo stood to rinse her dishes and put them in the dishwasher. She asked, "So, do you agree to my plan for the day?"

"Sounds like a good plan," Stacy said with a smile. "I'll run out and pick up some food for lunch and some other things we need. Why not invite Nic back with you for lunch?"

Before Jo could respond, her cell rang. She took the call while Stacy finished stacking the remaining breakfast dishes in the dishwasher, and put the butter and jams into the fridge.

"Hold on a minute, will you?" Jo covered the mouthpiece. "This is my friend Meg. You know, the one who got hurt the night I got shot? She wanted to know if we could get together for lunch. Would it be okay with you if I invited her over? I'd like to see her and thought you might enjoy meeting her."

"Sure, the more the merrier."

Jo finished up her call, and she and Stacy dressed to go out for their walk. They paused in front of the apartment. "Jo, you get started. I'll get the chair and catch up to you." Stacy ran across the street to get the companion chair while Jo started up the block. Although Stacy had no problem catching up with her, she noticed that Jo had already gone half a block and was not limping yet.

They walked the same distance they had the day before, but Jo didn't need a massage when they sat on the bench. It was much colder than it had been the day before, so they didn't linger there any longer than it took Jo to gather her strength for the return trip. "Feeling up to making the return trip?" Jo asked, "Ready to go back?"

"Sure, if you are. It's too chilly to sit here too long today."

They stopped in front of the shop. Stacy touched Jo on the arm. "We need some things from the store. Want me to wait until you finish talking to Nic?"

"No, I've had enough walking for now." Jo grinned. "If you don't mind going without me, I'll meet with Nic, and when we're finished, we'll see you at home. We won't be long."

"Okay. See you later." Stacy smiled and gave Jo a quick wave as she headed off down the street bound for the store. Upon returning home, Stacy prepared lunch and read as she waited for her guests to show up.

Nic and Jo arrived first. Nic greeted Stacy with a warm hug. "Thanks for inviting me over for lunch. It's nice to get a break in the middle of the day to be with friends."

It made Stacy happy that Nic considered her a friend. When the doorbell rang, Jo went to the top of the stairs to call down at Meg to come in.

While Jo was waiting for Meg, Stacy asked Nic, "Did you and Jo finish up your discussion about the class?"

"Yes. Jo has some good ideas already, and I think once she stops thinking it to death and gets involved in the teaching, she'll lose the nervousness. She'll be fine. She has an easy way with people."

Jo and Meg joined the other two in the living room. Jo introduced Meg to Stacy before they all migrated to the kitchen for lunch. They talked about a variety of topics including the weather, Meg's recent injury, and Jo's progress with her walks.

With Jo's encouragement, Nic told the story of her first meeting with Mallory and Amanda.

"Dana had sent them an email saying 'Nic will be coming. Expect a tall, dark Italian. Please let Nic into my house and take care of things until I arrive a few days later.' Since Dana had never dated a woman before and it seems she'd never referred to me using a pronoun, always by name, they were expecting some tall, dark Italian *man* to show up but not for a few days yet. I got there ahead of schedule. The day I appeared at the door they were expecting a furniture delivery. I showed up, and they thought I was delivering the chair they'd ordered. So it was one of those 'who's on first moments!' It took them several minutes to finally figure out that I was the tall, dark Italian that Dana was dating. Mouths were certainly hanging open that day. When the guy who was actually delivering the chair arrived, we were all laughing hysterically. He thought we were all nuts and didn't hesitate to tell us so. I have to admit that for the first few minutes after I met them, I would have agreed with him." Her laugher, a low-pitched melodic sound, blended with the others expressing enjoyment of her telling the story.

The meal went well. Everyone took turns contributing to the conversation until they finished eating. With the meal concluded, Meg asked Jo if they could speak privately.

"Jo, use the office," Stacy offered. "I'll chat with Nic and finish up here."

* * *

Meg and Jo went down the hallway and into the office. "So how are you feeling?" Jo asked.

"Much better now, thanks. You saved our lives I hear."

"Well, I'm sorry I didn't get him before he hurt you."

"How's the leg?"

"It's doing okay. It's better than it was for sure. Stacy massages it for me every day. She does a massage technique that she learned back when she was in high school helping a kid with CP. It's worked a miracle for me. When she does the massage before bedtime, I can actually sleep through the night and, after the morning massage, I'm reasonably comfortable during the day."

"So what's the story? She's your massage therapist? And why are you living here with her?"

Jo chuckled. "No, she's an author."

"So, what's the story? You're dating her?"

Jo shook her head. "No, she's straight. It's a weird story. I can't believe I got hooked into doing it. Regardless, I'm actually having a good time with her." Jo related what she was doing for Stacy. "So that's the story."

"You're right. I can't believe you're doing this." Meg shifted in the chair, seeming ill at ease. "Jo, I have a question to ask you. You know I lost most of my memories for the week before the incident. I've been getting things back little by little. I don't remember much about the day it happened. I do remember most things, I guess, before that. Can you fill in the blanks? Like, why we were at the hospital?"

"You don't remember anything about that day at all?" Meg looked down and Jo noticed that her face had colored. *Uh oh, I had hoped I wouldn't ever have to address this with her again.*

Meg sighed and looked up to meet Jo's eyes. "I have these flashes of things that may or may not have happened. Will you tell me the truth? Did we make love, or is it wishful thinking on my part?"

Jo really didn't want to have to hurt Meg a second time over the same rejection, but she was left with no choice. "We did. But, in the end, we agreed it was a mistake."

"I agreed that it was a mistake as well? I find that hard to believe. I've been in love with you for months. I remember I couldn't wait for you to come home. I think I planned to tell you how I was feeling."

"Yes, you told me that." Jo described, as gently as she could, the events of that day. "So, we agreed we'd stop by the hospital and then have a quick dinner. I can't say you were overjoyed about my telling you I just wanted us to stay friends and not pursue anything beyond that. You accepted it, and we were moving forward as friends."

Meg's eyes filled with tears. "So we made love and then you told me you didn't want me. I guess the sex wasn't that great, huh?"

"Meg, don't do this. Please. The sex was fine. I do care for you, very much. I love you, but as a friend only. Think about it. We're good friends, we catch a game together now and again, we bowl, and play cards. We've never shared anything more than casual conversation. I need more than what we share to base a relationship on. I'm sorry."

"Okay. I guess I'll see you around then." She abruptly stood to leave, obviously still hurting and visibly angry.

"Meg, please don't leave like this."

"Jo, I can't stay. I think I need some time." She strode down the hallway.

* * *

While Jo and Meg were in the office talking, Nic asked Stacy how things were going with her project.

"Pretty good, I think. I've learned a lot of general information from Jo along with some specifics that I might be able to use in my book. I'm still considering whether the blackmail angle that I happened upon will work well in the book."

"So, Jo is being helpful to you?" Nic stretched out her long legs, relaxing into the conversation with Stacy.

"Yes, very. The bonus is that I think we're actually becoming good friends. Jo's very comfortable to be around, and we seem to be pretty compatible." Stacy grinned. "I think she thought the whole scheme was hair brained at first. I get the feeling she's actually not minding it now."

"You've been very nice to walk with her and to get her the chair. It gives her the confidence to go farther."

Since they were making small talk, Stacy thought she'd ask Nic a question she was curious about. "Can I ask you something?"

"Sure, anything."

"Well, this morning Jo and I were talking, and she mentioned these rules she lives by."

"Ah yes." Nic exhaled a long sigh. "The infamous rule number one and rule number two."

Stacy smiled and leaned forward, resting her weight on her elbows. "Yes. Right. Everyone, I'm sure, would agree that rule number one is admirable. We'd all be better off if everyone followed that rule, wouldn't we?"

Nic nodded her agreement.

"I'm curious about her rule number two, though. Apparently that's not a rule that all lesbians live by. Obviously, you didn't follow it if you were Dana's first and only relationship with a woman. Why do you think Jo is so adamant about that rule? I know she was burned once. It just doesn't make sense to assume that would ever happen a second time, does it? I mean her rule just isn't logical."

Nic tugged at her left ear as she decided how to respond to Stacy. "I'm not sure I know how to answer that. Some lesbians won't have sex with straight women at all. Other lesbians like to bring women out and only want sex with straight women. Some won't date a bisexual woman, and still others will have a relationship with any woman with a pulse. You'll have to ask Dana how she felt. For me, plain and simple, I just fell in love. I suspect the same happened to Dana, before we could think about if it was right or wrong, if she was straight or lesbian. We each just wanted to be together, and that was all that mattered to us. I'm not sure Dana has decided yet if she's a lesbian or just in love with me."

"Does that bother you?"

"No, not as long as she continues to love me. I don't care how she identifies."

"Thanks, Nic. I'm thinking that my character in my book might have had a first time relationship with another woman and for some reason, she ended it. I'm trying to figure out if blackmail is the best angle to use or to just have the conflict be because she maybe decided to go back to her boyfriend. You know, like maybe the ex-girlfriend killed her because she went back to her old boyfriend."

Nic's eyebrow arched. "Maybe the boyfriend killed her because she left him for a woman. Why make the lesbian the heavy like everyone else does?"

"Good point. That would be another angle I can use. You know, to add to the suspense. Thanks, Nic. I'll think about that."

Stacy and Nic's conversation stopped when Meg came out of the office and strode down the hallway. Not looking very happy, Meg stopped long enough to thank Stacy for lunch and say goodbye. It seemed like Meg couldn't wait to get out of there. Her ire was evident in the look on her face and her abrupt manner.

"Wonder what that's all about?" Nic said. She didn't wait to ask. After checking her watch, she said, "Oh, I'm sorry, Stacy. I have to get back to the office, so I'd better be going as well. Will you tell Jo that I said goodbye? I don't want to be late. Thanks for lunch." She leaned down and gave Stacy a warm hug.

"Thanks, Nic. You gave me a something to think about for the book. I may explore your angle instead of what I was originally thinking. It could be more interesting in the end."

Nic put on her coat. "Will I see you two later?"

"No, I don't think so. Jo offered to help me with my survey. Maybe tomorrow."

"Ok, I'll see you then. Thanks again for lunch. I really enjoyed it."

* * *

Stacy gave Jo some privacy for another half hour. As time ticked by, she needed to get started on her survey. She made her way down the hallway and knocked on the open door. "Hey, Jo, may I come in?"

"Sure." Jo was lying on the bed.

"Is everything okay?"

"It will be."

"Want to talk about it?" Stacy crossed the room and stood next to her desk, facing Jo.

"Is it part of the deal?"

"No, I just thought you looked upset and so did Meg when she left. It's really none of my business. I was just trying to be a friend." Stacy turned to leave.

"Wait, I promised I'd help you with your survey. Want to get started?"

"Are you up to it?"

"Sure, I'm fine."

Stacy pulled out the folders containing the surveys she'd printed out earlier. She explained the process she needed to follow. "So, if you can just use this form to tally the responses from questions one to ten, I can devote the time I need to read the written responses and make some sense of them."

"Okay. Let's do it." Jo said rubbing her hands together.

"Feel like catching a movie later?"

"Let's just see if we get all the work done that you have to do first, then we can talk about it." Jo smiled. "It can be our reward."

They worked together in silence for an hour and a half before Jo stood up and stretched. "I'm done," she announced.

"Already? Great!"

"I need to walk around a bit and shake some of the kinks out of my leg." Jo rubbed her stiff leg.

"You want to go outside?"

"No. It looks too cold. Want some tea?"

"Sure. You mind making it while I wrap up here?"

"No problem. I can exercise my leg a bit while I wait for the water to boil. Do you have much more to do?"

"No, I'm almost finished. Maybe another ten or fifteen minutes."

Jo checked the time. "Want to catch the five o'clock movie? *The Tourist* is playing. I'd like to see it because Angelina Jolie is in it. I assume you wouldn't mind seeing Johnny Depp."

Stacy noticed that Jo's normal good humor had returned. She wondered what had happened between her and Meg. Instead of asking, she responded, "No. I'd much rather watch her. I loved her movie *Salt* as well as her Laura Croft movies."

"That's odd. I thought all straight women loved Johnny Depp."

"Now who's being stereotypical?"

Jo laughed. "You're right." She turned and limped down the hallway to make the tea.

Ten minutes later, they were sitting at the kitchen counter drinking the warm liquid. Stacy made an effort to try to find out what happened between Meg and Jo. "Meg seems nice. You know you can have your friends over any time you want."

"Thanks. You're dying to ask me about what happened, aren't you?"

Stacy's dimple appeared as she grinned and hung her head in mock embarrassment.

"Okay, here's the ugly truth. She's been a friend and I like her very much. I'm not sure she'll be back. She was a little upset when she left. It seems she got most of her memory back, and she's a little miffed over a couple of things."

"So when we talked about relationships, you didn't mention her."

"No, because I wasn't in a relationship with her."

"Apparently, she thought she was in one with you." Stacy stirred her tea absentmindedly.

"Yeah, and therein lies the rub. I'm not particularly proud of this. The day of the shooting, we uh..."

"You slept with her."

Jo nodded. "Yes, but..." Jo paused, averting her eyes. She slowly returned her gaze to Stacy's. "Look, no excuses. I got home from a long trip. She came over and met me at the door with a kiss I didn't expect. I hadn't been with anyone for at least two years, and I guess I'd have to admit that I just didn't resist the temptation she offered. Not to make excuses, I guess I was tired and I really didn't think about the consequences of my actions. I can't even blame what happened between us on too much alcohol. I just plain made a poor, spur-of-the-moment decision and didn't stop it when I should have."

"So you aren't in love with her?"

"No." Jo's tone and demeanor indicated she was sincere. "I mean, sure, I care for her. Not in the same way she cares for me, I guess. I do like Meg, you know, but just as a friend."

"However, she feels more for you than friendship."

Jo nodded. "It seems so. I made a huge error in judgment—a gargantuan mistake. Meg's a good person. Unfortunately, I'm not in love with her. I regretted my actions the minute it was over. Here's where the trouble starts. She knew how I felt. Right after the, well you know. We discussed what happened, and I was completely honest with her. She wanted more, I didn't. She said that she wished I wouldn't feel that we'd made a mistake. She hoped that our being intimate would help her 'get me out of her system' as she put it. She seemed okay after our discussion. We even ended up making plans to go out for dinner. Then all that happened at the hospital and she lost her memory."

Stacy studied Jo's face. "Judging from her demeanor when she left earlier, it would seem that she's remembered what happened."

"Yes, more or less. Unfortunately, she just has flashes of the," Jo used her fingers to make quotation marks, "good parts, and none of the conversation we had afterwards. It seems she doesn't remember the part where I told her it would never happen again. So unfortunately, I had to tell her, to reject her all over again. She was definitely upset. Interestingly, more upset today than she was the first time that I had to tell her that what had happened between us that day was never going to happen again."

"Oh, I see. So Meg thinks you dumped her and moved in with me?"

Jo nodded. "I'm afraid that may be having some impact."

"Oh, poor Meg. So did you straighten her out?" Stacy hated the thought that Meg would think that she had 'stolen' her girlfriend.

"Well, as much as I could. She was upset when she left. She knows that I wouldn't lie to her. I'm sure she'll be okay once she has some time to think about it. I'll call her in a couple of days."

"Maybe you need a third rule. Do not sleep with your friends."

"It's generally not an issue. However, your suggestion will surely bear consideration."

"So you hadn't been with anyone for two years? I thought when you said you hadn't been serious with anyone for over two years, well, you know." Stacy shrugged. "I thought I was the only celibate person in the world." There was a lull in the conversation as they mulled their own thoughts. "The world really is a paired place, though, isn't it? You ever sit and watch the world go by? It's like Noah's Ark, two by two by two. Sometimes I just hate being alone, but being with someone I don't enjoy is worse. So I choose the lesser of two evils."

"Maybe you just haven't met the right guy yet, Stacy."

"Yes, I've told myself that same lie. I'm just not sure I believe it any more. Maybe some of us aren't meant to get on the Ark two by two." She picked up her cup and set it in the sink. "We'd better get a move on if we want to make the movie."

They caught the show and afterward grabbed a burger before making their way back to Stacy's place where Stacy again massaged Jo before she fell asleep.

Chapter 12

NIC LOCKED UP THE office. She glanced up at the darkened windows of Stacy's apartment to see if anyone was at the window. Still curious about what had happened between Meg and Jo that afternoon, she started for home. *Was Meg jealous of Jo's relationship with Stacy?*

Once in her car, as Nic began the short drive home, she reviewed her thoughts about Jo and Stacy. They seemed to really have settled into an easy and comfortable routine. Jo was more relaxed and easy going than usual when she was with Stacy. She teased more readily, actually seemed happy, was surely lighter, and seemed less burdened. She couldn't be sure that was because of Jo's relationship with Stacy or a product of her no longer working on the force. If only Stacy was a lesbian, they would be a perfect pair. In fact, Nic sensed that Stacy might actually have a bit of an attraction to Jo. The premise Stacy had begun with was to learn about the lesbian 'lifestyle.' From Nic's perspective, it seemed that she was more carefully studying Jo specifically. Nic was amazed at how well Stacy seemed to understand Jo's personality and motivations in such a short span of time.

Arriving home, Nic entered the house and quickly began dinner. She knew that Dana would be pulling into the driveway in a few minutes. She lit the candles she'd set on the table and opened the wine. The slamming of a car door announced Dana's arrival. Nic met her lover at the door with a kiss. "I missed you so much today."

Dana smiled. "Only half as much as I missed you."

"Now, how could you possibly know how much I missed you? I thought of you every minute of the day that we were apart. So I missed you more."

Dana wrapped her arms around Nic's neck, pulling her down for a slow, soft kiss. "I thought about you twice each minute of every hour today."

Nic laughed. "Okay, you win. And if you don't stop kissing me like that, we're going to burn dinner again."

"I'm starting to be used to the taste of charred food," Dana replied. "Sometimes, I get something for lunch and just long for the taste of dried out and blackened food."

They laughed together as they walked hand in hand to the kitchen where they prepared their plates before they sat at the dining room table to eat.

Later that evening, as they lay entwined together, Dana asked, "Do you remember television?"

Nic was enjoying the feel of Dana's hand trailing slowly up and down her side. Despite the fact that they'd already made love, it wouldn't take much to get her interested again. Nic could never seem to get enough of her lover. She was deliriously happy and no longer able to imagine her life without Dana. She was counting the minutes until they could develop the business enough that they could both afford to do that job full time and could spend more time together. "What do you mean, do I remember television?"

"Can you even remember the last time we watched it?"

Goosebumps raised on Nic's thigh as Dana's hand traced a path there, trailing down the outside of her thigh across and over the top of her leg before lightly journeying upwards. Skirting along the edges of the soft curls at the apex of her legs and ending with her palm brushing Nic's already erect nipple, Dana's hand idly began the journey once again.

"Umm. TV? Watched TV? No. Why?" Nic's breathing rate had increased, indicating that the blood was hurrying to other locations on her body, leaving her brain not functioning at its full capacity.

"Well, I was thinking that if we're ever short of cash, we could sell it."

Nic smiled and rolled over, pinning Dana to the bed. She stretched Dana's arms over her head and kissed her way from Dana's palm to her naval. "I love the way you feel, the way you smell, the way you kiss me," she murmured against Dana's stomach. She moved up to Dana's breasts, paying careful attention to waiting until Dana began to move beneath her before kissing her way down to satisfy her lover's need for her. "I love the way you taste."

"Umm, that feels good, but I want you up here. I want you to come with me." Both ready, they entered each other and joined in mutual release.

"That was nice," Dana whispered into Nic's neck, her breathing still coming in short bursts. "I love you, you know."

"Yes, I know. I couldn't live without you loving me, I think. I can't imagine how I even existed before you chose to love me."

Dana rested her cheek on Nic's chest. "You've turned my world upside down. I've never longed for anyone before you. The minute you leave me, I count the seconds until I can be with you again. At first, I fought my feelings. I couldn't help myself and eventually I realized that nothing else mattered. I'd fallen in love with you."

"Did you struggle with that emotion, with the fact I was a woman?" Nic wanted more information after her conversation with Stacy.

Dana thought back to when she began to fall in love with Nic. "No, I don't think struggle would be the word I'd choose to describe it. I mean, of course you know I thought about it because we discussed it. In the end, it really didn't matter. I was in love with you and, once we made love, there was no way I'd let you go. That first night we were together was magical." Dana smiled at the memory.

"Yes, it was."

They snuggled together enjoying their closeness.

Nic nuzzled Dana's neck. "I've been thinking that Stacy might be attracted to Jo, and if I had to wager on it, I'd bet that Jo would be interested if Stacy wasn't straight."

"Yes. I've considered that idea, too. I wonder if Stacy is aware of their attraction."

Dana slid to her side and Nic adjusted her position to face her. Sliding her hand up to Dana's breast, she circled lightly from the nipple to the outer edges with her fingertips. She slowed, returning to feel the area she had just traversed. "What's this?"

"What?"

"I feel something. Turn on the light."

Dana did as Nic requested. "Where?"

Nic again felt Dana's breast until she located the small pea sized lump. "Here," she said guiding Dana's fingers to the spot.

Dana fingered the area, her eyes filling with tears. "Oh Nic, what if I'm sick? It's too soon. It's not fair."

Nic wrapped her lover in her arms. "Don't jump to conclusions. Maybe it's a cyst. Don't think the worst. But know that no matter what it is, we'll face it together."

"I know. But it's just not fair."

"Let's call Mallory. She'll tell you who to see, and maybe she can get you in quicker."

"Good idea. What time is it?" She checked the clock. "It's only 9:30. Let's get dressed and go see her."

"I'll call them first to be sure they're receiving," Nic said with a wink.

A few minutes later, they walked across the yard between their houses. After knocking on Amanda and Mallory's door, they opened it and yelled, "We're here!"

Amanda greeted them at the door with a hug. "Mal will be right out. What's up?"

Mallory came down the hall adjusting her belt. She hugged her friends and led them into the living room. "Hey, Guys, you sounded anxious. What's going on?"

Nic spoke first. "We found a lump in Dana's breast."

Mallory quickly sorted and reviewed what advice she had to offer. "Okay. First, don't panic. Chances are highly in your favor that it's nothing, maybe a cyst. Have you ever felt it there before?"

Both Nic and Dana shook their heads.

"Well, I'd guess that your first thought is fear it's cancer. I just read a very informative article not too long ago. Statistically, according to them, for women your age a very low percentage, less than ten percent of lumps that are self-discovered are malignant. You're lucky in one respect, you have youth on your side. After menopause, the chance of malignancy increases pretty dramatically." Mallory squeezed Dana's hand. "So, take a few deep breaths and try to stay calm. Chances are very good that it's nothing to worry about."

Relieved somewhat by Mallory's encouraging words, Dana joked, "This is probably the first time in my life that I'm glad I'm still getting my period."

Mal smiled at her friend's upbeat nature. "Anyway, there have been great strides in treatment. We're learning more every day...so don't worry until we are sure of what we're dealing with. Let's not put the cart before the horse as my aunt used to say." She smiled and squeezed her friend's hand. "Let me get you the number of the doctor I'd recommend you see. I'll get in touch with him first thing tomorrow. I'll ask him to see you right away."

Dana exhaled. "Thanks, Mallory. I appreciate it." She reached for Nic's hand. "I feel a little better."

"How about a drink?" Amanda offered. "Know that we'll be there for whatever you need. For now, put it out of your mind until we know what you are dealing with. Okay?"

Dana nodded. "Thanks. I feel a bit more in control. But I'll take you up on that offer of a drink now."

The friends sat sipping their drinks and Dana began to relax as they chatted. They caught up on everyone's individual news, before turning their attention to talking about their friends.

"How are Stacy and Jo making out?" Amanda asked Nic. "Anything new to report with them?"

"I don't know. They seem awfully close for having only known each other such a short time. Jo seemed in good spirits today, and she and Stacy are living like an old married couple. They have this, what? I guess you'd call it a kind of choreographed routine in the kitchen. They start a meal, and without much communication, the table gets set, the silver dispersed, and voilà, suddenly there's a meal in front of you. They don't quite finish each other's sentences, but pretty damned near." Nic reached for Dana's hand. "I think you should talk to Stacy. She had a lot of questions today about Jo and that stupid rule number two of hers."

Dana wasn't thinking clearly yet, still having the worry about the lump in her breast in the back of her mind. It took her a few seconds to switch gears and get tuned in to what Nic was talking about. "Oh, you mean that thing she spouts about not ever getting involved with a straight woman?"

"That's the one!" Nic replied.

Mallory laughed as she said, "Gosh, Nic, you need to talk to Jo, to tell her she doesn't know what she's missing."

Nic smiled at the good-natured teasing. "Come on, Honey, I've had enough of their abuse. Let's go home."

They hugged each other in turn. Mallory promised to catch up with the doctor first thing in the morning. "Remember what I told you and don't worry."

Chapter 13

"CAN YOU BELIEVE WE'VE been doing this for three and a half weeks now?" Stacy asked.

"I know. Time has literally flown by." Jo's daily grilling by Stacy had transformed into them just having normal conversations. They'd both been busy. Stacy had begun working on a new project. She'd already sent out a new survey, and Jo had prepared for and begun teaching her class. Jo had a wonderful mixed group of students of all ages, so there was much to discuss. She'd created several games for them to play, each one designed to break the ice and get people talking to one another. Beginning with the second meeting, people had taken to showing up early for the class and chatting in English before the French class started, able to share much more information in their native language than they could in their halting French.

Stacy had finally finished the first book Jo had given her to read and was rapidly progressing through the second. Jo expected that she'd be asking the dreaded sex questions before too long. She closed her eyes against what she anticipated would be an uncomfortable discussion.

Following breakfast, they each prepared for their walk. "Better dress warmly, Stacy. I think the weather has turned colder again." They'd been enjoying an uncharacteristically warm week for mid-March. Looking out the living room window, Jo continued. "Judging from the way people are bundled up against the wind, it looks like it's pretty brisk out there."

Stepping outside and pulling the door closed behind her, Stacy gasped as the first blast of cold air assaulted her. "Brrr! You're certainly right about the weather. Winter is definitely back."

Jo chuckled.

"I'll go get the chair and you get started. I'll catch up with you."

"Okay." Jo grinned. "You might be surprised, though. Thanks to you, my leg feels great. You may have to run to catch up with me."

"Small price to pay, if you're able to leave me in the dust." Stacy gave Jo's arm a squeeze. Jo turned north to follow their regular route while Stacy jogged across the street and into the shop to get the chair. With a quick wave to Nic, Stacy grabbed the companion chair from the alcove and darted out the door to join Jo. Stacy didn't have to run, but she had to hurry. Jo was already a block away, nearly to the first bench by the time she caught up with her. With pleasure, Stacy noted that Jo wasn't limping yet.

"Need this?" Stacy asked when she caught up.

"Nope, not yet."

"Rest?"

"Nope." Shaking her head slightly, Jo grinned. "Not yet."

They walked along with Stacy pushing the chair and Jo just using her cane. When they arrived at the second bench, Jo sat. "I know it's cold. I just need a minute or two."

"Sure." Stacy sat down and pulled the collar of her coat up around her neck. "Whew! Chilly."

"Slide over here a little closer to me. I'll block some of the wind. Besides, I've been accused of being something akin to a built-in furnace. I've had complaints in the summer time because I always emitted so much heat. But no one has ever complained in the winter."

Stacy accepted Jo's offer. She slid over next to her and slipped her hand into the crook of Jo's arm, leaning against her. "Mmm, you are warm. Where does all that heat come from?"

Jo was surprised that Stacy was comfortable with what could be perceived as a display of affection rather than what it was, just two friends sharing heat. "Aren't you concerned someone will think we're lesbians?"

Feigning shock, Stacy asked, "Oh, no. You're a lesbian?"

"Okay, perhaps I should have asked, aren't you concerned someone will think you're a lesbian?"

"No."

"Why not?"

Stacy shrugged. "I don't know. The thought just never crossed my mind that someone might assume that. We could be sisters. I snuggle with my sister all the time. Anyway, why would I care? Anyone who would think less of me because they suspected I might be gay is not anyone whose opinion would have any value to me anyway." Stacy frowned. "Have you had negative experiences before?"

"I've been pretty closeted because of my profession so, in the past, I've not usually been physically demonstrative with another woman in public."

"Are we being physically demonstrative? I was under the impression that I was keeping warm. But, if you're uncomfortable, I can move farther away," Stacy said, expressing her annoyance.

"No, I've got nothing to hide now that I'm off the force. I was just thinking of your reputation." Apparently, Jo had struck a bit of a nerve.

Stacy seemed a little miffed that Jo had even mentioned her concern. Jo had always been under the impression that any straight woman would be worried about being accused of, or suspected of, being a lesbian. She filed the question away to ask later. Perhaps when Stacy wouldn't be so uncharacteristically irascible.

Feeling cold and ready to return to some warmth Jo asked, "Ready to head back?"

"Yes. Walk or ride?"

"Walk, I think. I still feel reasonably able to navigate. My leg's tired, but not painful like it was before. We may need to renegotiate our deal. I don't think massages were a part of the arrangement." When Stacy didn't respond, Jo asked. "What are you thinking?"

"Honestly, I was formulating and then discarding a variety of smartassed responses. I thought better of it and decided to bite my tongue. I'm sorry I snapped at you before."

Jo grabbed the handles of the wheelchair and started to push. Stacy slipped her arm into Jo's and tucked in close. Jo's furnace kicked into a higher gear. *Oh God! Rule number two—remember rule number two.* Then the other voice inside her head kicked in. *Don't be an ass. She doesn't mean anything by it. She's just keeping warm. She thinks of you as a sister or close friend.*

Nic glanced out the window and smiled at the picture created by the two people coming down the street toward the office. Stacy was cuddled against Jo, arms linked, much the same way she and Dana had walked together in Italy. She wondered if things were starting to happen for them or if they were legitimately just fending off the cold.

Stacy waved hello to Nic through the window, then turned for her apartment while Jo pushed the wheelchair into the store and deposited it into the nook.

"So?" Nic asked, one eyebrow elevated, expressing her curiosity.

"So, what?"

"So, how are things going with Stacy?"

"Good. She's a great person. I like her a lot. We're becoming good friends."

"Friends?" Nic glanced across the street at Stacy's window. "You two looked pretty cozy for just friends."

"I told her people would think the worst of her if they saw her close to me like that."

"Why do you say 'think the worst of her? Do you mean they might suspect her of being a lesbian?"

Nodding, Jo unzipped her jacket. "Yes, I told her people would assume she was gay and that we were lovers."

"And what was her reaction?"

"She got a bit peeved at me."

"Jo, do you ever think she might be interested?"

"In what? Me, or in a lesbian experience?"

"Maybe in both."

Jo shook her head. "Remember rule number two. I'm not interested in being any first timer's experiment or experience."

"Why not? It sure worked for Dana and me. I'm Dana's first relationship with a woman."

"Didn't you worry that this was a path she was walking for the first time?"

"You mean that Dana might be taking a detour from the straight and narrow, and that she'd return to the main road eventually?"

Jo laughed and pulled up a chair. "Yes, precisely."

Nic glanced out the window again, tugging at her earlobe as she composed her response. Nic turned to look Jo directly in the eyes. Her direct gaze told Jo that when Nic spoke, she could depend on the fact that it would be with honesty and candor.

"I will admit that when we first got together it concerned me. By the time Dana asked me to trust her, it was too late for me to back away. I was too far-gone. By the way I haven't been sorry ever, not once. I mean, look at the relationship we have, and look at what I would have missed out on. These past several months have been the happiest of my life. I've gained a partner, a friend, a lover, and all of you guys as friends. I'm starting a new business with people I love and trust. I'm my own boss and doing work I love. With Dana's support, I've come out to my mother, and she has continued to embrace me. You know, Jo, sometimes what feels very risky really isn't after all. Especially if you take that risk for and with the right person."

Jo didn't respond, but she carefully considered Nic's words.

Chapter 14

"I FINISHED THE SECOND book you gave me to read." Stacy slid Jo's book across the counter towards her. "Thank you."
"What did you think of it?"
"I enjoyed it very much. I felt like I really got to know each character. I loved the main characters' relationship and their playful banter. The dialogue was very natural, and it was an entertaining story. It made me laugh and it made me cry."
Jo waited.
"And it was hot. I couldn't wait for them to get together. It was a good love story. I can see why you like that author's writing. Her characters feel like people I'd like to hang out with." Stacy stood and carried their dinner dishes to the sink.
Jo joined her, helping to rinse them and stack the dishwasher.
"Will it disturb you if I use the office to do some work?"
"Not at all. I would like to bike a bit. Will the noise bother you?"
"No." Stacy wiped her hands and closed the dishwasher. "I don't have to make any phone calls tonight, so noise won't be an issue for me."
Jo had steadily been increasing her stamina. She rarely ever took the wheelchair on her walks anymore, and the previous day she'd circled the block instead of covering her usual route. Not only was her strength and stamina increasing, she was also much more optimistic that she would eventually be able to regain even more functional use of her leg.

When Stacy started down the hallway toward the office, Jo was amazed. Was she also just a little disappointed that Stacy hadn't wanted to discuss the sex scenes? She'd expected questions or, at the very least, comments. Stacy had said nothing other than 'it was hot.'

Jo followed Stacy down the hallway to the office. "Need help?"

"Not right now. Maybe tomorrow."

"Same as before, tallying the results for you?"

"Yup." Stacy glanced over at Jo several times. "You're awfully antsy tonight. Something wrong?"

Jo shrugged. "No I guess not. I guess I expected a different reaction to the book, that's all."

"In what way? It was a good romance. It was just a simple love story, so there's no deep discussion needed. I've read a hundred just like it."

"Well, not exactly like it."

Stacy's brow furrowed wondering what Jo was beating around the bush about. "Okay, spit it out. What are you pussy footing around about?"

Jo smiled inwardly at Stacy's choice of words. "Okay, I thought you'd have some questions or comments about the love scenes."

"Well, after reading that, what questions could I possibly have left? As to comments, I told you, I liked it a lot, good story, steamy sex. What more could or should I say?"

"So you didn't find the love scenes uh..." Jo searched for an appropriate word. "For want of a better word, distasteful?"

"God no! Why would I? They were great. I told you I thought they were hot. They described sometimes passionate, sometimes tender, and always loving and giving relationships. I wish my sexual experiences had been half that good." She paused for a moment before she asked the one question she did want an answer to. "Tell me something, Jo. I do have one question. Is sex with a woman really like it was described in that book?"

"Yes," Jo said simply. "It certainly can be."

"Then, I confess, I'm envious." With that statement, Stacy began working, leaving an amazed Jo with nothing left to say or do but to get on her stationary bike and start to ride.

Jo had increased her time on the bike daily. She now was riding up to fifteen or twenty minutes per session without a rest. She tried to do three, sometimes four, sessions every day. She was pleased and amazed that she saw daily improvement not only on the bike but also in her ability to walk farther and be more secure and stable in her stride. The twice-daily massages that Stacy was giving her had made a dramatic impact on her life, and she was so grateful.

Jo rode and Stacy worked. When Jo's leg started to ache, she stopped and went to take her shower while Stacy finished up what she had to do on the computer. She printed out the responses to her survey so she and Jo could tally them the next day.

Stacy prepared for bed, before she trudged down the hallway toward the office and Jo. It had become their routine for Stacy to get ready for bed and join Jo in her room. Stacy would give Jo her nightly massage while they discussed the events of the day. Sometimes they'd share secrets about their lives. The more they talked, the more she learned and came to accept that other than the fact that they had historically been on opposite sides of the fence regarding choice of their sexual partners, their lives were just mundane daily living experiences with many more similarities than differences.

Stacy knocked at the entrance to the dual function office and bedroom for Jo. Jo had taken to wearing a loose pair of boxers to bed. She still refused to wear additional clothing other than that. "I'm just too hot to wear more," she had stated definitively. She had little modesty, either. Jo yelled, "Come in," in response to Stacy's knock. When Stacy entered, Jo was just about ready to slide into bed, and she looked up with a wide grin.

Stacy smiled in return and her eyes swept Jo's body appreciatively. Jo had a great body. She was the first woman she had ever met or seen with a true set of six-pack abs. Stacy squelched the momentary impulse to rub her hand over the smooth skin covering the lean muscles. She shook herself mentally and asked brightly, "Ready for your massage?"

"Yes. Ready if you are."

"I'd like to try adding in something new tonight." Stacy smiled inwardly, assuming Jo's response to her previous thought of running her hand over Jo's taut stomach. That would certainly be something new.

"What's that?"

"I got Mallory's opinion on this, too. She talked with one of the physical therapists. She agreed that stretching might help decrease your spasms. I'd like to try improving your flexibility in that leg through the stretching routine we used to use on that little boy. Your Achilles tendon on that injured leg seems tighter than the other one."

"I'm game. You've made such an improvement in my life with the massages. I trust anything you want to try."

"Okay, let's massage first to loosen up the muscles. After that, we'll do some stretching." Stacy warmed the lotion in her hands and began a slow, sensual massage of Jo's leg.

"I think I overdid a bit on the bike. I'm sore here." Jo pointed to her inner thigh, running her pointer finger from just below her crotch to slightly above her knee.

"All right. Let's start there. Lie back and I'll see what I can do."

Jo reclined on the bed, seeming unaware of her near nudity. She was totally comfortable now with Stacy's presence when she was mostly unclothed, as well as with her touch.

Stacy, on the other hand was beginning to have quite the opposite reaction. No longer able to resist her desire to touch, Stacy lightly ran her fingertips over Jo's abs, eliciting a flash of some previously unseen emotion in Jo's eyes. Stacy felt the muscles involuntarily react.

"I covet your muscles here. Can you help me improve mine?"

Jo's voice was a bit husky when she responded. "Sure, we can work on that if you'd like."

* * *

Stacy started the massage at Jo's knee and worked her way upward on Jo's thigh. She couldn't put her finger on it. The massage tonight was different somehow. She could feel the heat radiating from Jo's body as she worked her way up her leg. "You need to spread your legs a bit so I can get the top part of this muscle that's bothering you."

Jo laughed, propping herself up on her elbows. "You're lucky I know you're straight and that I have rule number two to fall back on. Do you have any idea how that phrase 'spread your legs' sounds to me? Especially as you're sliding your hands up the inside of my thigh?"

Stacy laid her palm against the warm skin of Jo's thigh. "Do you want me to stop?"

Jo grinned. "No, I'll be good. I'm just saying."

Stacy finished up the massage and began the stretching exercise. "I want to stretch this hamstring." Stacy knelt on the bed. "Now I'm going to put your leg over my shoulder." Stacy lifted Jo's leg, keeping one hand on Jo's knee and the other on her calf.

"Umm, tight," groaned Jo.

"Yes, we'll take it easy. I don't want to hurt you."

Thinking on a whole different level than the words were intended, Jo thought, *it may already be too late.* Jo knew she'd already developed feelings for Stacy and that it would hurt when it came time for her to leave. It had come as a surprise to her that despite her original resistance to the idea of her living with Stacy, she'd become very happy with the arrangement. She enjoyed Stacy's perpetual optimism and good humor. She was bright, witty, and offered easy, enjoyable company. Yes, no doubt about it, it would be sad when it came time for her to leave. She could do nothing about it. Stacy was straight, and she was not. There was that one big compatibility issue. Still, Jo knew that she was beginning to want more than she could ever have with the enticing woman who was at that very moment torturing her leg.

"Ouch! The last time a woman had my leg over her shoulders, I remember it being a much more pleasant activity."

Stacy laughed. "You mean you're not enjoying this experience with me?"

"No, I didn't say that. I'm just saying that the previous experience was better."

"I'm sure I can improve on my performance, given an opportunity."

Jo just smiled, and when she gave no further response, Stacy said, "Okay, enough of that for tonight." She lowered Jo's leg to the bed. "Turn over and let me relax your leg muscles."

Chapter 15

TWO DAYS LATER, NIC and Mallory were at the office when Jo stopped in to run off some materials for her class.

"Oh good, just the person we need to see," Mallory said.

Jo grinned her greeting. "Why? What's up?"

"Can you cover the office tomorrow for us?"

Jo pursed her lips as she thought about her schedule for the next day. "Sure, no problem. You guys got something fun to do?"

Mallory looked to Nic for guidance about how much information she wanted to share. Mallory suspected Nic would be characteristically open and honest. However, Mallory didn't feel it was her place to reveal their destination.

Nic responded, "No, far from it. We found a small lump in Dana's breast, and we're going to see a doctor for a biopsy and some other tests. Mallory is coming with us, so we'd like you to cover the office for us."

Seeing Jo's look of concern, Mallory was quick to reassure her. "Dana will probably find that the lump is benign."

Jo tilted her head and searched Mallory's face. "Maybe. It's still scary."

Nic nodded her agreement. "Without a doubt."

Turning to Nic, Jo asked, "How is Dana doing with all this?"

Nic shrugged one shoulder. "Nervous, for sure, but holding up. She's anxious to get on with it and see what the doctor has to say."

"I can imagine." Jo covered Nic's hand with her own. "Just remember, anything I can do to help."

"Just keep us in your prayers." Nic gave Jo's hand a squeeze.

Stacy came in just as Nic said that. She immediately looked to Jo for an explanation. Jo looked at Nic who nodded her permission for Jo to give Stacy a quick summary of the information she'd just learned.

"Oh, Nic, if there is anything I can do to help, maybe help Jo cover the office, drive Dana to an appointment, make you dinner, anything. Please don't hesitate to ask me. And tell Dana I asked for her." Stacy reached up to give Nic a supportive hug. Nic held onto the hug for a few extra seconds, taking strength from Stacy's friendship and offer of help.

"Thanks, Stacy, your support is appreciated."

* * *

Nic and Dana lay entwined, waiting for the alarm to go off the next morning. They weren't talking about it, despite the fact that both felt anxious. "Remember, Mallory told us not to worry about it. So let's just keep positive thoughts," Nic murmured against Dana's hair.

"I know. I'm okay, really. I'm anxious to get there and get on with it, though. I know that together we can deal with whatever it is. It's the waiting that's tough."

"You know, Dana, we've been pushing hard the past couple of months. I hope we'll get good news in a couple of days. How about we get the group together and go out for a nice dinner and maybe some dancing if we get a positive result?"

Dana snuggled closer and nuzzled into Nic's neck. "That would be nice. Will you arrange it or should I?"

"You know, yesterday, Stacy offered to do anything she could to help us. How about I ask her to do it? She told me to let you know she'd be thinking of you."

"That's really nice of her. I like her very much. Her kindness shows in nearly everything she does, and she seems to bring out the best in Jo."

Nic ran her hands over her lover's back, snuggling her closer. "Yes, I agree. I think part of that is because Jo is really feeling better. Jo worked hard in physical therapy and has done so much afterwards on her own. Stacy's massages and their walking together have made a big improvement in Jo's leg. When she's not tired and uses her cane, Jo is walking without a pronounced limp now, and her stamina appears to be improving on an almost daily basis. Stacy walks with her every day, even though it probably isn't really necessary that she accompany Jo anymore."

"Do you have anywhere special you want to go for dinner?"

"No. Unless you have a preference, let's have Stacy pick a place for dinner and surprise us." Nic adjusted her position to allow herself to rub her cheek against the top of Dana's head, inhaling the aroma of the almond scented shampoo she associated with her lover. "I'll call her later today and ask her to make reservations for Saturday night and to let the others know. I'll also ask her if she'd be comfortable going to a gay bar with us to go dancing."

"What if we get bad news? It won't be much of a celebration."

"Naturally, my plan is that it'll be a celebration. But if it's bad news, we'll need our friends more than ever," Nic answered. "If we don't feel like celebrating, we can always cancel."

"That's true. Okay, fingers crossed." Dana rolled over, settling her back against her lover and pulling Nic's arm securely around her. "I hate to say it. We need to get up and get dressed. We're picking up Mallory in forty-five minutes."

"I know. Think we can just stay like this for a couple more minutes?" She wrapped her arms tighter around Dana. Reluctantly, a few brief moments later, Nic exhaled a long sigh. "Okay, I'm ready now. Let's go take our shower."

Less than forty-five minutes later, Mallory walked across the yard and got into Nic's car, joining her friends. Nic backed out of the driveway and headed toward the hospital and Dana's appointment. During the consultation following Dana's examination, the doctor was very reassuring. He did a fine-needle aspiration, telling her he would put a rush on it and hoped he'd have the test results in two days. He also sent her for a diagnostic mammogram. He referred her to get the mammogram from a friend of his. As a courtesy to Mallory, he had called and asked the doctor to make the appointment for Dana as soon as she could fit her in.

"She'll see you tomorrow, on Wednesday. She'll read the images and have a report for me the day after you have the test. That should give you as quick an answer as possible. I'll call you with the results the minute they come across my desk. I hope to have the results back from the biopsy on Thursday or Friday as well."

"Thank you, Doctor. I appreciate your help. And thanks for expediting things and getting the results back as soon as possible."

The three women left the doctor's office and headed for the parking lot. "I know this doctor he referred you to. She has a stellar reputation and I think you'll love her. She's not only professionally very respected, but she's a lovely person," Mallory said. "She's one of the few doctors I know who will read the results immediately and get the report out quickly. I used to go to a doctor who would read the pictures right after the test, then do a breast exam and show me the results right away. It seems not too many doctors do that anymore. At least this doctor is good about turn around time for her reports."

"Yeah, I am relieved that I'll have the results by Thursday or Friday. The wait won't be too long. The waiting is the hardest," Dana admitted.

Mallory hugged her friend. "I know, Sweetie. You'll know everything in a couple of days. Again, there's probably nothing to worry about. Remember, no matter what, you won't face it alone."

"I know. I appreciate that. Are you coming home with us?"

"Yes. I'm not working today. Amanda asked me to call her when we got done. She's making us lunch."

* * *

The meal long completed, they were still sitting around the table at two o'clock when Dana's phone rang. She excused herself so she could have some privacy.

Nic took the opportunity provided by Dana's departure to express her appreciation. "Thanks, Amanda, for having us over. I think tomorrow, after the mammogram, I'll take Dana into the city and go to a museum. I think it'll help keep her mind occupied."

"That's a great idea," Amanda responded.

Nic removed her napkin from her lap and placed it on the table, "When Dana comes back we'll head home. I have some translations to finish up. Maybe Dana will help me. We're starting to get more referrals from jobs we've completed. If we get too much more work, I'm going to need some help. Problem is, the work seems to come in waves. There are days that I'm looking for things to do, and then other days when I'm working as fast as I can to keep up."

"Maybe I should start putting out some ads for freelancers that you can call when you need extra help."

"Yes. Good idea. Between Dana and me, we know several we can contact, too. Also, I think that we need to do some follow up phone calls to those people who said they might be interested in contracting with us for a discount. If we could land just one of those companies on a fulltime basis, maybe Dana could quit where she is and come help me." Just for a brief moment, the worst scenario crossed Nic's mind. "That way, we could spend more time together." Her eyes filled, but she quickly blinked back the tears. She didn't want Dana to see her crying when she returned.

"Nic, keep it together just for a couple more days. We've all got to keep positive."

"I know. I'm trying."

Dana returned from her phone call. "That was my boss. Last week, I pitched him the deal we discussed. I offered him a discount for five percent less than it currently costs him to do all the translation work for his company's correspondence and the monthly and annual reports. I now have a new part time position with the company. I'm in charge of coordinating their in-house translation services effective first of the month," she said with an ear-to-ear grin. "We're going to need to hire some freelancers."

Dana walked behind Nic and slid her arms around her neck, kissing her on the cheek. "Being your coworker will have its advantages. We can do most of the translation at home."

"Maybe we need to make a company policy that only one of you gets to work from home at a time. Otherwise we'll not be meeting our deadlines," Amanda chided.

"We're going to head home, Amanda, before you can give us any more abuse. After we finish up that last report Nic's working on, we'll be off the clock." Dana grinned and wiggled her eyebrows.

* * *

Dana and Nic went to the radiology department the next morning at eight for Dana's mammogram. They were assured that her doctor would have the results on Thursday. "Now all we have to do is wait," Dana said as she and Nic left for the hospital parking lot.

Before leaving the building, Nic pulled Dana into an alcove where they were not visible and put her arms around her lover. "I love you more than you will ever know or believe possible."

"I know that. You show me that every day we're together."

Nic loosened the grip of her arms around Dana. "Ready to go?" Dana nodded.

Nic whispered in her ear. "Which museum do you want to go to?"

"I don't want to go to a museum. I want to go home and make love with you until Thursday when the call comes in from the doctor and we know if we're celebrating or commiserating on Saturday."

Nic responded by taking Dana's hand. Without another word she led her to the car to make their trip home.

Chapter 16

NIC CALLED STACY TO ask for her help in arranging what, hopefully, would be a celebration on Saturday for the six of them.

"I'd be more than happy to arrange a dinner celebration for Saturday evening. I'm grateful that I can help." She was pleased that Nic had accepted her offer to assist in any way she could. She was also delighted to be included with the group for Saturday's dinner. "Have you heard anything yet?"

"No. We're hoping to hear later today or tomorrow at the latest. If the news we receive from the doctor is positive, we'll celebrate by going out dancing after dinner to our favorite gay bar. I hope you'll join us there, although we'll certainly understand if you don't feel comfortable going there with us." Nic smiled. "The place we like to go is really quite respectable. We always have fun when we go there. They always have a great band playing on Saturday night."

"Thanks for including me, Nic. I'll take care of the reservations as soon as we hang up and will leave messages for everyone with time and address information. And I'd love to join in the celebration after you get the good news," Stacy said encouragingly.

Stacy did as she promised. She chose a small Italian restaurant she liked and phoned for reservations. After she had confirmed a dinner reservation for Saturday evening, she called everyone and informed them of the plans.

Jo was across the street covering the office, so Stacy was home alone catching up on some chores. *Laundry,* she thought, *I should do some today.* She went back to her bedroom, tidied up, and began to sort her clothes for the wash she intended to do later. Noticing the book on her night table, she picked up the second lesbian romance novel Jo had given her to read. She smiled at the recollection of reading it. This book was even steamier than the first she had read. Pushing aside the pile of clothes, she curled up on her bed and opened the book, flipping to the first love scene, and began to read. Some time later, when she got to the chapter where the two main characters were about to finally make love to each other, she glanced up to check the time. After the two earlier scenes that teased and built the sexual tension, she was already horny and wondered if she should take a break and give herself a chance to cool off. She couldn't remember the last time she had such a strong physical response to any of the romance books she was fond of reading by mainstream authors.

In general, her reaction to mainstream books had been to wonder why she didn't feel the way the women in those stories did about sex. She was no virgin. In the two more serious relationships she'd had, sex had been something she had tolerated rather than relished. She'd always written it off to the fact that, although she had liked her partners and had enjoyed their company, she hadn't been in love with them. She'd not dated a lot in high school, preferring instead to go out in groups instead of on dates. In college, she had watched and listened to her friends as they excitedly related their plans to spend the weekend with their boyfriends. She'd been a virgin until she was twenty-three, originally planning on not having sex until after marriage. After dating David for nearly a year, she finally decided to find out what all the fuss was about. Although he was a tender lover, his kisses and tender touches just didn't excite her. Once they'd had sex, he expected that each date would end in his bedroom in the dorm. She began to reduce the frequency of their dates to weekends, sometimes begging off at the last minute. She didn't blame him when he broke up with her. In fact, she was surprised he had held on to their relationship for as long as he had.

After college, she threw herself into work, and after work, she volunteered at a shelter for abused women in her hometown. Seeing the sorrow there was enough to deter her from any serious relationships. She did date occasionally, but always broke it off before things got too serious.

Monique, Stacy's best friend, had gotten married after high school to her high school sweetheart, Rob. They had two kids together, and she was pregnant with her third when she discovered he was cheating on her. Stacy had spent every available night with her friend, helping her hold things together. Following the birth, Rob did return to the family after he begged for and was granted Monique's forgiveness. A marriage counselor helped them work to patch things up, with time and considerable effort on both their parts. Stacy was godmother to their daughter and missed the kids and her friend terribly when she moved to New York.

After Stacy moved north, she'd had a difficult time making more than casual friendships in such a large city. She had come from a beautiful small town in Virginia that was comprised of about eight city blocks. The town itself was what would be described as upscale. It was surrounded by horse farms and populated by families gifted with substantial financial resources. A reasonably popular girl in her small high school where she knew everyone by name, Stacy had stayed friends with several of the girls in her group. Her hometown was a place where you knew everyone's name and most of everyone's business, as well. She kept in regular contact with several of her buddies from college as well. One in particular, Maria, she was especially close to. They kept in contact frequently, talking on the phone at least twice a month. Thinking about Maria reminded Stacy that she really needed to give her a call.

Stacy was terribly lonely when she first came to the city, finding it difficult to find a group of friends to hang out with. She concluded that she was happier in a smaller environment. In search of a new peer group, she began attending church where she met a woman about her own age. She introduced her to some other women friends of hers. Stacy did do things with them occasionally. However, she never developed any close relationships like she had at home or at college.

Eventually, Stacy became friendly with her neighbor, Don. They became good friends and soon were seeing each other every night, sharing dinners, watching television, and going to shows and movies together. She was happy having him as a buddy. One night he brought home a jug of sangria and some Mexican food to celebrate his promotion at work.

"That's the good news," he'd told her. "The bad news is that I'm being transferred to Philadelphia in two months." She was upset that she would lose her friend. They drank most of the bottle of wine that night. Late in the evening, he kissed her and confessed that he had fallen in love with her.

In her none too coherent state, and afraid of losing her best friend, she'd gone to bed with him. Neither was prepared with a condom, and when he withdrew, just before he ejaculated onto her stomach, she couldn't believe how stupid she'd been. They were both awkward the next day, and she suspected they were both relieved when she found and moved into her current apartment. He'd emailed a few times after he moved, but their correspondence eventually died a natural death. Once settled in, she had made an appointment for her annual GYN appointment and asked to be tested for STD's. She was relieved to know the results were negative. She had been celibate ever since, concluding that sex was just not worth the trouble.

Reading the lesbian novels Jo had given her had certainly incited a different response within her. As she read further in the book, the lead characters finally declared their love for each other and fell into bed. Her hand found its way between her legs, and she came when the characters in the book did.

Stacy let the book fall onto her chest and closed her eyes. She imagined herself locked together in passion with another woman. Not with just any woman, just with Jo. *Whoa, where did that come from?* She rolled out of bed and went into the bathroom. Returning to her office, she inhaled deeply, appreciating the scent of Jo that lingered there. Even in the dead of winter Jo always smelled fresh and clean, like fresh air, soap, and sunshine. Stacy sat at her desk and looked out the window. She could see Jo sitting at the desk across the street in the window of the store and watched Jo pick up the phone and make a call. After a short conversation, Jo smiled just before she hung up. *Jo has a beautiful smile*, she thought.

As if sensing she was being watched, Jo glanced up at the apartment window. Stacy didn't think that Jo could see her because of the way the blinds were angled. She watched as Jo reached for the phone again and punched in numbers on the handset. Stacy was surprised when the phone on her desk rang. A smile came instantly to her face when she heard Jo's voice.

"Whatcha doing?" Jo asked, not bothering with identifying herself.

"Watching you through the window." She smiled when Jo's eyes instantly flicked upward.

"I can't see you."

Stacy reached for the string and pulled, raising the blinds to the top of the window.

"Oh, there you are," Jo said standing up and moving to stand at the front of the store. Gazing up, she said, "That's better." They didn't speak, just looked at each other across the street. "It's kind of lonesome here. How do you keep yourself from going crazy over there, working by yourself every day? I don't think I could do it."

Stacy smiled as she formulated her response. "Well, the best solution I've come up with so far is to find this engaging lesbian to share my abode. I've been very happy with the arrangement and will be sad to see her go."

"I can virtually guarantee that she feels the same way. Don't you think you'll stay friends? I mean, doesn't she work close by?"

"Yes. It won't be the same though, will it?"

"No. I'm sure she'll miss those long talks." Jo placed a hand on the glass a little bit above her head as she searched for Stacy's face in the window of her office.

Stacy could almost imagine the caress. "Not to mention the walks and the massages."

"And the back rubs and the scratches."

"Yes. Don't you think they've been pretty one sided?" Stacy said mischievously.

"Yeah. That's most likely because your lesbian friend is concerned that you might think she's making inappropriate advances towards you if she offered to reciprocate."

"Really? Oh, I wouldn't be worried, because I know that my friend has these rules she lives by, you see. Rule number two dictates that she'd never get involved with a historically straight woman, so I'm quite sure I'd be perfectly safe."

"Well, rules are often broken, and..." Before she could finish, the phone rang. Jo looked at the caller ID. "It's Nic. I'm going to put you on hold. I'll be right back."

Stacy didn't want to wait. She hung up and quickly ran through the hall and hurried down the stairs, racing across the street against the light. Jo was just hanging up the phone when Stacy rushed through the door.

Tears filled Jo's eyes as Stacy approached her. "It's just a cyst," she whispered into Stacy's neck as Stacy pulled her into a warm embrace.

"Then why are you crying?"

Jo sniffed and pulled away. She plucked a tissue from the box on the desk to dry her eyes and blow her nose. "Relief, I guess."

"Come here." Stacy opened her arms and Jo moved again into the comfort of Stacy's embrace. Jo settled, allowing herself the luxury of being held longer than was truly necessary. *If only*, she thought to herself. She pulled away, putting the desk between them. "Thanks. I'm glad you came over."

Stacy glanced over at the clock hanging on the wall behind Jo. "Two more hours and you can come home."

Some emotion flashed for an instant in Jo's eyes. It was gone too soon for Stacy to decipher its meaning. "Yes." Jo replied adding a smile, not trusting herself to say more. She had nearly told Stacy in their phone conversation that rules were often broken and she wanted to break rule number two with her. *Maybe things work out for the best,* she thought.

When Jo said no more, Stacy said, "I'll see you at home later?"

Jo nodded giving her a smile. "Yes, I'll see you there."

* * *

Stacy crossed the street and slowly climbed the stairs to the apartment. Lately, she was finding it difficult to read Jo. This afternoon while on the phone, they had been teasing and playful. She suspected that Jo was feeling the same way she was. Then again, after the phone call, when she had held her, she seemed comfortable. When she pulled away, she had virtually run to the safety of her position behind the desk. *What are you feeling, Jo? And me. What am I doing?* She wished she had someone to talk to, a sounding board.

Other than the women at *Oui, Madame*, the few women friends she'd made in the three years since she'd moved to the area, were casual. Very different from the deep friendships she'd made in high school and college. Although she'd remained close with her two best friends high school friends and her two closest college friends, she wasn't sure any of them would understand or be able to offer her any helpful advice about her feelings of being attracted to another woman. She wasn't even sure how any of them felt about homosexuality. After reviewing her options, she decided that Dana might be the best person to talk to, but she didn't want to bother her today. Anyway, she didn't have her number, only Nic's.

Stacy certainly knew she responded to Jo on many levels, the first being friendship. She loved the time they spent together talking and sharing their thoughts and feelings. They'd spent nearly every waking hour together since Jo moved into her apartment, and Stacy had never tired of her company. More than enjoying Jo's company, she had to admit that Jo's well-muscled and toned body attracted her. During the massages, she probably received as much enjoyment from giving the massage and being able to run her hands over the taut body as Jo did.

There were times like last night, when Jo was nearly naked, that Stacy actually struggled with keeping her hands on the parts of Jo's body on which she was supposed to be focusing. In addition, there were the sex scenes in the books that excited her more than she dared to admit even to herself.

There was no doubt in Stacy's mind that she found Jo attractive. She could drown in the color of her eyes. There were times when she had to will herself to look away. Then there was that mouth. She could imagine herself kissing Jo, softly at first. The kiss would deepen, with their tongues darting and inciting, as hands roamed each other's bodies, exploring first to find the most sensitive parts then returning to caress them later. She let her mind wander, just imagining being with Jo. The feeling of warmth between her legs and desire to be touched left no doubt in her mind that she wanted a sexual relationship with Jo.

Stacy mentally shook herself. *That's enough of that. Let's keep this a little more based in fact and a little less based on lust. Okay, what do I know? I know that I want her as I've never wanted anyone before. I miss her when we're not together, I thoroughly enjoy talking to her, and I melt inside when her eyes meet mine from across the room. Would I say I'm in love with her? It's too soon to be in love, isn't it?*

Before she could come to any conclusions, she heard Jo coming up the stairs and felt the excitement as her heart rate increased. *Oh boy,* she thought wryly, *this is something new and exciting.*

"Hello," Jo called from the top of the stairs.

"Hello," Stacy said, hurrying down the hallway to greet Jo. She approached her and much to Jo's shock, pulled her in for a quick hug. "I missed you today. Do you realize that is the longest time we've been apart in about a month?"

Jo returned the hug, then stepped away to hang up her coat. "I know. I was glad when we talked today. I was bored." They settled at the counter in the kitchen. "At least I was productive before that. I have my class all planned out, and I finished up my lesson plan for that kid I'm tutoring. He's a good student."

"Are you enjoying teaching?"

"Yes, very much." Jo surprised herself with her knee jerk reply. As she thought about it more she realized that she did, indeed, enjoy teaching.

"When do you take the certification test?"

Jo shrugged. "Amanda has handled the application, so I'm not exactly sure. It's sometime early next month that I go for the test. I still have to do some studying on history and culture. I think they expect you to know that stuff. Nic should be able to give me some guidance on the types of questions they'll ask me. She's coming in tomorrow, so I'm not working." Jo smiled at Stacy. "You know, we haven't taken any time this week to do anything fun. Maybe we could have lunch and go to the Museum? Anything you'd like."

Stacy's eyes held Jo's. "You do mean anything I'd like and not 'anything my heart desires,' right? I mean, you granted me one wish as I recall—anything my heart desires. I'm just checking that I'm not giving that up for picking a restaurant or museum."

"You are the crafty sort, aren't you? I was definitely not trying to wiggle out of my promise. I gave you my word, and I'll keep it willingly."

"Just checking," Stacy said with a giggle. "Gotta keep you honest, you know."

"I'm never anything but."

"Hmm, what about you, Jo? Anywhere in particular you'd like to go?"

"I asked you first."

"All right, I need to get a haircut before we do anything else. I'm getting shaggy. I'll call and see if I can get an early appointment. Then we can walk a little and maybe do lunch. I haven't been to the Metropolitan Museum of Art for a long time. Want to do that?"

Jo was worried about all the walking. "I'd love to do all of that, but maybe it'd be too much walking for me."

"Will you allow us to use the companion chair? I love what we have planned. We could use the break? We've been cooped up here for the better part of a month. It'll be fun just to get away together and have a fun day."

"Let's do it. You don't mind having to push my sorry butt around the city?"

"Jo, there's nothing sorry about your butt, and I'd be happy to push it around the city."

"Can you do me one favor?" Without waiting for Stacy's response, Jo quickly asked. "When you get your hair appointment, can you see if you could get one for me, too?"

"Sure. You getting it cut short like in the photo on your mantle? You look so cute with that hairstyle."

"I haven't worn it that way since I joined the force. That stupid hat they made you wear always gave me a cowlick right in the front." Jo used her three fingers, placing them at the peak of her forehead extending upwards. "When I took my hat off, it seriously undermined my authority." Jo grinned. "So I started wearing my hair just pulled back. The hat fit better, and I didn't have hat hair anymore."

"Well, there's no hat now."

"Why are you so interested in me having short hair?"

"Because I think you look hot with short hair. Not that this style is unbecoming," Stacy raised her eyebrows, arching one slightly, "but shorter is hotter."

"Are you trying to butch me up?"

"No, actually, I thought you looked more feminine with the shorter hairdo."

"Really?" Jo thought for a moment, recalling the shorter hairstyle. She had liked having short hair. When her hair was shorter, it had a lot of body and a slight wave to it. "Okay, short it is. Let's see if we can get an appointment."

They spent a quiet night together, ending it as usual with a stretching and a kneading of Jo's sore muscles.

* * *

Stacy massaged Jo's leg again the next morning before they each showered and dressed. "Temps will be near or slightly above fifty today. It'll be virtually spring-like," Stacy exclaimed excitedly. "I'm just going to wear a light jacket today."

"Let's take the truck, okay? The chair will fit more easily in the back. I'll take out the bed extender, and we can just slide the chair in and out. We can lock the cover, so it'll be secure when we're not using it."

"That sounds like a plan. Will you trust me to drive to the hair salon? That way I can drop you in front of the store and we won't need the chair."

"Sure." Jo handed Stacy the keys to her pickup. "You get my wheels and I'll get the chair."

* * *

Whistling a tune as she dressed, it suddenly came to Jo that, for the first time since she'd left her home after the shooting, she was happy. Moreover, it occurred to her that it was only since Stacy had become a part of her life that she felt this way. In her heart, Jo knew she would miss Stacy's constant presence in her life and that leaving would be hard to do. She finished getting dressed as she looked forward to their afternoon together.

The hairstylist listened to Jo describe the cut she wanted. The resulting haircut was very close to the way she'd worn it many years before. Instead of it being trimmed neatly at the neckline, the stylist had feathered it, leaving it wispy and brushed up in the back.

"This is a more hip and current cut than just trimming it off," the stylist told her.

"Ok, we'll give it a shot," Jo agreed. "But if I don't like it, I reserve the right to come back and have you cut it shorter back there."

"Deal."

Stacy was already finished and waiting for Jo when she went to the cashier to pay. "Jo, you look amazing."

As they left the store together, Jo looked up and down the street to see if she could see where the car was parked. Stacy had dropped her at the door earlier. "It's about a block and a half up." Stacy pointed. "Want me to go get it?"

"No, let's walk. My leg is feeling so much better. It's so much stronger and I have more stamina, thanks in large part to you."

Now, when taking their daily walks, Jo was able to walk twice around the block near the store without a rest if she used her cane. Stacy's presence gave her confidence, and she had grown to depend on Stacy to know when to link her arm through hers to add the stability she needed. She rarely took the chair any more, reserving its use for times when she had a lot of ground to cover, like today. Sometimes she'd reach for Stacy's hand and tuck it into the crook of her arm just because she missed having it there, more than for the need of her requiring it there for stability. She wondered if Stacy suspected. Jo did that today, and arm in arm they strolled down the street.

Stacy glanced over at Jo. "Hot."

"What?"

Stacy smiled. "I said hot. You definitely look hot."

Jo blushed. "I'm not sure I know how to respond to that. If I say you look hot, too, I'll sound insincere. I'm not. You are nearly irresistibly cute. I don't mean just today, I mean every day."

"Too bad. I mean the nearly part. You know, *nearly* irresistible." The playful conversation ended all too quickly. "Here's the pickup," Stacy said, handing Jo the keys.

"Want to eat near here or in the city?" Jo asked as she drove.

"Let's grab something around here before we get into the city. It'll be quicker and cheaper to eat here and parking will be easier. We're going out for a big meal tomorrow night, then to the bar."

"Good idea. You have any suggestions, Jo?"

"I'd love a burger."

"Okay by me."

"Take a left on Main. Let's go to the Shack."

The short trip to the restaurant ended with them finding a parking place right in front. They enjoyed their lunch together, laughing and teasing as they ate. The comfortable ambiance, good food, and speedy service all combined to make for a pleasurable experience.

* * *

They were running a little later than they expected as they pulled into the parking lot at the museum. Working together, they removed the companion chair from the back of the pickup.

Jo locked the vehicle before settling into the chair. "This feels weird. I can walk," Jo said as she settled into the chair.

"We both know that. This will be quicker and easier. Once we're in the museum, you can walk if you want, or maybe by that time you'll need to push me." Stacy touched Jo's face. "You look beautiful." She whispered, stroking Jo's cheek lightly with her fingertips. Quickly, she moved behind the chair waiting for Jo to settle before she headed toward the exit sign, pushing the chair.

A short walk later, they entered the museum. "Do you want to take a tour or just wander?" Jo asked.

"Let's just wander today. I'll push and you direct the way." They meandered through paintings, then sculptures, and ended up getting lost in the armor section. They finally figured out where they were on the map and navigated to an area of more interest to them. They stopped in the cafe for a cup of tea and a sweet when their energy waned towards the end of the day.

"What do you want to do for dinner?" Jo asked.

"I don't know. Pizza?"

"Umm, sounds good. Eat in or take home?"

"Let's see how we feel when we get closer to home."

They opted to take the pizza home since both were tired after their long day. "Should we take the wheelchair to the shop?" Stacy asked as she parked the pickup about a block from the apartment.

"No, I can walk down to the truck and get it tomorrow if I need it. It was good to have it today, though. I think I'm just about finished needing it around town here. I have to say it was a lifesaver today. It would've have been impossible for me to walk as far as we went today. Either we'd have seen much less, or you'd have had to go without me and I'd have ended up sitting on a bench somewhere. Thanks for pushing all day."

Despite Jo offering to treat for both meals as a thank you, Stacy insisted on splitting the bills. Stacy carried the pizza, and Jo linked her arm through Stacy's free one. Once inside the apartment, they served up the pizza.

Stacy took the first bite of her slice. "Umm, good. Still pretty warm, too."

"Uh huh, and good, too. Thank you, Stacy, for a wonderful day. I can't remember the last time I enjoyed spending this much time with someone and still felt interested in more time together. I never grow tired of my time with you."

Stacy swallowed. "Our time together is growing short, you know."

"Yes, I'm aware of that. How would you feel about extending it? I have to go up and open my parent's cabin. I don't want you to think that the only reason I'm asking you to come with me is because I would feel more comfortable having someone with me, even though I would. I'd really like it if you could come. It's beautiful up there, and I'd like to share it with you."

"I'd be happy to come with you. I've got another survey to turn in by the end of next week. Maybe I can work over the weekend and finish it up early. Will you help me translate it?"

Jo smiled. "Sure. I'd be pleased to do something for you for a change."

Once the dishes were cleared, Stacy went into the office and began writing up the summary of her survey. Jo had already finished up the part she could help her with.

"Will I bother you if I ride my bike a bit? I got my second wind, and I could stand to work off some of that pizza."

"Not at all."

Depending on how much she had used her leg during the day, Jo was able to ride for fifteen to twenty minutes on the bike, nonstop.

"I've come to find that sound much less annoying." Stacy had to raise her voice to be heard over the hum of the bike.

When she finished on the bike, Jo chose to sit on her bed and read as Stacy worked. As she read, she couldn't help feeling a little sad that she would be leaving Stacy's house in less than two short weeks. Stacy had been picking away at her novel in her spare time, although she wouldn't let Jo read it.

"You can read it as soon as I'm finished," Stacy promised when Jo asked for what seemed like the hundredth time. "Stop asking me."

Jo grinned. "I really do want to read it. I like to bug you about it, anyway. You're cute when you're angry."

Stacy shook her head and returned her focus to the job, resisting the smile that threatened to emerge against her will. She worked only a half hour longer. Looking up from her work, she studied Jo as she read. She'd always found Jo attractive. Now, with the new haircut, it was difficult to resist running her fingers through Jo's hair and...Stacy shook her head, denying her thought. "I'm wiped. I'd better get out of here and into my bed. I think if I work awhile tomorrow and put in some time on Sunday, I'll be able to finish up."

"I'll translate each page as you finish. Maybe we can ask Nic or Dana to check my work for me. I still don't have the certification."

"Yeah, but you have the skill. Neither Nic or Dana has ever changed anything you've written."

"Maybe, I'd still feel better if they check the translation for us."

Stacy glanced at the time. "Will we be late on Saturday?"

Jo pursed her lips. "Well, figure dinner will be over about what...nine-thirty? Then we have to drive into the city so it'll be at least ten before we get to the bar. I'd imagine we should be home by one thirty or so. Why?"

"Jo? Think it'd be a good idea to take a nap tomorrow afternoon. I can give you a massage first, so your leg will be in tiptop shape. I want to see you shake your tail feathers."

"That's a good idea." Jo paused. "Will you fast dance with me?"

"If you ask." Stacy stood to leave. "Get ready. I'll be back to give you your massage."

* * *

Stacy massaged Jo's leg and they did the stretching routine. Before she went to bed, Stacy did the exercise routine Jo had shown her to firm her abs and tighten up her muscles. Finished, she fell into bed and was soon asleep.

Jo tiptoed down the hallway and quietly entered Stacy's bedroom. She was naked. Without disturbing the sleeping Stacy, Jo slid under the covers and spooned behind the sleeping woman. Stacy awoke, and although surprised by Jo's presence in her bed, she continued to feign sleep as Jo's breath warmed her neck. Stacy could feel the outline of Jo's breasts pressed against her back, and when Jo's hand began its journey under her pajama top, she could feel Jo's nipples harden at the same time her own did. She stirred to turn over. "Jo..."

"Don't move," Jo commanded. "You've made me feel good with massages night after night. Let me make you feel good just this once. Roll onto your stomach and let's get rid of this top."

Stacy did as she was directed. Jo began a slow and steady kneading of Stacy's tired neck muscles. It felt heavenly. She could smell Jo's fresh scent and felt relieved that she'd showered before she got into bed. Soon, as Jo's hands worked, Stacy stopped thinking and allowed herself to only feel. Jo's hands massaged and soothed their way down her back first. Jo began to use her nails ever so lightly, trailing irregular shapes and patterns across Stacy's skin. The path was unpredictable, leaving each square inch of skin hoping that it was its turn next. A groan escaped Stacy's lips. She was shocked to realize that her own voice had made that sound filled with such need. Jo's hands slid beneath the band of Stacy's pajama bottoms.

"Raise up. It's time for these to go, don't you think?"

Stacy complied and soon she was naked. She longed for Jo to press her body to her own. Instead Jo continued with the slow, deliberate strokes, caressing her lower back then traveling across her buttocks to her thighs.

Stacy was wet and wanting Jo to touch her. Jo avoided touching the front of Stacy's torso. She continued to deliberately stroke and scratch her way down Stacy's legs to her calves. When she finished the tour of the back of Stacy's body, Jo returned to again spoon against Stacy, allowing her lips to trace soft circles down her neck and across her shoulders.

Unable to stand it any longer, Stacy turned over, seeking to feel Jo's breasts pressed against her own, needing to press her core against Jo's skin. *How can I be this much in need when we haven't even kissed yet,* she wondered. Her lips sought Jo's mouth. As Jo's tongue probed she met it with her own, and the passion exploded between them. She couldn't get close enough to her. They rode each other's thighs, increasing the need for more intimate contact.

Jo rubbed Stacy's breast, pinching the already erect nipple. Curious, Stacy reached out to tentatively touch Jo's breast. Slowly gaining confidence, she replaced her inquisitive fingers with her lips and tongue. She was pleased with herself when Jo moaned in response. Jo pushed against her and turned Stacy on her back. Jo's lips, her tongue, her teeth were everywhere, kissing, licking, and gently biting. As Stacy's need grew, she could smell the scent of their mutual arousal. Jo's hand touched her. Stacy begged. "Inside, please. Now. I need you inside me."

Jo entered her, stroking gently at first. As their need grew, the tempo and urgency increased. A powerful orgasm shot through Stacy. She screamed out Jo's name in release. Stacy's own voice woke her. She sat up in bed with a start. Feeling the empty space next to her in bed, she was disappointed to find it cold. She stood, slipped into her robe, and made her way out to the kitchen to get a drink of water. She pressed her cool damp fingers to her neck before splashing water on her face. Her dream had certainly settled any remaining questions. There was no room for doubt. She wanted Jo. She wanted her naked, and she wanted her intimately. She got her laptop from the dining table, took it into the bedroom with her and once settled began to type. It was four o'clock when she finished and closed her laptop.

The next morning, Jo was already awake when Stacy joined her in the kitchen. Jo was puzzled when Stacy seemed to be avoiding her eyes.

"Are you okay?"

"Yes, I had a very realistic dream that woke me up last night."

"Want to tell me about it?"

"Not right now." Stacy blushed as the memory flooded her mind. "It was certainly memorable. I promise I'll tell you about it sometime, just not right now. I need to get busy. I've got a lot of work left to do if I want to finish up early."

"I have to run over and see Nic. I need to find out my schedule this week. I know I have the class and the tutoring. I don't know what days she needs me to cover the office. Want to come? It'll only take me a few minutes."

Torn, Stacy debated only for a moment knowing she should start on her work. In the end, she decided to steal some time to go see Nic. "I haven't talked to Nic since she and Dana got the good news. I'd like to say hello."

The duo walked across the street and exchanged greetings with Mallory and Nic. After Jo and Nic had the schedule worked out, the four women made small talk. Mallory asked Jo how the massages and stretching were working out.

Jo casually threw an arm over Stacy's shoulder pulling her close. The gesture didn't go unnoticed by either Nic or Mallory who exchanged a look. Jo was unaware of the silent communication between Nic and Mallory, but Stacy saw the exchange and wondered what it meant.

Jo praised Stacy's massage abilities and virtually gushed about how she had helped her leg improve much faster than she'd been led to believe it would.

Jo turned to Stacy. "I've got a few things to do here. I'll be five minutes more max, I promise. Do you want to wait for me?"

"All right. Then I've got work to do."

"I know. I'm going to help you. Be right back." She grinned, gave Stacy's shoulder a squeeze, and headed toward the back of the shop.

"You certainly have an admirer there," Mallory commented. "Jo seems much happier."

"You mean about her leg?" Stacy agreed. "Yes, she is,"

"I don't think that was precisely what Mal meant," Nic said with a wink. "Look, Stacy, I don't mean to butt in here. It's just that you've been good for Jo. We all love Jo and want to see her happy. We all feel the same way about you."

Mallory was surprised when Nic didn't say more. So she decided to give Cupid a hand and put in her own two cents. "We all agree that it's too bad you're straight. Truth is, we all think you and Jo would be perfect together."

The two women standing before her had just put into words feelings that had gradually been coming into focus for Stacy. She decided to confide in them. "Don't assume that because I've always played for one team that I haven't actually given it some thought. I've grown to care a great deal for Jo and would be open to..."

How should she put it? What would she be open to, sex? A relationship? She wasn't sure yet. She finished her thought simply with, "I'd be open to more. But Jo has this rule."

Mallory rolled her eyes and Nic shrugged.

"Rules are meant to be broken, aren't they?" Nic cautioned, "Be sure that, if you decide to act on your feelings, you won't change your mind. Before you act, you need to feel that your heart would shatter if she walked out of your life."

"Believe me, it's not a decision I would ever make lightly. I would never hurt her. That's the last thing I'd ever want to do to someone I love." Her hand shot up to cover her lips. Shocked by her own words, she shook her head, eyes wide. "I don't know where that came from."

Nic reached out and lightly touched Stacy's chest where her heart resided. "From here," she said quietly.

"But how, Nic? She isn't interested in me as anything more than a friend. If I try to tell her how I feel, she'll just quote that damned rule and tell me no."

"I'm going to give you a little hint here. It's extremely hard to say no when your mouth is busy doing something else. Kiss her. Kiss her with all you're worth. If she has the feelings for you that I suspect she has, that'll do it." Nic reached over and squeezed Stacy's hand.

"Thanks, both of you, for the advice." Stacy sighed. "I appreciate your support and understanding."

Knowing it was soon time for Jo to return, Mallory gestured with her head to the back room. "We'd better be talking about something else when the object of your affection returns." She slid over and wrapped an arm around Stacy's shoulders. Giving her a quick hug, she changed the subject. "So, we're all set for tonight?"

Stacy's eyes twinkled with excitement. "Yes, I actually planned to mention to you, Nic, how happy I am that we're having a celebration tonight."

"Aren't we all?" Mallory looked at Nic. "How do you want to organize getting there?"

"Well, none of us has a car that will hold six of us. So, two cars I guess."

"Well, Amanda and I and you and Dana are right next door to each other, so why don't we all travel together and meet you and Jo at the restaurant? Jo knows where the bar is, so we'll just move there after we finish dinner."

Jo joined them for the conclusion of the discussion about the logistics of transportation for the evening, and the plans were set. "So, we'll see you there at the restaurant."

* * *

Stacy had been typing for nearly four hours straight. It was two-thirty. They had taken a fifteen-minute break for lunch. Stacy was so focused on what she was doing that she was unaware of Jo's scrutiny.

Jo appreciated the profile of the wonderful woman she had come to care deeply for. *She's so darned cute.*

Stacy's hair hung over her brow as she leaned forward to see what she was typing. She blew upward to move the hair from her field of vision, and when that failed, she impatiently brushed it aside and tucked it behind her ear, barely missing a beat on the keyboard. She paused to check her notes before she started to type again, rubbing the tension in her neck with her hand

Jo, sitting on her bed, had her computer settled on a pillow on her lap. She was a couple of pages behind Stacy in her translation. A smile came to Jo's face. The woman could type like nobody's business.

With a flourish, Stacy hit command P to print the last page of that section of her report. "There, done," she exclaimed.

"The whole thing?"

"No, unfortunately not. I'm at a good stopping point for today. Maybe two or, at most, three hours more tomorrow." Stacy leaned back and rolled her shoulders.

"Good. I'll be able to finish tomorrow, too. Then, you can get the report in the mail and we can get on with our little getaway. I'd like to leave after I teach my class on Thursday. I can move the tutoring around, and that'll give us a good three days there."

Stacy stretched her neck first left, then right.

"Come here." Jo closed the laptop and set the computer on the table behind her. She patted the space between her legs.

Stacy stood and approached the bed. "Where?"

Again, Jo patted the space between her legs. She slid to a more upright position. "Just sit here and let me make your neck feel better for a change. Then you can have your nap if you want. We have time."

"Oooh," she groaned, exhaling a long sigh. "That would be nice. I've always had bad posture at the computer. When I really get into something, I forget to sit up straight and lean forward towards the monitor. My neck and shoulders always suffer."

Jo raised both knees. Stacy sat on the edge of the bed then scooted back against Jo, settling comfortably between her legs, wrapping her arms around Jo's knees. Jo started to massage Stacy's shoulders through her sweatshirt. "Take this off, it's too thick."

As Stacy slid the shirt off over her head, Jo reached behind her for the lotion. She put some in her palm and warmed it as she had seen Stacy do every night and morning for well over a month. She began to massage the tender muscles of Stacy's neck and shoulders. Stacy's head began to loll as Jo soothed the sore muscles. "Umm, that's wonderful."

"Lean back against me and let me do your shoulders and upper arms."

Stacy followed Jo's instructions, leaned back, and willed Jo's hands to travel farther, to come down over her shoulders and cup her breasts. She wanted to remove her bra and flip over, to repeat the pleasures she had experienced in her dream the night before. Instead of moving down to where she wanted Jo's hands, Jo began to massage her temples, brushing her fingertips across her forehead. Stacy felt her eyelids close as she relaxed. Her head settled back against Jo's chest, and before she knew it, she was sound asleep.

A little over an hour later, they awoke. Somehow, Stacy had turned over and was straddling Jo's leg with her own while her head rested on Jo's left breast. Jo's arms were wrapped around Stacy. They awoke at the same time. Neither moved, each wanting to extend the intimacy even if it was only for seconds longer.

Jo was the first to speak, forcing nonchalance into her voice. "Have a good nap?"

Stacy sat up, sliding into a sitting position next to Jo. She had been so deeply asleep, that it seemed to be taking her longer than normal to begin to think clearly.

Jo recovered more quickly than Stacy. "Here's your shirt," she said, handing Stacy the sweatshirt she'd removed earlier to facilitate the massage. Jo was surprised when Stacy didn't put on the garment and rolled across her to get off the bed. *Is it my imagination? Had Stacy dipped a bit so their breasts would brush each other's as she slid across?*

"That was the soundest sleep I've had in, well, I can't remember when." She extended her hand to help Jo off the bed. "Come on. I'm going to dance your ass off tonight. Take your shower and we'll do your leg. I want you in tip top shape for the evening's activities, so you can't beg off."

"I won't beg off. I told you I'd fast dance with you."

Stacy wasn't worried about the fast dances. She wanted to slow dance with Jo. She wanted to pull her close and bury her nose in Jo's neck. She didn't know what it was about the way the woman smelled. Jo should simply bottle her scent.

With her shower completed, Jo blew her hair dry before she dressed in her bra and panties. As she strode towards her bedroom, she felt filled with anticipation for the evening. For once, she wouldn't be a fifth wheel when she went out with her friends. She was pleased to be seen with Stacy, and wished with all her heart that Stacy wasn't straight. Jo suspected that it wouldn't take much effort on her part to get Stacy into bed with her. There had been too many clues. She was obviously comfortable touching her. The recent sleeping incident proved her point, at least in her own mind.

Stacy was sitting on the foot of Jo's bed waiting for her. Jo watched as Stacy's eyes swept over her body making her slightly self-conscious.

"Face up, please." Stacy directed, pointing to the bed.

The massage was different tonight. Instead of seeking out knots and rubbing to the point that it felt good when she stopped, Stacy made long slow strokes up and down Jo's thigh before working on her calf. "Flip over, please."

Jo complied. Stacy repeated the long slow stretching of the muscles in the back of her leg from top of her thigh to her ankle. Jo figured if Stacy continued much longer, she'd have to change her underwear again before they left. When Stacy started to massage the inner part of her thigh, she finally commented, "You're doing something a little different tonight."

"Yes," she replied in the soft, silken drawl Jo loved. "I want to stretch out those long muscles for you in preparation for the workout I plan to give them tonight."

Oh God, thought Jo. *I know she doesn't mean that the way I wish she did, but it still made her hot to think of the possibilities.* "Okay, I'm good. You'd better hurry and get ready. We don't want to be late."

Jo dressed in the only good outfit she had brought with her, dark pants and a soft blue-grey blouse with split cuffs that rolled up one full cuff. Not fancy, just very comfortable and dressy enough for the restaurant. She heard Stacy leave the bathroom, bound for her own bedroom. Jo fooled with her hair until it looked pretty much the way the stylist made it look the day she had it cut. She liked her new short hairstyle. It was easy to care for and gave her a more feminine appearance. Her dark lashes needed no makeup. She did add some gloss to her lips.

Chapter 17

JO CAME OUT OF her bedroom and headed down the hallway before stopping dead in her tracks. Stacy was leaning against the kitchen counter waiting for her. Her hair was styled and she'd applied a light coat of eye makeup that made her crystal clear green eyes stand out even more than usual. She had on black pants and a red blouse that had a collar that stood up slightly. However, the neckline is what drew her focus. Two buttons were left open, drawing attention to Stacy's full, luscious breasts.

"Stacy, you look amazing. You take my breath away."

"Thank you, I could say the same about you. The color of the blouse brings out the color of your eyes." Stacy wanted some sort of physical contact with Jo. She approached her and slid her hands up to make an unnecessary adjustment to Jo's collar. A small smile curled her lips. "There, perfect." She reluctantly withdrew her hand and turned to get their coats.

They went down the stairs, Stacy first. Jo followed, locking the door behind her. Jo had a strange sense of excitement in the pit of her stomach. They'd decided that because she was familiar with the location, she would drive to the restaurant. Jo would drive to the bar after dinner.

Stacy slid her hand into Jo's, as was her practice. Instead of looping it up into the crook of her arm, Jo continued to hold Stacy's hand as they strolled slowly down the street toward her truck. Stacy had butterflies in her stomach. *Is this the way I would feel all the time, if she were my girlfriend?* Somehow, the small gesture of Jo holding her hand instead of slipping it through the crook of her arm made the evening they were about to share different somehow. Holding her hand was more intimate than strolling arm in arm. Jo was walking easily, with no visible limp. Stacy felt proud to be seen with this impressive looking woman.

They pulled into the parking lot of the restaurant and Jo pointed out Dana's car. "They beat us here and we're ten minutes early."

When everyone was seated, Amanda put a hand on Mallory's shoulder. "Tonight is our treat in celebration of Nic and Dana's good news." Everyone was relieved to know the lump was a cyst and nothing to worry about.

The waiter came by to take the drink orders. Everyone ordered a cocktail. After the drinks were served, each woman raised her glass as Nic made a toast. "To everyone here. When I fell in love with Dana, I hit the mother lode. I found the love of my life and the best group of friends anyone could have." She raised her glass to a round of 'hear, hear,' from everyone at the table.

The dinner was delicious. Service was family style, so everyone got to taste some of each of the dishes they'd chosen. Amanda had ordered two bottles of full-bodied merlot to be served with the dinner selections.

The evening was proving to be an enjoyable time filled with laughter. By the time the waiter served dessert, they were all looking forward to moving on to the next event. While they waited for dessert to be served, Jo had her hand resting on her thigh, an old habit from when she had to massage it if she sat for more than a short time. Stacy slid her hand over Jo's and leaned in to whisper, "I'm having a wonderful time."

Jo squeezed Stacy's hand in return. "Me, too. Wish there could be more evenings like this one."

Jo and Stacy waited in the parking lot of the bar for the others to pull in. They found a table that would hold all of them and ordered a round of drinks. Jo, who had only had one drink at dinner and a sip of the wine for the toast, ordered club soda. Dana, who was the other designated driver, did the same. The band was setting up, and within fifteen minutes of their arrival, they had started their first set. The bar filled quickly, a steady stream of women in all types of attire showing up to party with their friends and women they hoped would be friends, or at least intimate acquaintances, before night's end.

The band started with some line dances to get people up on their feet. Before long, the floor was crowded with women doing all different sorts of dances. Stacy watched in fascination, feeling a sense of exhilaration at the energy created by the women surrounding her. Nic and Dana were the first from their table to take to the floor. Stacy watched her friends as they moved together, eyes locked in an unspoken passion they shared. Soon Mallory and Amanda joined the dancing, leaving Stacy and Jo at the table.

Stacy bounced along with the music as she glanced around the room. She was a bit surprised to see two women along the wall kissing each other unabashedly. They soon followed each other into the restroom. Jo reached for Stacy's hand.

"Not everyone has so little respect for her partner." She had to speak loudly into Stacy's ear to be heard. "Are you ready to dance?"

"I thought you'd never ask." They moved to the floor and joined their friends. They danced three fast dances together, moving closer with each song. By the end of their third dance, they were moving like lovers. It would be hard to determine who was having a better time, Stacy or Jo.

"I need something to drink," Jo said. They returned to the table where Jo took a sip of her club soda. Stacy took a sip of her rum and coke. The band changed the tempo, slipping into their first slow number of the evening.

"Dance with me," Stacy requested, holding her hand out to Jo.

Jo took her hand but didn't move. "I'm not so sure that's a good idea."

"Why? You can't be afraid of a little old country girl such as myself," Stacy chided thickening her accent.

"You don't think so?" Jo laughed. "You're the hottest woman here. I'm just thankful I'm not drinking, or I'm not sure I could control myself."

"Nobody's asking you to control yourself. I'm asking you to dance with me."

"Stacy..." Jo started to shake her head.

"Jo, remember the 'anything my heart desires' promise? This is what my heart desires. I want you to dance with me tonight. I want to feel like you are dancing with me because you really want to."

"I want to more than you'll ever know." Jo stood up and led Stacy to the dance floor, taking her into her arms and pulling her tight. She vowed that, just for tonight, she'd relax her guard and enjoy the lovely woman who had her nose nuzzled in her neck. At the risk of being redundant, she repeated in her head that she was so glad she was not drinking.

Stacy and Jo danced well together, their bodies close, two moving as one. The first song melded into another as they moved around the floor. Focused only on each other, they were unaware of the scrutiny of their friends. One other pair of eyes closely fixed on them as well.

They danced three slow dances in a row, only stopping when the band took a break. Heading back to their table to join the group, they were still unaware that their comfort level on the dance floor and the way they moved together had garnered several comments from their friends while they danced. Stacy looked across the room to the bar, hoping to catch the eye of the overworked waitress. She desperately wanted some water or club soda.

"Jo, isn't that Meg over there at the bar?"

Jo's eyes focused on a furious looking woman seated at the bar, glaring in their direction. She gave Meg a wave. Meg simply glared back in return, making Jo wonder what Meg was thinking. Meg finally staggered to her feet and weaved her way across the dance floor.

Nic leaned over to speak into Jo's ear. "This looks like trouble."

Meg didn't say anything at first. She just stood at the edge of the group staring at Jo. "I never pegged you for a liar, Jo." Her speech was thick and slurred from the alcohol she'd consumed.

Jo stood up. Meg, nearly half a head taller, towered over her. "Meg, please don't do this. Don't make a scene. Our group is here celebrating a happy occasion. It's really important to me that you don't ruin our evening."

"I'm not making a scene, Jo. I'm just standing here wondering when you became such a liar."

Nic stood up. She was tall enough to look Meg in the eye. "Meg, Dana and I are here to celebrate a happy occasion and I'm asking you politely, one final time, to save this conversation until you're sober."

Jo implored the drunken woman before her. "Come on, Meg, come outside with me and we can talk there."

"Is your new girlfriend coming, too?"

Trying to ignore the comment, Jo said, "Come on, Meg." Jo turned and headed for the door, hoping that Meg would follow.

Nic grasped Meg by the arm. She squeezed enough to gain Meg's attention through her alcohol-clouded brain. Wincing, Meg allowed Nic to guide her outside.

Jo was waiting in front of her truck. "Meg, I don't know what your problem is. I'm here with my friends, trying to have a good time, and you're ruining our evening. I'm not sure I understand why."

Nic backed away to allow the two women some privacy, although she remained close enough to come to Jo's defense against the taller woman should that become necessary.

"Problem? Why wouldn't I have a problem? You told me that woman you are pawing out there on the dance floor was straight and that you weren't involved. You were doing some sort of research project. Liar!"

"Meg, I haven't lied to you. I've told you before that we are not now, nor have we ever been intimate. She's not my lover. She's straight. Meg, you are way out of line here. I've told you twice already that you and I will never be more than friends. I'm warning you that if you don't back down here, you'll jeopardize our friendship, too."

Meg's emotions turned on a dime. She switched from belligerent to weepy and dissolved into tears. "I'm sorry, Jo. It's just that I can't seem to get over you. I love you, Baby." Jo sidestepped Meg's attempt to wrap her in a sloppy embrace.

Jo looked to Nic for help. Nic stepped in and said, "Meg, did you come here with anyone?"

Meg shook her head.

"Well, you can't drive home like this." Nic looked around to find someone to help.

"I'll take her home," Jo said. "Give me your keys, Meg."

Meg searched her pockets, finally producing the keys to her pickup. She handed them to Jo as she weaved unsteadily on her feet.

"Come on, let's get you into your truck. You can sleep off a little of this overdose of alcohol." Nic and Jo helped Meg into the passenger seat of her truck. By the time they got Meg loaded into the vehicle and closed the door, Meg was already passed out. Jo pressed the key fob, locking the doors of the truck. Nic and Jo returned to their friends who had, by then, settled their bill and were waiting for the two of them to return.

"I'm sorry, people, Nic and I got her loaded into her truck. I'll drive her home." Jo turned to Stacy. "I hate to ask you this...do you think you could follow us in my truck?"

"Sure."

"I'm sorry."

Amanda jumped in. "It wasn't your fault. You and Nic handled it very well. In her condition, it could have turned ugly."

Stacy took Jo's hand. "She's right. Come on, let's get her home."

Outside in the parking lot, everyone hugged goodnight. "I'll see you on Monday, Nic. Thanks." Jo waved to the others. "Goodnight, everyone."

Stacy hugged each of the women in turn. "I had a great time, thanks for including me. Dana, I'm so glad you got good news."

Jo added, "Yes, I hope this little incident won't make us forget that this was a happy occasion we were celebrating."

Nic pulled Jo aside. "Do you think we need to follow you?"

"No, she'll have slept some of it off by the time I get her home. I'll be okay. But thanks for offering."

Nic gave a wave to her friend and joined the others for the trip home.

Jo unlocked Meg's truck and slid into the driver's seat. She needed to move it forward about six inches in order to reach the pedals. She checked to see that Stacy was ready before they pulled out to make the fifty-five minute drive to Meg's home.

Meg woke up about ten minutes from her house. She was extremely contrite that she had ruined Jo and her friends' celebration.

"Look, Meg. I've told you this before. I didn't lie to you. Stacy and I are not involved, although I will admit that if I thought there was a remote possibility, I would decide to move in that direction. If I make that decision to be involved with her, you need to recognize that I'm completely free to do so. I've told you that I'm not interested in a relationship with you at least twice now. I made a big mistake that day I slept with you. I apologize that I didn't say no before that happened. For one last time, it will never, ever happen again. I can't make it any clearer than that."

"I hear you. Please don't stop being my friend, Jo."

"I hope that won't be necessary."

Jo parked the truck in front of Meg's house and helped Meg get to the door. She slid the key into the lock, opened the door, and flicked on the lights. She handed Meg her truck keys. "Go take a couple of aspirin and drink a big glass of water. You're going to have a headache tomorrow that I wouldn't wish on anyone."

Jo watched Meg go into her house. Stacy pulled up behind Meg's truck and Jo walked over, opened the door, and leaned in. "Want me to drive?"

"No, I'm fine. Get in. Let's go home."

Jo settled into the passenger seat of her truck. "Well, that was a dramatic ending to an otherwise enjoyable evening. I'm sorry Meg ruined our fun."

"It wasn't your fault that she got soused and acted like an idiot. I have to admit that I can't blame her. You're just so darned irresistible. I'm sure she just couldn't help herself."

Jo laughed. "Yeah, right."

Chapter 18

STACY PARKED ABOUT A block from the apartment. As they made their way home, she noticed that Jo was favoring her leg though not quite limping. She linked her arm through Jo's knowing she had neither her cane nor the wheelchair to lean on as they walked home.

Once inside, Stacy checked the time...one thirty-five. "If you can get ready for bed before I fall asleep, I'll give you a quick massage."

"Oh yeah, I'd really appreciate that. I have to admit that my leg held up pretty good considering the work out we gave it." Jo grinned, meeting Stacy's green eyes with a warm gaze of her own. "I had a wonderful time with you tonight."

Stacy was the first to move. She started across the room with a destination of Jo's arms around her and Jo's lips on her own. Before she was half way there, the phone rang.

She turned to look at the offending object. "Who could that be?" Jo's immediate concern was that it was Meg calling.

Stacy rushed to pick up the phone before the end of the second ring. She checked the caller ID before answering. Concerned, she pushed the on button and said, "Mom, what's the matter?"

Jo was worried by the serious expression on Stacy's face as she listened to her mother.

"Where is he now?" Stacy asked.

After listening to her mother, Stacy told her that she would be there as soon as she could. She ended with, "I know, Mom. I will. I'll grab a couple of hours of sleep first. I'll leave here around dawn."

"Be sure you rest first, Honey. Promise me. And drive carefully on the way down."

"Don't worry, Mom. I'll be careful, I promise."

Stacy turned toward Jo, tears in her eyes. Jo quickly reached for and drew her close. "Tell me what happened."

Stacy took a moment seeking the comfort that Jo offered her before she pulled back to say, "It's my dad. Mom thinks it's a heart attack. He's stable now. Mom wants me to come."

"I'll come with you. It'll be easier if both of us drive."

Stacy contemplated Jo's offer. After careful consideration, she declined. "No, I'll be okay. I really appreciate that you'd be willing to come with me. You have obligations here—both to your class and to the kids you're helping. I'd love it if you'd come home with me. However, I'd prefer it to be a time when you'll be able to see more of my hometown than the hospital waiting room. When we go, I'd want it to be a vacation. I want you to meet my family and my friends and see my favorite places. Besides, if you're willing, you could be more helpful to me here." Stacy sought Jo's eyes.

Jo nodded. "Anything you need. How can I help?"

"I need to get that survey in by Friday. I'll be spending a lot of time at the hospital. I'll finish up what I need to do on the report and email it to you. Will you take care of the last parts of the translation and then submit it for me? I'll email the information you'll need to do that when I send the last part of the report."

"Okay. I'd rather go with you. However, if you think I'll be more useful here, that's what I'll do. I'd do anything you ask."

"Do you mean that?"

Jo frowned. "Of course."

Stacy needed Jo, but not for sex right now. She wanted the closeness and the intimacy they'd shared earlier during their nap. Stacy knew she'd be away for at least several days and when she returned, she and Jo would vacation for a few days. If she could not convince Jo that she loved her enough that her stupid rule number two didn't apply to her, Jo would move back to her home. She hoped they would be friends. Their time together, as they had come to know it, would end.

Stacy crossed to stand in front of Jo. "I need you to hold me tonight. Just hold me. I need to get some sleep before I drive home. Can you do that for me?"

Jo smiled and pulled Stacy towards her, holding her 'til she felt her relax. "Let me change. I'll be in as quick as I can."

Stacy returned to her room and prepared for bed. She put on clean pajamas and slid into bed. As Jo had promised, she came in a few moments later. She was wearing a tee shirt and boxers.

"Which side do you want me on?"

"Which would be better for your leg?"

"Maybe I should be on your left side. That puts my good leg next to you." Jo walked around the bed and slid in.

Stacy rolled toward Jo. They settled into a comfortable position with Stacy's head on Jo's shoulder and her leg casually resting on the thigh of Jo's good leg. She needed to touch Jo, to feel her skin. She slid her hand under Jo's tee shirt and heard her sudden intake of breath. Jo's skin was soft and smooth to the touch, and Stacy had an almost uncontrollable urge to allow herself the luxury of sliding her hand over Jo's belly then up to her breast. It just felt so natural to her to desire that. In her heart she knew she loved and wanted Jo. Now was not the time for them to make love. She wanted to give Jo time to absorb that she loved her and time to allow herself to love her back. She wanted Jo for a lifetime, and she didn't want their first time together, if there was to be one, to be rushed. "I want to tell you something, Jo. Before I do, I want you to promise me something."

"Anything."

"Don't say a word. I want to tell you something, and I need you to give me your promise that you won't say anything in response right now and that you won't move." She stressed 'won't move' to make it clear it was an imperative. "Promise?"

"Okay, I give you my word. I promise to hold my tongue and to be still although you're worrying me. What is it?"

Stacy snuggled closer, sliding her hand up Jo's side, her thumb resting just below Jo's breast. She wanted more, so much more. She rose up and quickly kissed Jo's mouth as she slid her hand up to cup Jo's breast. True to her word, Jo didn't move. Her only reaction was a quick intake of breath and a clenching of her hands.

Stacy could feel Jo's heart beneath her hand. She took a deep breath and risked her heart. "I love you, Jo. I love your heart and your kindness, your bravery, your determination. I love your looks, your smile, your body, and I love the way we can talk about anything and everything. I love the way you tuck my arm into yours, and the way you made tonight special by holding my hand instead. I know you have your rule against straight women. I swear to you Jo, I want no one other than you. If I were to live a hundred more years, I wouldn't leave you for anyone, male or female. There's no way for me to prove it to you. I'm sorry that I have no way to erase my history. I'm asking you to trust in me and believe me. I've never lied to you, Jo, and I certainly wouldn't start now with something this important. While I'm gone, I'm asking that you think about what I've told you and see if you can't add some sort of codicil to that rule of yours that might allow you to open your heart to me...to accept me into your life. I love you, Sweetheart, with all my heart, and it's my hope that you'll find some way to love me back."

Stacy started to pull her hand away from Jo's breast. Jo reached up and stopped her by gently placing her hand on top of Stacy's. Jo pressed her hand down, willing Stacy to not move. When she felt Stacy's hand relax, she slid her hand under her shirt to hold Stacy's hand in place against her breast, against her heart. Stacy sighed and snuggled against the woman she loved. She was soon sound asleep.

* * *

Jo remained awake for a long time listening to Stacy breathe. Was it possible that she could have this lovely woman? Could she trust that there wouldn't come a moment of realization after they had made love, after Stacy had answered her final questions about what it was like to love a woman, and after Jo completely surrendered her heart that Stacy would change her mind and realize that she just couldn't be with a woman? What would happen if Stacy's friends disowned her or if her parents turned away from her? Would she still want Jo then, or would history repeat itself?

Jo knew that it was too late to protect her heart. She knew that she already loved Stacy. Still, their love was new. If she turned away now, no doubt it would hurt. If they didn't go any further, maybe it would hurt less than it would if they were together for some time before Stacy had a change of heart and left her. Jo didn't think she could stand to face that rejection from Stacy. It was at least two hours later when she fell into a deep and exhausted sleep, still unsure of what she would decide.

Stacy woke up around three hours after she'd fallen asleep, still snuggled against Jo, her hand still cupping Jo's breast. She could feel the steady beat of Jo's heart beneath her fingers. Carefully she slipped her hand out from under Jo's shirt and reluctantly slid gingerly out of bed.

She went into her walk-in closet and pulled the door closed. She quickly packed her overnight bag with three days' worth of clothes and a few extra pairs of underwear before she quietly crept down the hallway to shower and dress for the day. She sat at the kitchen counter to write a note to Jo.

> Jo,
> It's so early. I didn't want to wake you. I wanted to get started, to get a jump on traffic. I'm anxious to get to the hospital, to my mom and dad.
> Thank you for keeping your word last night, well, really this morning. I feared that if you spoke, you would deny that you love me, and right now, with all that's happening at home, I couldn't face it if you said that. I love you with all my heart and with all I have to give. You once offered me 'anything my heart desired' and I foolishly wasted that promise last night to get you to dance with me. Even so, I wouldn't want you to come to me that way—not because of a silly promise, or through some sense of obligation. I want you to come to me because you want me as much as I want you, because your life is better with me in it than without.
> One of the things I have told you I admire in you is your bravery. Take the risk, Jo. Be brave and allow yourself to trust me, to love me. I promise it will be worth it. Scout's honor.
> I'll call you when I get there and have more information. I'll return as soon as possible so I can have my final lesson of what it's like to be a lesbian. It is one lesson I've dreamed about more than once. If making love with you in real life is half as good as it has been in my dreams, I can't wait.

Stacy reread her note and signed her name. She had bravely put her feelings out there for Jo to accept or reject. There was nothing more she could do. She resisted her desire to go back and kiss Jo goodbye. She quietly left her apartment and started her journey home.

Chapter 19

JO AWOKE AROUND EIGHT-THIRTY. She listened for Stacy but was only greeted by silence. She put her hand to her breast, recalling the mixed emotions that Stacy generated when she slipped her hand under Jo's pajama top. Already her heart ached. All the thinking she'd done before she surrendered to sleep had given her no clearer a picture of what she'd decide. She touched her lips, recalling the kiss Stacy had placed there last night. Jo kept her promise not to speak or move despite the gargantuan effort it took. As Stacy's mouth gently covered her own, Jo had wanted nothing more than to pull Stacy into her arms and make love to her, to confess that she was already hopelessly in love with her, although too afraid to make a commitment. Her skin had hummed with the need for Stacy's touch, and her heart ached with the need to confess her desire. Running her tongue over her lips, she imagined she could still feel Stacy's soft mouth on her own. *She thinks I'm brave. The truth is I'm a coward, through and through. How could she possibly love me? I'm an idiot.*

Jo rolled over, inhaling Stacy's scent on the pillow. They had been too overwhelmed last night for her massage, so Jo was stiff this morning. Beginning her process for getting out of bed, she pushed herself to a sitting position and massaged her leg as best she could. She stood up and stretched out her tendon. *Not too bad.* With some effort, Jo made the bed before heading for the kitchen, calling Stacy's name as she went. She checked the bathroom and the office before she returned to the kitchen to make tea. *I can't believe she left without waking me.* As she turned toward the counter, she saw Stacy's note.

Jo read the letter quickly from beginning to end, then went back to reread every line again as her tea water heated in the microwave. She paused when she came to the sentence *I want you to come to me because you want me as much as I want you—because your life is better with me in it than without*. The microwave chimed and Jo carried the note and her tea to the counter. Sliding onto a stool, she rested her fingers on the note, unconsciously tapping her fingers as she thoughtfully reviewed the past weeks they'd spent together. How her life had changed with Stacy in it. She replayed the conversations they'd had, the massages, the walks, the work they'd done together. Stacy and Jo had shared their hopes and fears with each other. Jo had to admit that she was never bored when she was with Stacy. All those things aside, if she was honest about her feelings, she knew already that she was in love. One thought still nagged. What if they moved forward and then Stacy changed her mind about being involved with a woman?

Jo finished her tea and went into the office to do her exercise routine. To finish her workout she rode the bike. She completed three sets of eight minutes each with less rest than normal between each set. Checking her stats, she pumped her fist and uttered, "Yes!" She was pleased with the progress. Stacy had been faithful with the massages and more recently with the stretching. Jo had hoped that she would consistently improve if she were dedicated in her exercise program. Not naive enough to think that she'd return to her former level of mobility, she still maintained hope that she'd be able to return to most of her activities if she recognized her limitations. She was fortunate to have found someone who loved her despite her handicap. Someone who was patient with her inability to do some activities and willing to help her work to be the best she could be.

Stacy thinks I'm brave. In my mind, I've been an incredible coward. Last night and in her note, Stacy laid her heart on the line and I'm sitting here analyzing my risk. Jo thought back to when she'd held Stacy tight against her as they moved together around the dance floor, then recalled the response she felt when Stacy touched her breast last night. She knew the soft and gentle touch was not meant to urge her to respond sexually so as Stacy had requested, she had held herself in check. There was no doubt in her mind that she wanted Stacy. She didn't want what they had already shared to ever end, and she sensed that if they took their relationship to the next level, there would be no pulling back for her. *Could I be more of an idiot? I'm scared, but I need to stop this nonsense and just tell her that I love her and want her, no matter how much I've tried to fight it. That's the simple truth.* Jo returned to the kitchen and wrote, 'I love you, too,' on the bottom of the note Stacy had left for her and left it on the counter.

The silence in the apartment was deafening. She missed Stacy already. When she checked the time, she knew Stacy was still on the road and wouldn't be able to answer her phone. Regardless, she wanted to tell her she loved her and couldn't wait for her to return. *Maybe telling her I love her will remove one concern, allowing her to focus fully on her father.* Deciding to send a text, Jo got her phone and typed. *'No doubt about it, I love you, too. Can't wait to give you your final lesson in your current course of study.'* She smiled to herself as she typed the final line. *'The final exam is hands on!'*

Jo glanced at the time. Their friends would want to know about Stacy's trip home and the reason for it She didn't want to wake them if they were all sleeping in after a late night last evening, so she decided to text them instead of calling. She sent Nic a separate text saying she'd be in to the office Monday morning by ten. Jo explained that she needed Nic to check her translation for Stacy as soon as she arrived because she'd promised to get Stacy's documents into an email in a timely fashion.

Jo tidied up her breakfast dishes, then took a shower, and got dressed. Nobody was at the office today, so that was not an option. She decided she'd go back to her house and clean.

* * *

Stacy arrived in her hometown at two that afternoon. Despite her exhaustion, she wanted to talk to Jo. She wished for about the hundredth time that she'd allowed Jo to come home with her, but there would be time for that if Jo would allow herself to love her. *Jo and those damned rules.*

Stacy wanted to call to tell Jo she'd arrived safely. As she flipped open her phone to make the call, she saw that she had a text. She clicked on it. Her hand flew to her mouth, her eyes closed, and she said a silent prayer of thanks. *She loves me.* Tears of relief and joy came to her eyes, and she exhaled for what felt like the first time since she'd written the note. *Was that just this morning?* Although she knew she needed to get in to see her Dad and Mom, what she needed more was to hear Jo's voice. She dialed Jo's cell number.

Jo spoke before Stacy had an opportunity to greet her. "I love you, Stacy Alexander."

"I love you, too. I wish I'd let you come with me."

"I wish you had, too. I want to meet your family and I want to make love to you. Not necessarily in that order."

They shared their laugher, each clutching the phone close, each wishing they could be together.

Stacy released her seat belt so she could adjust her position in the seat. "So, I have to pass a hands on exam, huh? I hope there'll be opportunities for ample practice before the final."

"I'm available for individualized instruction for the right student."

"I'm glad. I only want one instructor, just you, no others."

"I'm counting on that." Jo hesitated before she said the next sentence, wording it carefully. "I couldn't stand it if you went back to one of my competitors."

"I know that. You don't need to worry. I'm positive that no one can compete with you. I'm one hundred percent positive. I have no doubts. I'm glad you decided to believe me."

"Me too." Jo paused, breaking the tone of the conversation to change the topic. "I don't want to stop our conversation, but I'm concerned. How's your dad?"

"I just arrived here and got your text. I haven't been in there yet. As much as I hate to do it, I have to say goodbye for now. I'll call you later tonight with a complete update. Don't forget that I love you."

"Not for a minute." Jo was grinning ear to ear. "It makes me happy to think about it. I love you, too. I hope your Dad will be okay."

They reluctantly hung up as Jo pressed her hand to her heart, remembering the feel of Stacy's hand resting there as she slept.

Chapter 20

STACY ENTERED THE HOSPITAL and got directions to the CCU where she found her mother in the waiting room. "Hi, Mom."

Her mother looked up, her face beaming at the sight of her daughter.

Stacy hugged her mom. "How's Dad?"

"He's doing much better. It turned out it was angina. They did an emergency angioplasty early this morning. If everything goes well today and he remains stable, he may be released tomorrow. The doctor said your father needs to lose some weight and increase his exercise. According to the medical team, as long as he doesn't take a turn for the worse before morning, he's good for another ten thousand miles."

"That's certainly a relief."

"I'm sorry I made you race down here, Honey. Still, it's good to see you. Can you stay a while?"

Stacy sat next to her mother, taking her hand in her own. "I'll stay until he comes home, but I have a project due Friday. Some friends will help me submit it if I don't get back in time to do it myself. But there's another project I've been working on that requires my attention, too." She smiled inwardly, thinking of Jo. "I'm eager to get back to it as soon as I know Dad is okay."

"I'm happy to hear you've got some friends who will help you. I worry about you up there alone."

"I know. I've met some new friends that I like a lot, some very nice people. I'll tell you more once we know Dad's all right."

That afternoon, Stacy's sister, Melody, arrived. The family received a good report from the doctor who again confirmed that, if all was well the next morning, he would release his patient to their care sometime Monday.

"Come on, Sis, let's go get Mom a cup of coffee and catch up."

Stacy and her sister found their way to the cafeteria, which was relatively unpopulated on a late Sunday afternoon. The sisters each picked a drink and a snack before they settled in a quiet corner for their catch up chat.

"You look tired. Hard trip down?" Melody asked.

"Not really. More likely it's the late night I had last night."

"Oh? Do something fun?" Melody peeled back the wrapper from her cupcakes.

"Yes, in fact I did. I went out dancing after dinner with some friends."

"I haven't heard much from you this past month or so. Guess you've been busy. How's the book coming?"

Stacy unscrewed the cap from her bottle of water. "Actually, quite well. I've been busy doing research on an aspect of my story I knew nothing about. I decided to hire someone to tutor me on the subject. She moved in and has been very helpful to my research."

Melody's brow furrowed. "Moved in? What subject needs someone to move in?"

Okay, Melody, here we go. Good thing you're sitting down. "Lesbianism."

Melody's eyes snapped up. She searched her sister's face. "This is just research, right?"

Stacy took a deep breath. "No, as it turns out, I don't think it is. I've fallen in love, Sis."

"With a woman, I assume?"

"Yes." Stacy held her breath and waited for her sister's response to the unexpected news.

Melody's closed hand came to her mouth, more in contemplation than in shock. "Gee, Stacy, when you tell Mom and Dad, you might want to lead into this a little more gradually. Are you sure?"

"Yes, I have no doubt that I love her. Her name's Jo, by the way. I didn't expect it. Mel, I'm happier than I've ever been. It's very new, the realizing I'm in love part, I mean. We just confessed that we love each other last night, well, this morning really. We started as friends, and my feelings developed from there."

"So, you're a lesbian now? I don't understand how. You've always dated men."

"I'm not sure exactly how it happened, either. I just fell in love, probably for the first time in my life. I wish I'd brought her with me. You'll love her. I know it." Stacy paused, giving her sister some time to process all the new information. "I feel a little guilty. I want to be here for Dad and Mom but, now that I know Dad will be okay, I can't wait to get back to Jo."

"Tell me about this woman, Jo."

Stacy grinned. "Well, first off, she's amazing." Stacy filled in her sister on Jo's background. She described her new friends across the street, told her about Jo's shooting injury, and how she had saved at least two people's lives. "Besides all that, she's gorgeous. She's got these grey eyes that I could drown in, and a killer smile. And her body, Melody..."

"Okay, stop right there. Too much information!" Melody laughed.

"Don't worry, I'm not going to talk about sex." Stacy pursed her lips. "Technically, we haven't really done that yet."

"So how do you know you're a lesbian?"

"It's not really about sex, Sis. I mean, sure, that's part of it. I want her. I've never ever felt this way about anyone before. I'm just sure. I can't explain it, really. There's just not one doubt in my mind."

Melody glanced down, processing her sister's words. Slowly she raised her gaze to meet her sister's and smiled. "So when do we get to meet this amazing woman who has such power over you?"

"I don't know, maybe in a couple of months when we've had a chance to be together for a while. I'll bring her down. I'm sure you'll like her Melody, she's a good person."

"Look, maybe you shouldn't tell Dad right now."

"I know." Stacy took her sister's hand. "So, do you still love me, Sis? I know this is a big adjustment in your thinking about me."

"Of course I still love you, you idiot. Why would you ask me such a thing? Did you doubt that?"

"Maybe, just a little. You're the first person I've told. One of my friends, Amanda, told her family and they disowned her. Her parents both passed away not speaking to her. She and her brother are finally in contact thanks to Amanda's partner." Stacy gathered up the two drink containers and napkins preparing to stand. Almost as an afterthought Stacy asked, "What do you think Mom and Dad will say?"

"I don't know." Melody rested her elbow on the table and put her chin in her palm. "They know these two gay guys, Leonard and Bruce. I've never heard them say anything negative about them. Then again, neither of them is their kid. Honestly, I just don't know. Do you want me to come home with you and Mom tonight? I'll stay with you while you tell her if you think it'll help."

"No, you told me to not tell them like I told you. I think I'll tell them I'm in love first with a wonderful person named Jo. I'll try to figure out how to break it to them more gently than I did to you."

Stacy stood up, gathering her cup and napkin for the trash. "We'd better get back to Mom. She'll think we've abandoned her."

On the way back to the CCU, Melody asked her sister, "Wouldn't it be wise to wait until you and Jo have been together longer, you know, have a really established relationship? I mean you've only known her a few weeks. What if this doesn't last? Then you won't be gay any more, right? Maybe they don't need to know right now."

"No, I don't think it works that way. I love Jo, and I want to be with her. Even if something happened to Jo, I won't automatically become straight again. I've learned that's not where my interests are. Being with Jo, holding her, feels right. I've never felt that way before. I've finally found out where I belong."

"Stacy, I'm just saying that you need to be sure before you tell our folks."

"I am sure. I promise though, I'll be more measured with the news." Stacy grinned as she smacked her sister on the arm. "You'd better wipe that deer in the headlights look off your face."

"You're not going to say anything now. Right?"

"No, I'll tell Mom in private. I won't make you have to witness my confession." Stacy laughed at the look of relief that shot across her sister's face. "Come on, you big coward. Let's go."

They returned to their mother, coffee in hand, and took turns visiting their father one more time before they all headed home. Stacy and her mother waved goodbye to Melody as they headed for their separate vehicles.

* * *

"I'm starving, Mom. Are you hungry? Can I make you a sandwich or something?" Stacy pulled open the fridge and various cupboards looking for sustenance. "Want half a sandwich?"

"I'm not really hungry, so a half will be more than enough. I think I'll have some chips. I need to get rid of the snack foods before your father comes home. It'll be good for me, too. I could stand to lose ten pounds myself." She reached for the chips and opened the bag, nibbling as Stacy made a sandwich.

Stacy looked at the clock. It was only six thirty. It felt like she'd been awake forever. She did want to call Jo and, despite what her sister had said, she wanted to tell her mother about her new relationship before her father came home. Because they were alone, tonight would be a good time. Maybe her mother could break the news to her father after she'd returned north. She wanted them to meet Jo, and she wanted them to know about her relationship before they met Jo.

"Mom, I want to talk to you. I have some news to share with you."

"Good or bad?" Stacy's mother asked, turning towards her daughter with a smile filled with love on her face.

"Well, I'm going to start with the good news. The rest, I think you'll have to be the judge of whether you think it's good or bad."

Her mom sat wiping her hands on a napkin she plucked from the holder on the table. "Okay, I'm ready, let's hear this good news."

"Mom, I met someone, and I've finally really fallen in love. It's the head over heels kind."

"Oh Stacy, that's wonderful. Who is he, and when did all this happen?"

Stacy buttered the bread and spread the mustard as she talked. "Well, we met about five weeks ago when I ran into a block on my story I'm working on. I got an idea that maybe my victim who was murdered was being blackmailed. I wanted to learn more about my victim's lifestyle and why there might be reason to blackmail her. About the same time, I met a group of women who opened a new business across the street."

"These are the friends you told me will help you with your report."

Stacy smiled. "Yes. Actually, I met Jo first. Jo and Nic helped me with the translation of my report. Later, I met the other partners, Dana, Mallory, and Amanda at the open house for their business the next day. They opened this translation service and language school right across the street from my apartment. I shared my problem about my story with them. Oddly enough, Amanda is an author, too. They suggested that Jo would be a good resource for my research."

"So are you dating Nic or Jo?"

Stacy took a deep breath, delaying the rest of the conversation as she folded up the lunchmeat and put the meat and cheese back in the fridge. "Now, Mom, don't get ahead of me here! Nic is already involved with Dana. But, I did fall in love with Jo even though, technically, we've not done what you'd consider dating."

"How can you fall in love with someone you haven't dated?"

"You know, Mom, it just happened." Stacy explained that Jo was now retired from the police force because of the shooting at the hospital. There were tricky times, although she managed to avoid using the feminine pronoun in reference to Jo as she described her bravery, resulting injury, and pain.

Stacy put the sandwich she'd made on the table, separating it onto two plates. She pushed one towards her mother. "So, because of the leg injury Jo suffered and my need to get so much information about my subject, I decided to offer Jo a place to stay in my office."

Mrs. Alexander paused before taking a bite. "You let a complete stranger move in with you? Are you crazy? Some man you didn't even know a week?"

"I know it sounds crazy, Mom, but you haven't heard the whole story. Bear with me a little longer, and I hope you'll be relieved. Anyway, Jo moved in and we began to talk. While we worked together on my project, I helped Jo exercise and take daily walks. Then I came up with the idea that massage would help, you know like with the little boy I helped in high school, remember? So we started massages, twice a day, and there's been a big improvement in Jo's leg since then."

"Oh God, Stacy. Now you're telling me you're rubbing this strange man's leg. No wonder he never dated you. He didn't have to. I thought I'd raised you better than that."

"Mom, really. Nothing has happened between us sexually. We just fell in love."

"I want to meet the man who could live with an attractive girl like you, who is massaging his leg all the time, who hasn't made a pass at you. There has to be something wrong with him. Is he gay? Is that the news you're avoiding telling me?"

"Technically, yes."

Her mother interrupted. "Dear God, Stacy! What are y'all doing getting involved with a gay man? That's just asking for heartbreak, girl."

"Okay, Mom. Here's the part I've been avoiding telling you..."

"Oh, Stacy. He's illegal. He's in the country illegally and is looking to you to get him a green card."

Stacy actually laughed. "No, Mom, there is no guy, there is nobody illegal. Jo is a woman. I fell in love with another woman."

Stacy's mother's mouth literally dropped open. "Well, that's not news I'd ever thought I'd be relieved to hear. Honey, are you sure? How can you be so sure?"

"I can't explain it, Mom. She makes me feel..." Stacy paused searching for the right words. "I guess it makes me feel like I'm home. It just finally feels right."

"Not everyone will agree with you, you know. Did you tell your sister?"

"Yes." Stacy put her uneaten sandwich on the plate and leaned forward.

"And?"

"She says she still loves me. I'm hoping you'll be able to tell me the same thing."

"Don't be ridiculous." Stacy's mother rose, came around the table, and gave Stacy a hug. "Of course I still love you. You're my daughter. I won't say I'm overjoyed. I hope you know that the thing I want most is to see you happy."

Stacy gave her mother a few minutes to process the information she'd just learned. "I want you to believe me when I say I've never been happier. I love her, Mom."

Stacy and her mother talked a little while longer as they finished their meal. She told her mom all about her new friends and answered all her mother's questions about Jo.

Standing up, Stacy said, "Mom, I'm bushed, and I want to call Jo tonight before I go to bed. I also have some work to do and a couple of calls I want to make. We can talk more tomorrow morning. Okay?" Stacy leaned down and placed a kiss on the top of her mother's head. Gathering the paper plates and napkins, she cleaned off the table and turned to go to her room.

"Stacy? Can we wait to tell your father about this? Maybe it'd be better if you bring Jo down and we tell him after he meets her. Otherwise, we can come up for a visit. Would that be okay?"

"Sure. That's a great idea. Please don't worry about me, Mom. I'm really very happy. In fact, I'm happier than I've been in longer than I'm willing to admit."

"I'm glad you feel that way. I just..."

"I know, Mom. Everything will be fine. You'll know it as soon as you meet her."

"I can't help worrying just a little. It's a mother's duty."

Stacy laughed. "I know."

Okay, Honey. I love you."

"Love you too."

Chapter 21

STACY CALLED JO THE minute she was alone in her room.

"Hi, Honey. How's your dad?" Jo asked after the brief greeting they'd shared. Jo adjusted the phone and settled back in her chair.

"Hi yourself! He's doing much better. Turns out it was angina, not a heart attack. He might come home tomorrow if everything goes well overnight."

"How's your mom holding up?"

"Good, really. My sister was with her most of last night. Then she came back this afternoon. I had a good talk with both of them. I told them about us."

Jo was surprised. "What'd you tell them?"

"I told them I was in love. Really, the conversation with my mother was funny in some ways. I'll tell you about it when I get home."

"They were both okay with you being involved with a woman?"

"Seems so. Both of them told me they still love me. Mom asked me to wait to tell my dad. Makes sense."

"Stacy, I love you..."

"Do I hear a 'but' there?"

"No, not really. Uh, it's just..." Jo exhaled a worried breath. "Honey, are you sure about all of this? I mean, well, we haven't even slept together yet. How can you be so sure?"

"We've slept together. You don't snore and you don't have stubble in the morning."

"That's not what I meant and you know it."

Stacy's sigh indicated her exasperation. "I told you, I love you, and there will never be anyone else for me. Besides, I know that we'll be good together in bed. Do you disagree?

Jo knew in her heart they would be good together, too. "No. I do agree with you. It's just that I don't want you to be hurt. If you tell people and they don't accept that you've changed, it's really hard when people reject you. I don't want that to ever happen to you. It would be especially unfair if it happened before you're sure."

"Jo. I keep telling you I *am* sure. I'm happy I found you and that I'm finally in love. I thought it would never happen for me. Now that it has, I want to shout it from the rooftops. It's not my issue if people don't approve. It's theirs. If they don't approve of me and you, I don't want that type of person for a friend."

"And you call me brave. You are braver than I ever was. Until recently I lived in the closet."

"Would you rather that I not tell people about us?"

Jo mulled the question for a few seconds. "I don't know. It's just that I'm afraid you'll be hurt."

"I see." For a few blank seconds, no one spoke. Finally, Stacy said, "If I'd fallen in love with a man, everyone would be happy for me. Even you are reticent to announce that we love each other. Why? Heterosexuals take out newspaper announcements to tell the world they love each other and plan to marry."

"Yes, but that's a heterosexual relationship, it's one that society approves of—it's different for us. Although things are changing, there are still a lot of people who think what we feel, what we do, is wrong."

Stacy thought about what Jo had said. "Well, if people think that my being in love with you is something they view as wrong, they're just going to have to get over it. I know what I feel is right. And that's all there is to it."

"I keep waiting for you to change your mind about all this."

"I know you do. It's not going to happen. I'm not a schoolgirl, Jo. I've lived long enough to know what I want, and what I want is you."

"You amaze me. I want you, too."

"Tell me more about that. You said you knew we'd be good together. Tell me about what our first time making love will be like. I want every detail. Where will we be?"

"Well, maybe we'll be in your room. We'll have more room there."

"No, first you'll meet me at the stairs with a kiss when I come home."

"Okay, I'll meet you at the stairs with a kiss." Jo hesitated a moment. "You know you weren't fair on Saturday. You kissed me and made me promise not to move. Do you know that when you fell asleep with your hand on my breast I was awake for like two hours? I wanted you so much. Sadly, I was a coward. I was afraid to tell you how I felt, afraid to act on my feelings."

"Hmm. And here I thought you were being honorable, just keeping your word that you wouldn't say anything or move."

Jo laughed, getting into the fun of their teasing. "No. I was so shocked when you kissed me and then put your hand on my breast, I think it took me a couple of hours to finally admit that I was willing to ignore my life rules and act on my feelings. I mean I knew I was in love with you before that. I was still just being stupid."

"Okay, you're getting off track here. Let's get back to our first shared kiss. Next time, I expect you to kiss me back."

Jo exhaled a long sigh. "Remember, you can't blame me for that. That was your idea and yours alone. Hmm...this is tough. Okay. I imagine that, at first, it'll be soft, because I already know that you have soft lips. We'll start slow and sweet. First, I'll kiss you easy. Maybe nibble a little on your fabulous mouth. I want to sink into that dimple you torture me with. When I've had my fill of that, I want to kiss your neck then come back to your lips. I'll kiss you more seriously that time, and it'll build 'til one of us starts to explore with her tongue."

"That'll be me. I want to taste you."

"Mmm. Our tongues will meet and the heat will start to build between my legs."

"Mine, too."

Jo opened her collar. "So, I'll slip my hands under your shirt and explore your back as we continue our kissing."

"Umm, I love kissing." Stacy's voice was husky. "And I'm going to love kissing you. I keep thinking back to when we were dancing together. I could feel your breasts against mine. My nipples felt like stones."

"I know. I could feel them."

"Oh God, Jo, I want you so much." Stacy blew out a puff of air and wiped the perspiration that had accumulated on her forehead. "We have to stop this. I have work to do, and I'll be in no condition to do it if we keep talking like this. I wish I'd have let you come with me. I know it was sensible for you not to come. It made more sense for you to submit my report, and you need to work tomorrow. Maybe we should end this conversation while I can still stand up so I can finish up what I need to do on that report."

"How far is it to get down to where you are?"

Stacy laughed. "It's too far and too late. Just think how good it will be when we finally do get together."

Jo smiled, just imagining. "Yes, it will be. I can promise you that it will be."

"I'm counting on it. I'd better let you go. I'm sorry I can't rub your leg before you go to bed."

"I can rub it. It's just not the same without you doing it."

Stacy looked at her calendar. "I'll be home in a couple of days. I plan to rub your leg and a few other areas that I have high hopes will be a lot more fun and much more responsive."

Jo exhaled. "You're killing me."

"Maybe I'd better read that novel you gave me over again so I'll know what to do. What do you think?"

"I think you'll know. You have all the same equipment I have, so you should be familiar with what makes it work."

"I'm a little nervous," Stacy admitted. "I don't want to disappoint you."

"It's impossible. Just holding you last night made me happier than I've been in, well, I guess just about forever. Anything more than that will be like icing on the cake."

"Hope you're not on a diet, 'cause I plan to see that you get plenty of icing. Don't forget that hands-on final exam I have to pass. I'll need some one-on-one hands-on tutoring."

Stacy could feel Jo's grin over the phone. "I'm your girl, then." Jo glanced at her watch. "I'd better let you go. I'll talk to you in the morning when I get in to work. I'll talk to Nic first, and then call you a little after ten. Or is it better for you to call me?"

"Send me a text. I'll call you back as soon as I can."

"Okay, love you. Good night."

"I love you, too. G'night."

Chapter 22

NIC, DANA, MALLORY, AND Amanda got together for brunch at Mallory and Amanda's on Sunday morning, the day after their celebratory dinner and night out dancing.

"That was fun last night. Dinner was good, and we had fun at the bar afterward. I can't tell you the last time we danced so much." Mallory passed the salad to Dana. "We should do that more often."

Nic nodded and tugged her ear. "We've been so busy getting the business up and running that we've been working harder than we did when we worked for other people. You're right. We *should* do it more often. It was nice that Stacy and Jo came along. They are so cute together. They both seem interested in each other. I think Jo and that damned rule number two thing is kind of discouraging Stacy from saying anything."

"I don't know." Mallory winked at Nic and took the salad bowl she handed her. "They looked pretty cozy last night. That slow dance they were doing just before Meg came over was sort of steamy for two people who aren't in a relationship. They sure looked like they were more than just friends. Who do you think will end up getting hurt if they can't agree they want to move forward?"

Nic shrugged. "No telling. I'm reasonably certain that Stacy will make the first move. She asked me what she should do about rule number two."

"What did you tell her, Honey?" Dana rested her hand on her lover's thigh.

Nic grinned. "I told her that it would be hard for Jo to say no if her mouth was busy or something to that effect."

"Is that the tactic you used on me?" Dana pinched Nic's thigh.

"Ouch. No, as I recall, it was more like the approach you took. I'd promised you I wouldn't make the first move and I didn't."

Amanda jumped in. "Whoa! I can't believe I'd forgotten that Dana made the first move on you."

"Yes, I guess I did. Nic chased me until she let me catch her." Dana giggled. "However, it certainly wasn't without encouragement, for sure. We were so hot for each other it was just bound to happen. Maybe that's what will happen with those two."

Mallory changed the subject. "Hey, did any of you think that Meg's behavior was the least bit strange? Nic thought it was just because she was drinking. I got such a weird vibe over the whole incident. I've known Meg for quite a while, and I've never known her to act like that. She's always been so kind and gentle. She was just so different last night."

"Maybe it was a combination of booze and that knock she took on the head," Amanda suggested.

Dana looked to Mallory, "Is that possible for someone to have a change in personality like that after a shock to the head like she took?"

"Yes, absolutely. Meg had a serious concussion and suffered memory loss from the blow to her head. I was concerned when she apologized last night. Didn't she say something like she just couldn't get Jo out of her head, or she couldn't let her go?"

Everyone nodded. There was a lull in the conversation as everyone started to eat. Nic grabbed a slice of garlic bread from the basket and took a bite. "Umm, this is good Amanda."

"Thanks, Nic. Back to Meg. Her behavior seems a bit obsessive to me. I know she was drinking last night. However, she's already demonstrated memory loss caused by her injury. Minimal Traumatic Brain Injury, or MTBI, can also result in a lot of the symptoms she displayed last night. I don't know how much she had to drink before she confronted Jo. It's possible she might possibly be having some hypersensitivity to alcohol as well. I'm just saying that although Nic and Jo handled her very well, you have to admit that she was pretty threatening. She made me very uncomfortable."

Nic set her fork on the plate. "I don't know. She seemed really drunk. I hope she doesn't drink to that excess again. She obviously has trouble handling her alcohol and her attitude, especially where Jo is concerned."

Mallory frowned. "You know, she had a pretty serious concussion. Maybe next time I see her I'll suggest she mention any symptoms she's having to her doctor. I'm just saying that something about her wasn't right last night. It made me really uneasy."

Nic's phone signaled she had a text. She reached into her pocket to check it. "It's from Jo. Excuse me. I think I should check it." She snapped her cover closed after reading the text. "Mrs. Alexander called after we got home last night with some bad news. Stacy's mother told her that her father had chest pains, a possible heart attack. Stacy left for home early this morning, and Jo has already finished some translation for her that she wants me to check on Monday morning. She'll have more later in the week when they finish it."

Nic texted a response indicating she'd be glad to help out and to be sure to let them know if there was anything they could do for either of them.

Jo responded with her appreciation and that she'd see Nic at the office Monday morning at ten.

Chapter 23

STACY WAS TIRED AFTER her long drive down, the day at the hospital, and the strain of coming out to her family. Still, she wanted to call her friend Maria. After some small talk, Maria asked Stacy why she hadn't been in touch lately. "I'm glad to hear from you. I was about to send out the hounds!"

"I've been busy falling in love. Are you sitting down?" Stacy released a nervous giggle.

"Falling in love? Well...wait. Let me get my tea." There were some sounds of movement on the other end of the phone as Maria got her cup and settled. "Okay, I'm sitting down. This ought to be good. So who is he?"

"Well, it's not a he, it's a she. Her name is Jo."

After a brief pause, Maria said in an even tone a statement rather than a question, "Really...When did you switch teams?"

"Well, I just confessed last night that I'm in love with her. Then my dad had a heart attack and I had to leave for my parents home. I'm there now, so nothing happened, and she's still in New York."

"So I can't even ask you what the sex is like?" Maria chuckled.

"Nope, not yet. That's not all there is to it. She's a wonderful person. She used to be a policewoman, so she's in great shape. She has these four wonderful friends that I've become friendly with. To me, the most important thing is that we talk. We talk all the time." Stacy explained about her living arrangements over the past five weeks and how she and Jo had grown increasingly closer until she finally realized that she was in love with her.

"I have to admit I'm surprised. Had I known, I might have made a play for you myself. I always thought you were cute."

"What are you talking about, Maria? You're straight."

"For the most part. But I have taken a walk or two with the other team before."

"You never told me."

"Nope. It wasn't a subject that ever came up before." Maria explained that her first experience was in high school with her best friend. "Then the second time, I was drunk and this woman made a pass. I thought why not?"

"I can't believe you never told me. I thought we share pretty much everything."

"We do, but like I said, by the time I met you, all that was history." Maria blew on her tea. "Besides, you always seemed so sweet and innocent that I was afraid to tell you."

"Really?" Stacy absorbed this new information about her close friend. "I can't believe you never told me."

"Don't be hurt. Since I wasn't dating very much then, I think it probably just never came up." Maria paused, considering the question. "Truth is, I think I've always found women more interesting and I enjoy sex with women."

"I thought we knew pretty much everything about each other. You really surprised me. Well, at least it's a relief to know I haven't horrified you. Jo and her friends have told me stories about people they know whose families and friends disowned them because they came out to them. I told my mom and my sister tonight. I can't say they're overjoyed, although they both told me that they still love me."

"So tell me more about Ms. Right."

Stacy talked for a few minutes about Jo and the others. When she finished, Maria updated her on her own news. They both laughed when Maria admitted her news was relatively mundane when she compared it to Stacy's.

As their conversation wound down, Maria asked, "Will I see you this trip?" She lived about two hours north of Stacy's hometown.

"Not this trip. I'm only staying until my dad is okay and he can come home. I'm anxious to get back to New York."

"I bet you are!"

"Oh, stop. Why don't you come up for a weekend and meet Jo and my other friends?"

"I'd love to. Call me when you get home and get things all settled."

They bid each other goodnight with Stacy promising to call soon.

Checking the time, Stacy considered what to do. *Nine o'clock. Not too late to talk to Monique. The kids should be in bed by now. I probably won't get to see her this trip, so at least I'll touch base with her.*

Stacy dialed her old friend's number and was pleased when she answered with a cheerful greeting. Stacy told her that she was in town because of her father's health problem. Monique updated her about each of the kids.

"How's Rob? You guys doing okay?" Stacy asked.

"Yeah, for the most part. Rob's taking a more active role in the family and we seem to be doing better. How are you doing?"

"I'm really happy, Monique. I've met someone."

"Great. Tell me."

Starting with how she was stuck on her novel and she needed to do research, Stacy went on from there. She concluded with the fact that she had fallen in love with Jo. "She's a wonderful woman, Monique."

"So you're telling me you're a queer now?"

Stacy felt her face flush and her stomach clench with a sense of foreboding. "Queer? Yes, I guess I am." There was dead silence on the other end of the phone. "Monique? Is there a problem?" Stacy waited for Monique to respond. She waited as long as she could before she made a final appeal. "I'd hoped you'd be happy for me, Monique. If you'd just meet her, I'm sure you'd like her."

"I wouldn't count on that. I don't know how you could have sex with another woman. I mean it's unnatural. Ugh. It disgusts me."

Stacy could imagine Monique's curled lip and disapproving visage. "I have to say that I'm surprised by your attitude about this. I never thought that our friendship could be this tenuous."

"And I have to say that I never expected my friend would become a queer."

"Monique. You know me. We've been friends for years. I'm your kids' godmother. We've been through so much together. I'm your friend, same as always. How can you turn against me after all that history we've shared? And how can it be possible that I never knew you'd feel this way?"

"I don't think the subject ever came up before. Thankfully. We didn't know anyone queer in high school."

"So where do we go from here?"

There was a long pause as Monique considered her response. "I don't know. Maybe if you come to your senses you can call me and we'll see."

"No, I don't think so. If you can turn against me just because I fell in love with someone you don't approve of, I don't think our friendship was what I thought it was. I'm really sorry you feel this way."

"Don't blame me. You're the one who changed, not me."

"I haven't changed Monique. I'm the same person I always have been. I'm the same friend I've always been. There's just this one tiny little thing that's different. How can it matter so much to you?"

"It just does. Goodbye, Stacy."

"Goodbye." Eyes filled with tears, she hung up the phone. Stacy couldn't help feeling shocked at Monique's reaction. It amazed her that a friendship she had considered one of her closest could end, just like that. She wanted to call Jo and tell her what happened. Instead, she decided she'd wait until they were together to talk about it.

Too upset to go to bed, Stacy decided she'd work on her report until she settled down. She had anticipated it would take another two or three hours to finish it. She was pleasantly surprised when she was able to finish it in about an hour and a half. Attaching the report to her email to Jo, she added a note saying she'd had an unpleasant exchange with one of her friends and had learned something very interesting about another. Life is truly full of surprises, isn't it? She added that she was looking forward to talking with her around ten the next morning.

Chapter 24

JO WOKE UP AROUND seven missing Stacy. She got up and did her exercises, then massaged her leg. *Stacy certainly does a much better job of that than I do.* Following a quick breakfast, Jo checked her email, read Stacy's report, and printed it out so she could work on the translation. Flipping through the pages to the end, she realized it wasn't too long. She was supposed to meet Nic around ten at the office. Jo chuckled as she realized how spoiled she'd become by living at Stacy's apartment. She'd gotten used to just walking across the street in the morning. Hoping to avoid the traffic between her house and the office by leaving early, she hoped to finish up translating the report at the office before she had to meet with Nic. Once Nic had reviewed it, she'd submit it for Stacy.

Jo's cell phone rang, and she reached for it hoping it was Stacy. It was a surprise to discover Meg on the other end of the line.

"Hi Jo. Hope I didn't wake you."

"No. I'm just on my way to the office. I'm leaving here in a few minutes."

Meg sounded disappointed. "Oh. I was wondering if you could stop by and give me a ride to work. My truck won't start."

Jo hadn't been home in over a month. Puzzled, she asked, "How did you know I was here?"

"I saw your truck in your driveway when I passed by your place last night."

"Really? That's a bit out of your way, isn't it?"

"Yeah, a little. I've been driving by keeping an eye on your place while you've been staying with Stacy. I figured it was a good idea, you know, just to make sure your place was okay."

"Gee, Meg. That's very nice of you. I had no idea you were doing that. Thank you."

"No problem."

Jo checked her watch. Wanting to get the report finished and mailed, she knew she would be cutting it close if she picked up Meg and drove her to the doctor's office where she worked. Considering their tenuous friendship, she hated to leave her stranded. "Okay, I'm on my way. I'll be there in a few minutes."

"Thanks for coming, Jo. I've really missed you. It'll be good to see you."

"Okay, I need to hurry. I'm short on time. I'll be there soon."

Thinking it strange that Meg hadn't mentioned Saturday night, Jo rushed to gather her belongings. She was in too much of a hurry to consider it at length. After her initial worry about finishing the report, she knew she'd be fine. She should still have time to translate most of it when she arrived at the office. She'd finish it up while Nic was proofing the first part. In addition to her normal need for punctuality, because Nic was doing her a favor, Jo didn't want to be late for her meeting. She also had a tutoring session later in the afternoon, and she wanted to do some preparation for that. She had one other thing she wanted to do. She wanted to stop at the florist and send flowers to Stacy and her family from her and the others. She was stressed by the time she pulled away from her house bound for Meg's.

She fired off a quick text to Stacy. *Good morning. Miss you lots. I'm stopping off at Meg's to give her a lift to work. She has car trouble. May be a few minutes late texting you at ten. Love you.*

On her way to Meg's, she thought about what Stacy had attached as an addendum to her report. She'd apparently had a bad exchange with one of her friends. *I hope they'll be able to work things out.* She hated that their love had been the cause of the disagreement.

As she approached Meg's house, she was surprised to find Meg's truck parked in the street and her garage door opened. *That's strange. How could Meg have gotten her car out of the garage if she wasn't able to get it started?*

Jo pulled into the driveway and tooted the horn, expecting Meg to come trotting out. She waited a bit and tooted again. *Where the hell is she?* She drummed her fingers on the steering wheel, turning her wrist to check the time. *I told her I was in a hurry.* She checked her watch again and heaved a sigh. *Come on Meg. Geez, I told you I was in a hurry.*

She waited another minute. *That's it.* She yanked forcefully on the door handle, muttering to herself as she got out of the car and rang the doorbell. There was no answer. When she tried the knob, she found the door unlocked. Opening it, she stuck her head in. "Meg, come on! I'm going to be late," she yelled from the doorway.

Receiving no response, Jo entered Meg's house. It was a tiny place, consisting of an open kitchen and living room combination. A short hallway led to a single bedroom and a bath. The best part about the house was the double doors that opened to a small but beautiful back yard. Meg loved to garden, and she'd made a lovely little oasis out there. Jo walked to the doorway at the back of the living room, thinking maybe Meg had gone outside to get something. Not seeing Meg there, she turned and headed for the hallway.

"Meg," she called again. Meg's bedroom door was closed, so she knocked and yelled Meg's name again. She opened the door a crack. "Meg?" The door jerked open. Meg grabbed Jo's wrist and pulled her inside the room with such force that Jo fell face forward onto the rug, landing on her bad leg. The pain stunned her for a moment. As she shook her head to clear it, she felt something sharp in her leg and was puzzled about what it was. When she tried to get up, she felt a bit woozy. *Wow, I must have fallen harder than I thought.* She shook her head again to help clear it.

"Gee, Jo, I'm sorry. Let me help you up. Here, sit on the bed for a bit until you get oriented. You really took a spill."

Jo wasn't thinking clearly. She looked at Meg who had a strange look in her eyes. "We've got to get moving, or I'm going to be late," Jo told Meg, her speech slurring. Jo was feeling strange and couldn't seem to lift her arm to push against the bed to help her stand up. A few short seconds later, everything went black.

* * *

Jo started to become aware of her surroundings, unsure of how much time had passed. She was still feeling groggy and disoriented. Alone in Meg's bedroom, stretched out on the bed, she tried to bring her hand to her face to wipe it and found that her hands were restrained. Looking up, she saw that her wrists were immobilized by two sets of handcuffs the other end of which were attached to the headboard. *What time is it?* She glanced over at the clock. *Almost nine.* She tried to concentrate. *In a little while, Nic will begin to miss me, and Stacy will wonder why I haven't texted her at ten or so as I promised. Maybe they would touch base and someone will come to look for me. I have to keep Meg talking and occupied as long as I can to buy some time.*

As quietly as she could, Jo tested the handcuffs against the bars on the brass bed. *No, that didn't seem like it would work. Solid construction. Why couldn't Meg have bought a cheap bed? That would be a funny line if this were not such a serious situation.* Despite her situation, Jo chuckled.

Jo blinked, trying to clear her mind enough so she could figure out the situation. What could Meg possibly hope to achieve by taking her a prisoner? This was so unlike her friend. Meg was normally such a kind person. Something was obviously wrong with her. Jo thought back to Saturday night. Meg had obviously had too much to drink. Maybe that wasn't all, though. She seemed belligerent one minute and then hurting and deserving of sympathy the next. *Maybe she shook a screw loose when she hit her head.* Jo didn't know enough about brain injury to know whether it could cause someone to act like this. However, one thing about which she was certain—Meg was not acting rationally.

Jo's brain fog was starting to clear. She realized that when she felt the sting in her leg, Meg must have injected her with some sort of anesthetic or paralyzing agent. What did she have in mind for her next? She couldn't keep her here. Eventually her friends and Stacy would compare notes and figure out she was with Meg. It made sense that if Meg planned to keep her alive, she'd have to move her somewhere else, but where? Jo didn't have to wait long to find out. At nine thirty-seven, Meg opened the door to her bedroom as if it was the most normal thing in the world to have someone chained up there.

"Hello, my love," she virtually sang. "Awake I see. Do you feel okay? I got you some breakfast. I know you like those blueberry muffins from the bakery, so I went out and got gas and stopped to pick some of them up for you. I got you tea, too. It took me a little longer than I thought it would. Hope you weren't too uncomfortable."

Meg came over and sat on the edge of the bed. She reached out her hand and smoothed back Jo's hair. "I meant to tell you, I like your new haircut. You look rather cute with your hair cut short like that. Did your new girlfriend suggest that to you?"

"I told you on Saturday night, she's not my girlfriend. She's my employer. I'm working for her. She's an author, and I'm helping her with some of her research. Plus, she needed some things translated and I've been helping with that."

"You don't expect me to believe that you moved in with her to do research and translation, do you?" Meg broke off a piece of the muffin and fed it to Jo.

Jo suspected she'd never want to eat another blueberry muffin as long as she lived, assuming she lived to get out of this situation. The one advantage that she had was that Meg was unaware that Stacy knew where she was going. She was thankful she'd left her phone in her truck. If Stacy called or texted her, at least Meg wouldn't hear the signal and intercept the message.

"Well, you can believe what you want. Really, Meg, it's true. Stacy's straight. She's always been straight. You have no reason to be jealous of her."

"Don't I? I've seen you parading up and down the street arm in arm. I've seen her rub your leg. For a straight woman, she's pretty familiar with your body."

"She's trained in healing massage. She's helped me a lot. The walks help my endurance. I'm grateful to her. That's all."

"I watched you dance with her Saturday night. She was all over you like white on rice."

"Look, Meg, I swear to you, I've never touched her. I swear. I haven't made love with anyone since you."

As they talked, it seemed that Meg might be a little more in touch with reality. "Look," Jo said. "Here's how it happened that I moved in with her. It all started when she came into the office to get us to do a translation job for her. She was our first customer." Jo told Meg the story of how she got involved with helping Stacy with her research. "So it could have been any one of us. Because I was hobbling around and she lived right across the street, moving in with her just seemed the easiest thing to do to enable us to spend as much time as possible on her research project. Also, it was convenient for me to be so close to the office because of my leg and all."

"You know, Jo, you almost make it sound reasonable. Here, have some more muffin."

Jo swallowed. "It's the truth. We're done. I finished the job. You can see for yourself that I've moved back home. I'm telling you the truth. Besides, you know me. What have I always said?" She smiled at her captor. "You must have heard me state rule number two a million times. No straight women."

"I don't know, Jo. You've almost got me convinced. You really haven't had sex with her?"

Jo looked Meg in the eyes. She could honestly make the statement. "I can swear to you on all that's holy. I haven't had sex with Stacy Alexander. I swear that's the truth."

Meg broke off another piece of muffin and pushed it into Jo's mouth.

"Can I have some tea?" Jo's mouth was so dry that she was having a hard time choking down the muffin.

Meg held the cup so that Jo could sip her tea. Jo took the opportunity to glance at the clock over Meg's shoulder. In another ten minutes, it would be ten o'clock. Nic would be wondering where she was soon. At least she hoped Nic would be wondering.

"Well, Jo, I hate to leave you. However, I'm going to be late for work if I don't go. I'll be back for lunch at one thirty. I'll bring you a sandwich when I come back. I know you like that ham and cheese on combo rye with that horseradish mustard from Sid's Deli. I'll get one on my way back. It'll be around one forty-five. Why don't you take a little nap? I suspect you might have a bit of a headache from the medicine I gave you."

Meg leaned over and gave Jo a soft kiss on the lips. As much as she didn't want to, Jo kissed her back. *I hope Stacy will forgive me,* Jo thought irrationally. "Umm, sounds good." She gave Meg the brightest smile she could muster.

Chapter 25

MALLORY SAID TO NIC, "Where do you suppose Jo is? She's never late."

"I don't know," Nic replied. "She told me she'd be here by ten. It's already almost eleven, and we haven't seen or heard from her. You don't think Stacy's dad took a turn for the worst and she went down there to be with her, do you?"

"Jo is the most responsible person I know. She'd have let us know. I wonder if Stacy has heard from her."

"One way to find out." Nic got out her phone and dialed Stacy's cell number, hitting the speaker button.

"Hello, it's Nic. Everything okay there?"

They listened as Stacy updated them about her father's condition. She was brief in her description and ended by asking them a question. "I was wondering. I'm a bit worried. Is Jo there? She was supposed to call me at ten and she didn't. I've left several messages for her on her phone, and she hasn't returned any of them. Is everything all right?"

"Hi, Stacy. It's Mallory, too. We have you on speaker. We were wondering the same thing. Jo didn't show up here this morning. She was supposed to meet with Nic around ten and she didn't show up. You know that's not like her. We were wondering if you've heard from her."

"She sent me a text earlier this morning saying she was stopping off at Meg's to give her a lift to work. You don't think something happened to them, do you? Like maybe they had an accident or...?"

Mallory grabbed Nic's hand. "Don't know. For sure, we'll contact Meg and see if she knows anything. Don't worry. I'm sure it's nothing. She's probably just gotten tied up in something. You know her, she's always helping someone."

"Well, I hope that's it. I'm worried. It's not like her to be late without letting someone know. Please call me as soon as you know anything."

"That's a promise."

When Mallory disconnected the call, she turned to her friend. "Nic, something's very wrong. You know this isn't like Jo. I don't like it that Meg is involved in this somehow. I told you, she wasn't right on Saturday."

"Okay, let's not panic."

Mallory picked up her cell phone and her jacket. "I think I should take a ride by Jo's house and see if she's there. If not, I think we should check out Meg's place. If they're not at either place, we can call Meg and see if she knows anything."

"Wouldn't it be easier to just start by calling Meg?" Nic asked.

"Easier, maybe. I just have a real uneasy feeling about this. Can we try it my way, please?" Mallory implored.

"Sure. What do we do about here?"

"I'll call Amanda and ask her to come over and cover the office for us. We can put a sign on the door saying closed for lunch. She'll be here in half an hour or so. We'll be back in an hour if we don't find Jo. If that's the case, I think we need to call Jo's old boss. The Chief will help. Think we should call him now?"

"Let's wait and see what we can find out first." Nic got her jacket and keys.

Mallory called Amanda and wrote up the sign while Nic got the car. With the sign in the window and the door to the business locked, they drove as quickly as they could to Jo's house. Jo's home was secure and there was no sign of Jo's truck. Next, they made the ten-minute trip to Meg's house. The house was quiet.

"Neither Jo's or Meg's trucks are here," Nic observed.

"Pull in the drive, Nic. I just want to take a look around."

Mallory got out and went to the door. She rang the bell several times with no answer. On a hunch, she went around the side of the house and looked in the garage window. There was Jo's truck. Mallory had a sick, uneasy feeling. She raced back to Nic's car. "Jo's truck is in the garage. Let's look in the windows and see if we can see anything."

"Do you think that we should call the chief?" Nic wondered.

"Let's check first. Please."

"Okay. I'm not convinced this is the best approach."

"What if Meg's hurt her? Come on, Nic, the sooner we find Jo the better."

"Okay. I agree." Nic and Mallory went around to the back of the house to peer in. The living room was quiet and in order. They continued around the back to the side of the house.

Mallory yelled Jo's name. "Did you hear that?"

Nodding, Nic picked up a rock and broke a pane of glass in the back door, quickly reaching through to unlock the latch. She beat Mallory to the bedroom and burst through the door. "Oh my God, Jo. Are you all right?"

"I'm much better now. I'm sure glad you found me. There's something drastically wrong with Meg. She drugged me this morning and chained me up."

Mallory started to check Jo out. "Where is she now?"

"Well, after she fed me a muffin and some tea, she kissed me goodbye as if this was the most normal situation in the world and left for work. She's definitely off. Nic, can you see if you can find my handcuff key so we can get these off? There's one on a key ring in my glove box."

Nic found the key and hurried back. She unlocked the handcuffs while Mallory called Jo's old boss and Jo massaged some feeling back into her hands. Mallory put the phone on speaker so Jo could explain what happened.

Jo's former boss asked, "Where is Meg now?"

"She works for the Mitchell Medical Group over on Locust Street. Chief, she's not a bad person. She was injured a couple of months ago when I got shot. I think this is something related to her injury. I don't want to press charges. I just want her to get the help she needs."

"That may be out of our hands, Jo. I promise, I'll do what I can."

"Let's get out of here just in case Meg leaves work early. Then I want to call Stacy and tell her I'm okay. "

Concerned it wasn't safe for Jo to drive after being drugged, Mallory drove Jo's truck, and Nic drove Jo in her car. Mallory insisted that Jo get checked out at the hospital before she allowed her to return home. The doctor pronounced Jo 'none the worse for wear' and told her to go home and get some rest. While Jo was leaving the hospital with Mallory, her cell rang.

The call was from the Chief. He told her that he'd taken Meg into custody and were taking her to the hospital's psychiatric ward for an evaluation. "Meg broke down in tears when we arrested her. She said she didn't know what was wrong with her. She just couldn't help herself. She is totally fixated on you. I think you were lucky that Meg's inherently a good person. She seems to not have meant you any harm. She just wanted you to be with her, and apparently she saw this as her last resort to achieve that end."

"She's sick, Chief. Do what you can for her, will you?"

"Sure, Jo. I promise."

* * *

After Jo's release from the hospital, they returned to the office. "I'll go over to the apartment with you, Jo," Mallory offered.

"I'll be fine. Stacy is on her way back. She plans to be home tonight, hopefully before midnight. Her dad's doing much better and is resting peacefully."

Nic squeezed Jo's shoulder. "I have a feeling this is going to be quite a reunion when you two get together." Despite Jo's protests, Nic convinced her that she was capable of tutoring her student in high school French. "We'll take care of things here. I'll also take care of the report. Go and get some rest. I'm sure you could use it."

Jo hugged and kissed her friends in turn. "How can I thank you? You saved my life today. There for a while I was afraid I'd never see any of you again. What a bizarre day."

"Now, there's an understatement if ever I've heard one." Mallory draped an arm over Jo's shoulder and gave her a squeeze.

"Nic, that document I need you to proof for me is in a blue folder on my backseat."

"Don't worry. I'll take care of it for you. I'll drop it off after I meet your student."

Jo blushed and then winked at Nic. "No hurry. Stacy and I will pick it up tomorrow."

Chapter 26

MALLORY WALKED ACROSS THE street with Jo and noticed that Jo was limping a bit. "How about a massage?"

"Thanks, Mal. That would help a lot. I fell on this leg when Meg pulled me into the room. It was such a shock when she grabbed me and pulled that I didn't have time to turn on my other side. I hope I didn't do any more damage."

"Come on, let's see if we can work out some of those kinks. Maybe you're just bruised. You go get ready and I'll be in there in a few minutes."

Jo went to her room, slid out of her clothes, and dressed in a tee shirt and boxers. When Mallory entered the room, she pointed to the lotion. "That's what Stacy uses."

"Okay, lay back and relax. I'll see what I can do." Mallory massaged most of the kinks out of her leg. "Maybe you should take some pain meds. Do you have any here?"

"Yeah, in the kitchen."

"Let's get you some tea and something to eat with that pill."

"Anything but blueberry muffins," Jo grinned. "I don't think I'll ever think kindly of them again."

* * *

Jo's leg felt better after the rub down that Mallory gave her. The two friends sat across from each other in the kitchen as they waited for the water to boil. Jo ate some cheese and crackers and took the pills. The tea was soothing, and she admitted she felt better after eating. "What a weird day."

"Yes it was. Chances are good you'll never have another like it. What do you think will happen to Meg?"

"I don't know. I hope that they'll just hospitalize her, instead of sending her to prison. At least she'll get the treatment she needs there. I mean, obviously she's suffered a greater injury to her head than anyone suspected."

"At least if they hospitalize her, there are meds and psychiatric care that can help her."

"It was very disconcerting when I learned she'd been watching me on my walks with Stacy. I never even suspected. Geez, I'm a cop, or at least I was a cop. I should have been more observant."

"Well, you had no reason to suspect she was watching you, and maybe you were less vigilant because you've been busy falling in love. Haven't you?"

Jo nodded. "Stacy's a wonderful person, Mal. I've spouted that rule number two crap for so long I actually believed it. Thank God, she didn't let it stop her. She risked everything to tell me she loved me. She's even told her mom and her sister that she's in love with a woman and came out to two of her friends. All that before we've really even kissed. That's gotta count for something, don't you think?"

"I'd suspect that you should get some rest." Mallory stood up as she prepared to leave. "I think you might need it when your girl gets home to you."

"I can't wait to see her. My last thought before everything went dark this morning was of her and how unfair it would be if I couldn't get to be with her any longer than we've had." Jo shook her head. "I've got to go to bed and get some sleep. I feel exhausted."

"Okay, hope that massage helps. Need me to do anything else?"

"No, you've saved my life today and given me a massage. What more could a girl want?" Mallory put her hand to her cheek, pointer finger raised. She tapped her finger on her cheek and looked towards the ceiling. "Hmm, let me think."

Jo slapped Mallory playfully on the arm. "Go on and get out of here. Thank Nic for taking care of my student when you see her." She gave Mallory a warm hug. "And thank you for rescuing me today."

"It's only fair. You saved my life. I owed you. Okay, call if you need anything."

Jo followed Mallory out to the stairs. Mallory left and Jo started back down the hall toward her room. She was ready to get into bed when she changed her mind, turned around, and headed for Stacy's bedroom. She wanted to feel closer to Stacy while she waited for her to come home. She slipped into Stacy's bed. *Stacy will be tired when she gets here. She had only a few hours of sleep on Saturday night, then drove all the way to Virginia and now all the way home.* Jo smiled at the last thought she had of the woman she loved just before she drifted off to sleep. *I'll be happy even if all I get to do is just hold her tonight.*

* * *

Mallory walked across the street to the office. Amanda was sitting at the front desk while Nic tutored Jo's student. Mallory asked, "So did Nic bring you up to date on everything that happened?"

"What a weird day. You were so right about Meg. I hope they can help her."

They talked a little more about Jo's harrowing experience and Meg's medical condition. Mallory gestured with her head at the phone. "Any calls today?"

Amanda pointed to the notepad she'd made notes on. "I had a couple of small jobs come in. I got a call from one of the companies that Nic reached out to. It looks like we might get a contract to do their work. I told them she'd call them back so she could work out the details with them. Yesterday, I signed contracts with two more freelancers. I think we should be good to go when Nic closes this deal. Jo is studying for her certification exam. We're on our way. We're not turning a profit yet, although we're way ahead of our projections."

"Honey, you've done a great thing for all of us, opening this business. Nic has shouldered a lot of the load so far. In a couple of weeks Dana will come onboard full time, and things will be easier for all of us. Adding Jo's class has been a success. That bunch she's teaching will probably be here forever. We may have to charge them rent." Mallory smiled. "You do know that they're now bringing sandwiches to class. It's like a party in there."

Amanda laughed at Mallory's observation. "I know. She's made her class fun, and I think she's learned that she enjoys teaching. She's a natural. Have you watched her teach?"

"Just a few times for a short while. I agree with you. Although her classes are very structured, she thinks up fun activities that get everyone actively involved."

Amanda and Mallory stood facing each other across the reception desk. Amanda shook her head. "We've been so lucky. I can't wait for tomorrow. Things get better and better every day. How do you feel about things?" Amanda leaned on the counter to seek her partner's eyes.

"I agree with you. I'm deliriously happy." Mallory's love showed in her eyes. "Wanna marry me?"

Amanda spoke softly. "Name the day."

"I've been thinking maybe Labor Day weekend. We'll all be off. It's a holiday, so none of our family and friends who come will have to take any time from work."

"I like it. I like that time of year, too. It's not usually beastly hot." Amanda grinned playfully. "And we'll have ample time to practice for the honeymoon."

"I never knew you had such a wicked streak when I hooked up with you. Let's talk with Nic and Dana. It's their day, too. I think they've been too busy to even think about the wedding."

"Yeah, they've been too busy practicing for the honeymoon, too." Amanda's laughter was interrupted when she heard Nic's voice.

Nic emerged from the back room and bid Jo's student goodbye. As the door closed, she asked, "What's so funny?"

"We were just talking about the wedding," Amanda said.

"Yeah," Mallory added, "and about practicing for the honeymoon."

"I see. When are we going to do it? The wedding, not the practice."

When their laughter died down, Mallory replied. "We wanted to ask you and Dana what you'd think about Labor Day weekend."

"We're done here for tonight. Let's go get Dana and go out for dinner. We can talk everything over then. If you guys will lock up, I'll give her a call."

The three women left, chattering with excitement about their plans.

Chapter 27

STACY WAS EXHAUSTED AFTER making the trip in record time. The clock on the dash showed that it was nearly nine-thirty by the time she pulled into a parking place about a block from her apartment. She gathered her belongings and headed for home. Her heart was beating in expectation of seeing Jo. Nic had called her earlier to let her know that Mallory had taken Jo back to the apartment and that Jo was planning to take a nap. Nic said that Jo seemed okay, just tired, and she had cautioned her to drive safely.

Stacy opened the door to the scent of leather, the familiar smell of home. She listened. Hearing nothing, she climbed the stairs quietly and deposited her bags at the top of the steps. The light over the stove in the kitchen was on, giving a soft illumination to the main living area. She draped her jacket over the back of the stool and saw the note she'd left Jo two days earlier, still on the counter. She picked it up and read Jo's response. Her heart swelled. *She loves me, too!*

Quietly, Stacy got a clean oversized T-shirt from her suitcase then went down the hallway and into the bathroom. She took a quick shower and brushed her teeth. When she was finished there, she put on the shirt and headed for the office and Jo.

The blinds were open. The streetlight provided enough illumination to show her that Jo was not there. *She must be in my room—no, our room, now.* Stacy hurried down the hallway, through the living room, and into her bedroom. The nightlight was on, and Jo's regular breathing indicated that she was sleeping. Stacy stood near the bed, unsure if she should wake her.

"Stacy?"

"Yes, it's me." Stacy moved to the side of the bed. "Sweetheart, I was so worried." She leaned over and kissed her. It felt like the most natural thing in the world. Jo kissed her back softly, pulling her down so she was lying across her on top of the covers.

Jo just held her for a few seconds. "I was afraid I'd never see you again, never get to hold you like this."

"You're safe now, and I'm here." Stacy sighed as she laid her head on Jo's chest.

"How was the drive? Tired?"

"Exhausted. How are you feeling?" Stacy pushed up to rest on her elbows to better study Jo's face.

"Better now that you're here. I missed you so much. Come on, get in here with me, I'll warm you up. You feel cold. Why are you wet? Is it raining?"

Stacy stood up and stripped the shirt off, not feeling shy. "I took a shower." Completely naked, she slipped out of her panties and slid into bed with Jo. "Hey, that's not fair," she said pulling on Jo's T-shirt.

"Easily remedied." Jo slipped off her shirt and boxers.

Stacy settled against her. "Oh God, you feel so good."

Jo rolled to her side and kissed Stacy's cheek. "That dimple has called my name from the minute I met you." She kissed her softly on the mouth, feeling Stacy respond. "I love you," Jo whispered.

"What about rule number two?"

"I'm not worried about it anymore. What about you?"

Stacy smiled, showing her dimple. "Well, I for one don't plan on getting involved with any straight women." She tried to keep a straight face as long as possible before she finally gave into laughter.

"Well, that's good, I guess." Jo, sobered, kissed Stacy, a long, slow, thorough kiss that took Stacy's breath away.

Their mouths met, their tongues played together, and Stacy's world went on fire. Her body came alive. She could feel Jo pressed against her the whole length of her body. Stacy's hips strained against Jo, wanting release from her increasing passion.

Jo pulled back and looked into Stacy's eyes. "I want to make love to you, slow and easy."

"I want you, Jo."

Jo bent to kiss Stacy's lips, then trailed kisses down her neck. She inhaled the scent of Stacy's skin, tasting it with her tongue, and felt herself respond to her lover. She slid her hand up over the soft and tender skin of Stacy's breast, rolling the already erect nipple beneath her palm. Stroking Stacy stoked her own passion. She lowered her lips to suck Stacy's nipple into her mouth and tongued it until Stacy moaned softly. She rolled Stacy on top of her, allowing Stacy to settle against the thigh of her good leg. She pushed up, raising her knee to provide a better angle for Stacy to move against.

"Jo, you feel so good."

Jo ran her hands down the muscles of Stacy's back. Massaging as she moved the length of Stacy's body as far as she could reach, she trailed her nails over her smooth skin as she reversed the path of her hands.

"That feels wonderful." Stacy rose up and slid a little lower along Jo's body. Her lips found Jo's breast, causing a quick intake of breath. Stacy tongued one nipple as she tentatively explored the other with her palm. "You feel so good," she murmured.

Unable to hold herself back any longer, Jo flipped Stacy onto her back and began to make love to her in earnest. It seemed to Stacy that Jo was everywhere at once. Kissing here, touching there as she stimulated her into a desire she had never known before. As Jo slid her hand between Stacy's legs, Stacy felt a need deep inside her unlike anything she'd ever experienced.

"I want you inside of me." Her breath was coming in ragged gasps. "Please, Jo, please. Now."

Jo knew that in the future she'd make Stacy wait longer. But, spurred on by her own sense of urgency and need, Jo gently entered her lover for the first time, finding her slick, wet, and ready. As she began to stroke slowly at first then with an increasing tempo, Stacy urged her on with matching thrusts of her pelvis. Jo lowered her mouth to Stacy's breast and, after sucking the aroused nipple into her mouth, she began to tongue it at a matching pace with her hand movements until Stacy climaxed, screaming out Jo's name.

Jo was on fire. She wanted more of this wonderful, responsive woman. She began to trail kisses down Stacy's body finally settling between her legs, tasting her. She teased her lover with her tongue as she rocked against Stacy's leg until they both came. Jo collapsed against Stacy's stomach, softly kissing her there before she rested her head. Stacy stroked her fingers through Jo's hair.

"Well, that ended any hope of escape for you," Stacy said, a smile curling her lips. "Now you're stuck with me forever."

Jo slid up to kiss Stacy's lips. "So was it everything you imagined?"

"Uh huh. And more." She rolled Jo over, settling on top of her, adjusting her hips so that they were straddling each other's legs. She began to press her leg against Jo's core.

"I thought you were tired."

"I was. However, I haven't had a chance to make you feel good yet. I've wanted to touch you for so long. I love your body."

Stacy began to make love to Jo. She slid to her side, freeing her hand to trace a path across Jo's stomach, caressing the muscles she had yearned so often to touch. She kissed and traced nearly every inch of Jo's body. She couldn't believe the response she felt inside herself as she slid her fingers into the opening waiting between Jo's wet folds. She began to stroke. Stacy had already had two orgasms and, as she stroked her lover, she felt her own excitement rise again.

Sensing that Stacy's need was as great as hers, Jo shifted position so she could slip her fingers into Stacy. They moved together in a shared rhythm until they both came. Jo wrapped Stacy in her arms and they cuddled together, both spent.

Stacy's hands trailed up Jo's side, coming to rest on her lover's breast. "I love you."

"I love you, too. Want to talk, or do you want to sleep?"

"Talk, I think, then sleep."

"Okay, you start. What do you want to talk about?"

"You." Stacy raised her lips for a kiss.

Jo shifted lower in the bed and complied. They looked into each other's eyes. "What about me?"

"I can't get enough of you. I can understand now why Nic and Dana are always, as someone put it, sneaking off for a quickie."

Jo grinned. "Can you now?"

"Loving you is like coming home to a familiar place. It just feels so right. I thought I'd be nervous, but I wasn't. Everything seems so natural."

"No regrets?"

"No." Stacy paused. "Well, one. Only that it took me this long to find you."

"So what do you want to do with the rest of our lives?"

"You mean besides make love with you every chance we get?"

Jo touched Stacy's cheek. "Yes, besides that."

"I don't know. More of what we've been doing, I guess. I've been really happy with you here with me. From now on, it'll be better because now I know you love me. No more trying to figure out what I'm feeling. No more worrying about your rules and how you wouldn't allow yourself to love me back. No more wondering if my heart would break when time came for you to leave me. I just want to enjoy being with you. I want you to come home with me and meet my family and my friends—the one I have left there, at least."

"What do you mean? You told me you'd tell me more details about that."

Stacy told Jo about her exchange with Monique, including how hurtful the exchange had been.

"I'm sorry, Honey, that she felt that way and hurt you."

"On the bright side, I learned something about who my true friends are. Maria is eager to meet you. She wants to come up for a visit."

"That'll be nice. When do you want her to come?"

"I don't know. We have plenty of time to decide. Maybe you'd rather go home with me to meet my folks and you can meet her there?"

"I'll do anything you ask me to do."

"Hmm, let me think about that offer," Stacy said, encircling her lover and pulling her close.

"I can tell I'm going to enjoy being your partner!" Jo whispered just before she kissed her.

Chapter 28

NIC AND MALLORY WERE working on the schedule when Jo checked in late Tuesday morning. She apologized for her late arrival with a sheepish grin.

Mallory threw an arm over Jo's shoulder and gave her a squeeze. "So you two finally stopped beating around the bush and told each other how you feel?"

"Yes, and I've radically revised my belief system. Did I mention I'm happier than I would've ever imagined I'd be about it, too? Also, I wanted to thank you for covering my tutoring session yesterday, Nic."

"Not a problem. He's a nice kid. I helped him prep for his exam he has coming up."

Jo came around the counter and glanced at the schedule Nic had in front of her. "I have another tutoring session this afternoon and I have my class tonight. I came to run off some stuff I plan to use for my class. Stacy and I plan to go to my parents' cabin this weekend after I teach my class on Thursday night. We'll leave Friday morning."

Nic tried to persuade Jo to take off the rest of the week, starting that minute.

Mallory supported Nic's suggestion. "Really, Jo, you should consider Nic's advice. You don't seem to recognize what a really traumatic event you've been through. I think you've been too busy with Stacy's return," she said with a wink, "to let what happened at Meg's really absorb and settle in."

"No." Jo shook her head denying the statement. "I know it was scary, believe me. I just don't want to dwell on it. By the way, I talked to the chief this morning. They put Meg in the psych ward. Mal, can they help her?"

Mallory shrugged. "It depends. Between therapy and drug treatment, I think Meg has a chance of resuming a normal life. There's no doubt that this will be a life-altering event for her. I'm guessing that she took the drug she used on you illegally from either the ambulance or the doctor's office where she worked. That alone could end her career. However, since it's her first offense, she might just get probation with careful monitoring since what she did can be linked back to the head injury. I think the penalties vary by state. It's sad that this all came about from her head trauma."

Jo pulled the desk chair over and sat down. "Yes, the guy I shot was certainly not the only victim of that stupid fight those two guys had. It's just so senseless. Regardless, I feel I would have a hard time trusting Meg again. I have to admit the whole experience with her scared the crap out of me."

"All the more reason to get away for a while. Please," Nic said. "I'll cover your schedule the rest of the week. Take Stacy away and enjoy each other."

The two friends argued back and forth, with the final compromise being that Jo would meet her obligations for that day and she would allow Nic to cover her Thursday obligations.

Nic put her hand on Jo's shoulder. "If I see you two back here before Monday, I'll be really upset. You've had a rough several months, Jo. Take the time and have some fun."

Stacy showed up just in time to hear the last few sentences of the discussion. "Hey, we discussed this earlier. We think it would be fun if you all joined us at the cabin."

Nic declined the offer. "Someone has to stay here and hold down the fort," she chided. Feeling obligated to pass on the invitation, Mallory called Amanda after Jo and Stacy left.

"I don't know, Mal." Amanda responded. "Do you think they really want company? Isn't it sort of a honeymoon for them?"

"I did ask them that. They assure me that the place offers ample privacy for them, and they will be happy for the company after having this week together. What do you think?"

Jo and Stacy were thrilled when Mallory called them later and announced that she and Amanda would come up for the weekend. "We'll come in Friday night, after I finish up here."

"That's great. The more the merrier. Tell Nic to just come on up after work on Saturday if she and Dana change their minds."

* * *

Jo and Stacy left on Wednesday morning for the roughly three and a half hour trip to the cabin Jo's family owned near Edinborough. Although it was already April, there would probably still be snow on the ground and it would be chilly.

"The place was handed down from my grandfather to my father," Jo explained as she navigated through the light traffic on her way to the cabin. "My parents have been talking about selling it. I think it's getting to be too much for them to manage. My sister loves bringing her family here to be with Mom and Dad for the Christmas holidays. Now that her kids are almost grown, they're less interested in being here, so I don't see them coming up very often. They're at an age when they'd rather be with their friends than their family."

"How do you feel about them selling it?"

"I'd hate to see it sold." Jo checked over her shoulder before passing the slow-moving vehicle in front of her. "I'd love to buy it from them. Right now, I have enough on my plate with my own home, at least until I pick up some more hours. I love being there."

"What do you enjoy about it?" Stacy glanced over at Jo, enjoying watching her as she drove. The intense look of concentration on Jo's face made her feel completely safe.

"It's a great getaway. It sits on the lake. My grandfather built the house, and my father and brother-in-law, Jake, renovated it about fifteen years ago. The house has three bedrooms and two and a half bathrooms. The porch is useable in the summer for sleeping as well. It's weatherproof, has storm windows with screens, and two daybeds. There just wasn't enough room for all of us. My Dad and Jake decided to finish off the second floor above the boathouse. Now, there are another two bedrooms, a bath, and a small sitting room out there. In the summer, there's an outdoor shower, too. My favorite feature of the cabin is the huge porch that wraps around three sides of the house. We screened in one side a few years ago."

"And it's situated on the lake, you said. Is there a boat, Jo?"

"Yeah, it's right on the lake. There're a couple of kayaks, a canoe, and a rowboat. Hiking and fishing are good in the area, too. There's some great trout and bass fishing up here."

Stacy smiled, "My dad would love that. He's an avid fisherman."

"Maybe that would be a good place for me to meet them," Jo suggested.

"Let's do that when it's warmer, maybe this summer. It's too cold now. So, you don't use it from Christmas 'til now?"

"No. The house has electric heat as a backup. Our main source of heat is from wood stoves. We've always been afraid to leave it without draining all the systems down, just in case the electricity goes off. I've considered putting in solar panels on the roof of the boathouse. It's a big expense and, for as often as I get up there, I haven't felt it's really worth the investment."

Stacy thought about what Jo told her. "You know, maybe now that you're not working full-time, it'd be possible to use it more. We're not tied to the apartment. I can work anywhere. If I need to come in to see my publisher, it's not that far."

"That's a nice thought. Still, in the wintertime, it's pretty dead there. I enjoy it for weekends and holidays. I think living there full-time might be difficult, especially in the coldest months. Acceptance for our lifestyle wouldn't be the same as it is at home, either." Jo glanced briefly over at Stacy. "There's no hurry to decide. Wait 'til you've spent some time there and we can discuss it further. Our first big decision is what we're going to do about our current living situation."

"What do you mean?"

"Well, I have a house; you have an apartment. Our living together was supposed to be temporary. I don't want to assume that just because we slept together that you want me around twenty-four seven."

The sharply exhaled snort of air indicated Stacy's annoyance. "What're y'all talking about?" Her southern accent became more pronounced with her anger. "I didn't just sleep with you, I committed to you. Don't even think of trying to push me away. Are you having second thoughts about us?"

Jo apologized. "No, no, Honey. I'm sorry. I didn't mean to upset you. No. How could I have second thoughts? It's just that I didn't want to assume anything."

"Look, I've waited a lifetime to find someone to love. We happened to do things a little strangely, living together from day one before we even knew each other. Regardless of how we got started, I can't imagine my life without you in it all the time, every day. Can you? Can you see us returning to living apart?"

"No, I thought I'd go stir crazy on Sunday without you." Jo grinned. "Monday, not so much. I was pretty busy. You know, I was tied up most of the day."

"Oh stop. I don't think I'm ready to laugh about that experience quite yet." Stacy slid her hand up Jo's thigh, coming to rest in the hollow where her leg met her torso. "I did think about you a lot. I have to admit that my thoughts ran more along the lines that I might never see you again instead of how much I missed you." Jo laced her fingers with Stacy's.

"I'm sure." Stacy squeezed Jo's hand. "Okay, that's settled. For a bit there, I almost forgot about your house."

"Well, it's not on a lake or anything like my folk's place. Still, it's not like living in a city or town like you do. I have a nice back yard, a two-car garage, two bedrooms, and a bath and a half. There are advantages to your place. Proximity to the office, for one. I like knowing I'm able to look out the office window and being able to see you."

"Yeah, but with two of us there full time, wouldn't it be crowded?"

"Less so now. You'll get the office back if you'll let me sleep with you!" Jo winked.

"I think that could be arranged." Stacy grinned.

Jo glanced at Stacy briefly. "Was that our first argument?"

"Argument? Why?"

Jo shrugged, a sly smile curling her lips "Because if that was an argument, we get to have make up sex."

Shaking her head, Stacy said, "Believe me, we won't need make up sex. I think we're going to give Nic and Dana a run for their money. I can't keep my hands off of you. I adore making love with you. I never thought that touching someone else would or could excite me like it does. And when I slid inside you that first time, it almost made me come."

"Geez, Stacy, give me a break or we're going to have a wreck."

"You mean you don't like to talk about me making you feel good? I love kissing your breasts. You're so responsive. And your stomach, those abs. Oh my God, how much longer 'til we're there?"

"Almost. Keep that thought. I'm driving as fast as I can."

Twenty minutes later, Jo wound her way down a narrow road and through the dense forest. She took a smaller road filled with ruts that wound down towards the lake. "I'm glad we brought your all-wheel drive truck," Stacy said.

"There it is."

"Jo, it's beautiful." The log home blended perfectly into the forest. The view of the lake was wonderful. "How much land?"

"Just under ten acres. Like I said, we've owned it a long time. We couldn't afford to buy it today. We're lucky that taxes aren't that bad yet." Jo parked the car. Before she did anything else, she leaned over and kissed her lover. "I thought we'd never get here. I want you so much." Their second kiss left them both breathing hard. "If I don't stop now, we'll never get things done that need doing. Let's get things opened up and the water turned on. Don't forget where we were so we can start there." Reluctantly Jo turned away and put her hand on the door handle.

"Let me unpack the car while you do what you need to do with the water."

"Okay, that'll help a lot. Put the stuff in the first floor bedroom. That's the warmest one." Jo got out of the car and zipped her jacket.

Stacy put on her coat and grabbed their overnight bags. She made two trips back and forth to bring in the food they'd bought at the country store. "Jo," she called. "Can you help with the ice chest?" Stacy shivered against the chill.

"Give me a minute. I'm almost done here."

They'd bought ice because the fridge wasn't turned on. "I'm not sure we needed ice. It's still pretty cold here."

"I'll get the stove fired up in a couple of minutes. Let's get the food in the fridge. Is that the last of it?"

Stacy nodded. "Yep."

A few minutes later, the heat started to spread inside the house from the wood stove. Jo cranked up the electric heat to take the worst of the chill off the rooms. "I'll leave it off upstairs. You can go see the rest of the rooms if you want."

Stacy looked the rest of the house over while Jo fussed with the fire. Standing on the balcony overlooking the living room, Stacy could feel the heat from the fireplace rising to warm the room below. As she descended the stairs, she could feel the difference in the temperature downstairs. "Umm, starting to warm up in here. Feels good," she said coming up behind Jo and wrapping her arms around her lover.

Jo turned, taking Stacy in her arms. "I can make it a lot warmer, if you're interested."

"Always. Now and forever, day after day."

Jo kissed Stacy's dimple. "Nights, too?"

"Definitely the nights."

"I love you."

"Come show me how much."

Chapter 29

THE TWO NEW LOVERS had a wonderful few days together. As the week progressed, the weather warmed up. Jo showed Stacy the living area above the boathouse. "This is lovely up here, really cozy. You said there are five bedrooms. Right? That means you can sleep ten?"

Jo led Stacy to the balcony where they stood in the sunshine. "Yes, five. However, technically we can sleep fourteen. We have a futon in the corner of the little sitting room that can be used in a pinch. Plus the sofa in the living room is a sofa bed. We usually just put kids there because it's not private. We've also been known, during the summer when we've been crowded, to sleep people on a blowup bed on the porch. It'd be too brisk in this weather."

"I love the view from the balcony up here. In the sun, it's actually warm enough to sit outside for a while."

Later that afternoon, they dressed in layers and went for a rowboat ride. When they returned, they made up a room for Amanda and Mallory on the second floor.

Friday night a little after nine, Amanda and Mallory arrived. Mallory was filled with news about Nic teaching Jo's class the night before. "She loves the people in your class."

Jo agreed. "Yes, I'm really enjoying them. It's a nice group of people, and despite everyone's differences, they all seem to like each other. Don't you wish the world could be that way all the time?"

"Guess who I got a note from, Jo." When Jo couldn't guess, Amanda continued. "My brother."

Amanda turned to Stacy. "I think you know that my brother and I have been estranged. I haven't heard from him in something like eleven years, ever since I came out to my family. My parents died having never spoken to me again after I told them about myself." She looked away to hide the pain. "Now, my brother's oldest kid is going to be eighteen. She's finishing up her freshman year of college. He has twin fifteen year olds, too."

"I'm sorry. That must have been so hurtful. I'm so glad my family didn't react that way. I haven't told my father about Jo yet. I thought it better to let him get over his angina first." Stacy sighed. "Thankfully, my mother and sister were okay with my news about my new partner. They're not thrilled, not by any stretch of the imagination, but they still love me. I know they'll be happy for me eventually, especially after they meet her and see how happy we are together."

Angry on Amanda's behalf about the shabby way her brother had treated her, Jo asked, sarcasm evident in her tone, "What prompted him to write? Does he need a kidney or something?"

Amanda laughed out loud. "Gosh, I never thought of that! No, I don't think so. Remember, a few weeks before Christmas, when Mallory called him? They had an interesting discussion." Turning towards Mallory, Amanda said, "Tell them, Hon."

"Well, the conversation began on pretty shaky ground." Mallory's brows arched as she recalled the difficult conversation. "He called me a dyke. I told him that would be 'Doctor Dyke' to him. It made him laugh, and I guess that was a good thing. As our conversation continued, it seemed the harder I came back at him, the better he liked me. It ended up that I told him that there were lots of Democrats and Republicans in Washington. They, despite their different viewpoints, were able to be good friends and manage to get along, providing they didn't discuss politics. I suggested he try that approach with his sister since they obviously only disagreed about just the one issue. He ended up telling me he'd think about it."

"So that was the end of it?" Stacy asked.

"No." Mallory leaned back in her chair, took a deep breath, and finished the story. "I was surprised when I got an email from Spencer. He started by emailing me jokes about Democrats about a week after our conversation. His first personal note simply said, 'Put that in your pipe and smoke it!' I responded in kind with jokes about Republicans. I think I added a snotty little note at the end of my next email. Eventually, as we continued to exchange emails, I started just adding a little personal note about mostly nothing, maybe a movie we saw, or a television program that we'd watched that was interesting. You know, mundane little day-to-day things that happened in our lives like our favorite tree died or our plumbing leaked. Just the regular stuff you might complain about to a friend. In the past four months, we've written four or five times a week.

"Not one word of me in all this chatter, mind you." Amanda interrupted Mallory's story, her comment causing everyone to laugh.

Mallory continued. "Anyway, when I got shot, I told him how Jo had saved my life. Later, I told him about Meg going off the deep end and kidnapping Jo."

"Bet that went over great. He must love this." Jo turned to Stacy. "First he disowns her because he disapproves of her sexual preference, and now there's the added component of shootings and kidnappings."

"Yeah," Mallory agreed. "Funny thing is, I was pretty philosophical in one of our exchanges. I've always said to him that life is fragile and can be gone in an instant. Poof! Like a box of talcum run over by a truck."

"Now there's an analogy that certainly paints a vivid picture." Everybody laughed at Stacy's comment.

"I guess so." Mallory shrugged. "For whatever reason, it seemed to have a special impact on Spencer. I got a call the other day from him. I couldn't believe it when I saw his name on my caller ID. I answered the phone with just my name. I said, 'Mallory Barnes.' He said, 'Is this Doctor Dyke?' I laughed at him and said, 'Is this Mr. Bigot?'"

"It made him chuckle," Mallory said. "It's weird. The ruder I am to him, the better he seems to like it. I can't figure him out." Mallory was obviously enjoying relating the story. "Anyway, back to my story. Spencer said that he'd given a lot of thought to what I'd said about life ending unexpectedly. He said he wanted to talk to his sister, although he didn't know how to do that after so long."

Amanda interjected that she thought maybe her sister-in-law had been working on him to make amends. "Perhaps it helped and everything finally sank in."

"Hon, your brother, after our correspondence where I detailed all that had been happening in our day to day existence, also said he realized that our lives were really not that different from the life he lived. He told me that when his sister," Mallory touched Amanda's hand, "had told their parents and him that she was a lesbian, he envisioned that she would be promiscuous, drinking, and running around with all sorts of women. He never realized that she'd settle down in two stable relationships and lead as mundane a life as he did."

"Assuming one doesn't consider the shootings and kidnappings." Jo added with a snort.

"Yes, I guess." Mallory grinned, looked around the table at her friends. "So, I invited him to come up to visit us."

"And is he going to do it?" Jo asked.

Amanda took up the rest of the story. "Mallory says he's saying he'll come. We had such a nice Christmas with Nic's mom and Mallory's folks. We're thinking that we might do a Memorial Day or a Fourth of July family thing."

"You know," Jo said. "We've been thinking about inviting Stacy's family up here, too. Let's do a family thing, and all of us come up here and invite our families to join us. There are lots of things to do that time of year here like fishing, hiking, swimming, and boating. It might make it easier than sitting there eyeball to eyeball with your brother one-on-one."

"Umm, maybe." Amanda glanced around. "That'll be quite a mob. Jo, can you fit everyone here?"

"I don't know," Jo said. "How many people are we talking about?"

"Well, I don't think Spencer will bring the kids. So probably just him and his wife," Amanda said.

"Okay, so that's two. The six of us is eight. Stacy's parents make ten. Nic's mom is eleven, and if her sister comes, that'll be twelve."

"What about your parents, Jo?" Amanda asked.

"No, it's their anniversary, and they always take a cruise then. I'll definitely mention this shindig to them. They might make an exception this year."

"Twelve we can do here with no problem. If the kids come, we can always throw up a couple of those blow-up beds. It's only a couple of days, so I'm sure they'd survive. If my parents come, we could be too crowded."

"Isn't that a lot of people for three and a half bathrooms?" Mallory wondered.

"The only time it's an issue is in the mornings. We usually have a crowd at Christmas, and that's the only time of day it's a problem." Jo thought a minute. "You know, the people next door rarely come up any more. They rent their cabin out to people they know. Maybe we could rent the place next door. Their house is similar to this house in square footage but laid-out differently—it has more bedrooms. If we can get their house, we'd certainly have no issues with space then. If you're serious about us doing this, I can give them a call tomorrow."

Amanda looked to Mallory who nodded. "Let's see if that's an option. Call them and, if it's something they're willing to do, we can talk more about it then."

"Do you think it'll be easier for your brother if there are more people, or will he be overwhelmed?" Mallory asked Amanda.

"He's pretty gregarious. I think it might be easier for him. With so many people, the topic won't focus on my homosexuality. It'll keep that subject more in perspective. He'll be able to see that none of us is to be feared, that we all have normal lives and families who accept us for who we are. Good examples for him, I think."

"One problem," Stacy said. "My mom knows about us and so does my sister. We'll want to tell my dad that weekend."

Jo took Stacy's hand. "How about we take care of that by bringing your parents up a couple of days early. That's assuming my bosses are willing to give me some extra time off." Jo winked at Amanda and Mallory.

"I can virtually guarantee that can be arranged," Amanda promised.

Mallory stood. "Well, I don't know about you two, but I'm ready to turn in. I'm bushed. It's been quite a week."

"Tell me about it!" Jo pointed. "Okay, you two are upstairs. I've put the heat on up there for you, and I'll stoke up the stove tonight so you should be comfortable. We'll see you in the morning."

Both couples talked separately about the potential family weekend, deciding that it seemed like a good plan. The next morning, the four women met for breakfast then went for a hike around the lake. After they returned to the cabin, Jo contacted her neighbor who said he was willing to rent the cabin. He gave Jo a price, which she reported to the others. She promised her neighbor she'd let him know before she left for home the next day.

On Saturday afternoon, the four friends sat on the deck and played cards, enjoying their leisure time together. "This is great up here, Jo. I'm loving our time here, aren't you Mallory?" Amanda asked.

"It's wonderful and so relaxing. It would be nicer for a long weekend than for the short amount of time we have here. Too bad we have to leave tomorrow afternoon. I'd love to be able to stay longer."

Amanda nodded thoughtfully as everyone agreed. Late in the afternoon, the four women went for a walk through town, stopping in at the Country Store to pick up another dozen eggs, some ham, and another loaf of bread.

"French toast for breakfast," Jo announced. "I'll get some lettuce, lunch meat, and cheese for lunch tomorrow."

"Maybe we can start for home tomorrow around four and stop somewhere on the way for dinner. It'll break up the ride."

"Great idea, Stacy." Amanda agreed. "Dinner will provide a great interruption to the long ride."

When they got back to the cabin, they were pleased to discover Nic and Dana's car in the drive and the two of them sitting on the rockers on the porch. "Thank goodness," Nic said, grinning. "We were afraid we were on the wrong porch and you were coming to take us away."

"Hey there! What a pleasant surprise." Jo exclaimed, hugging her friends in turn.

"We lost power at the shop. Someone knocked over a pole. They told us that we'd be without power until they could repair it. We just decided what the heck, and here we are. Hope that invitation is still open," Nic said.

"The door is always open for my friends." Jo opened the door and everyone went inside.

"We had a wonderful time sitting on the porch. It was starting to get chilly, though. It feels good in here." Nic rubbed her hand up and down her arm as she spoke.

"I'll throw another couple of logs on." Jo grabbed the log carrier and went to retrieve more wood.

The evening went quickly as the women brought Nic and Dana up to date on their plans for July. Nic looked at Mallory. "I know my mom would love to see your mom again. They really hit it off at Christmas."

Mallory added with a mischievous grin, "We'll put Nic's mom and my mom to work on your brother, Amanda. They'll get him in line."

Jo and Stacy made breakfast for the whole crew the next morning, after which they took the rowboat and canoe for a paddle and row around the lake. Later, as the temperatures rose, they enjoyed the sunshine on the deck as they talked more about the upcoming vacation together with their families.

"Look how long it took us to make breakfast for just the six of us," Dana commented. "Do you think we can feed all the people we want to invite? I mean, think about it, if we had eight or ten more people to feed, we'd have to start prepping for lunch right after breakfast and the same for dinner. We won't be free to entertain and enjoy our time with our families and each other if we're slaving away in the kitchen all the time."

"Maybe," Nic suggested, "if we keep the meals simple, we could manage it. I think you're right, though. If we can't be free to enjoy ourselves and spend time with our guests, there's no sense in inviting everyone up here. Maybe this isn't the best solution."

After a minute or two of silence, Jo laughed. "I can almost smell smoke from all these wheels turning. The solution is simple. Let's hire a caterer. I know a woman, Judy, who started her own catering business a couple of years ago. I've attended several events she's catered. Her food is excellent. She's single, so traveling here shouldn't be an issue for her. For big events, her sister helps her. Maybe we could hire the two of them for the weekend. It would certainly make our lives much easier."

Everyone agreed it was a wonderful solution. Dana volunteered to coordinate the meals through the caterer, removing one huge obstacle from organizing the weekend.

Jo called the neighbor and reserved his cabin for the July 4th weekend.

The final hurdle that the group argued about was who should stay where. Opinion was split about the suggestion Nic made that the family members should be left alone as a group in one cabin. "We can stay next door. That way our families can talk about us."

Jo expressed concern. "But they're our guests. Shouldn't we be there to be fulfill our roles of hostesses?"

Amanda pushed her hair back from her forehead and exhaled a sigh. "The caterer will be there during the day if none of us is around to take care of whatever anyone needs. If we're organized, surely one of us can be available to hang out there with any family member who isn't involved in an activity. After dinner we can stay until it's time for bed before we go next door. We can return early in the morning to help serve coffee and see that everyone is fed. It might not be a bad idea. It'd be a chance to support each other, too, without being under the careful scrutiny of our families."

"Let's not decide today," Mallory said. "Let's get the invitations sent. Once we have a final count, we can fight it out then as to where everyone will stay."

"Great idea." Jo added enthusiastically. Everyone seemed relieved that they had covered all the details of their family vacation. Everyone nodded approval of the plan. "If it's this hard to plan, imagine what it'll be like when everyone is here."

Having enjoyed relaxing together in the scenic location, all too soon it was time for them to pack up and leave for home. They agreed that they would meet at a restaurant Jo was familiar with that was a little more than half way home. They met for dinner before heading to their separate homes.

Chapter 30

THE NEXT COUPLE OF months sped by. Stacy's mom called her unexpectedly one day and told her she had found an opportune time to tell her father about her relationship with Jo. "So you might as well bring her down here to meet us."
"How did he take it, Mom?"
"He loves you, Honey. He wants more than anything to see you happy. It may not be what he'd have chosen for you, but it's your life."
"Mom, when you meet her, maybe you'll understand better. She's wonderful and we're very happy together."
A couple of weeks later, Jo and Stacy drove to Stacy's hometown in Virginia. Stacy's father and Jo hit it off when he discovered she liked to fish. Jo also met Stacy's friend Maria when they stopped in for an overnight visit on their way home.
As for Stacy's other hometown friend Monique, she was someone who, despite two attempts on Stacy's part, never responded again. She sent a note to Stacy saying that as long as Stacy was living her sinful lifestyle, she should no longer consider herself Godmother to her kids. Stacy was very upset by the hurtful rejection. "How can she hate me so much? I'm the same person I always was, except for whom I've chosen to sleep with, a fact that has no bearing on her life whatsoever."
Jo was at a loss for an explanation. The only thing she could do, was hold her lover while she shed tears of hurt and rejection.
Following Spencer's email exchanges with Mallory, he began a correspondence with his sister that eventually graduated into phone calls. Although Mallory wanted to take full credit for the recent and still tentative reconciliation, the truth was that Amanda couldn't shake the feeling that Spencer wanted something from her. Her suspicions

were confirmed when, during a phone call to firm up travel arrangements with Spencer, he asked, "Sis, do you think it's possible for us to find some time to talk privately during the family gathering? I have some questions to ask you."

"Sure. You can ask me now."

"No, I want to spend some time together first."

Squelching the laughter that threatened to erupt, Amanda asked, her tone serious, "You don't want me to donate a kidney to you, do you?"

"What? Are you nuts? No, forget I mentioned it. I'm sure we'll have time to talk about it during our vacation. By the way, I think Justine might want to come. The twins will be away at camp, so they won't be a problem. I know she's eighteen, but I don't want to leave her home alone with us so far away."

Amanda bit her tongue. Although she wanted to say, 'For God's sake, Spencer, she'll be away at college in a little over a month,' she refrained. Amanda couldn't imagine what Spencer wanted to ask her, and she remained just a little uneasy about the upcoming encounter with her brother. She readily agreed, however, to Justine coming, feeling excited at the prospect of seeing her niece again after so many years of imposed estrangement.

* * *

The preparations for the Fourth of July party were progressing smoothly. Nic's mother had accepted the invitation, as had Mallory's parents. After the exchange of several emails, Amanda's brother and his wife also had also sent a formal note expressing their appreciation for being invited and accepting the invitation for the holiday festivities. Jo's parents also confirmed after agreeing to book a later cruise, and Stacy's parents were looking forward to meeting Stacy's friends as well as Jo's parents.

Two weeks before the gathering, the friends met to discuss living arrangements for the weekend. They confirmed their original plans to keep Spencer in with the rest of the family. "So, let's plan out everything we need, and discuss where we'll put everyone," Jo suggested.

"First on the list is food," Amanda said, checking her notes. "Dana? Is everything arranged?"

"Yes, we're all set. We've booked the caterer. Like Jo said, she's bringing her sister along to help. Apparently, the sister is eighteen and will be going off to college this fall. She's happy to be making some extra money."

"Did you review the menus?"

"Yes, some of the meals will be done on the grill. We can have roast chicken one night, hotdogs and hamburgers on the holiday, and pasta the last night. She's prepared to cook any fish we catch." Dana turned towards Jo and winked. She knew Jo was looking forward to fishing with her father and hoping she'd bond with Stacy's father during the fishing outings on the lake. "Since we're all traveling up on Thursday or Friday separately, I figured we'd all fend for ourselves until Saturday morning, our first group meal. There'll be a couple of casseroles that will be easy to heat up and some sandwich stuff, too. Breakfasts will be quiche one morning, hot and cold cereal and an egg bake called Governor's Eggs the second day, and Danish and other assorted pastries on the fourth to allow some extra time to prepare for the lunch. Everyone can clean out what's left on Tuesday before we leave. We'll be sure there're enough scrambled eggs and toast for everyone as the main part of the meal before everyone leaves." With her tongue firmly in her cheek, figuratively speaking, Dana added, "I ordered a variety of snacks, too. The caterer will set up a table of snacks every afternoon with some iced tea or lemonade to stave off any threat of starvation until dinnertime and, of course, there will always be fresh fruit out for anyone wanting it."

"Great job, Dana." Amanda checked off the first item on her list. "Everything sounds like it's taken care of in the food department. One thing, let's remember to bring up any tray tables we have. We don't have any dining area big enough to seat everyone at a table. The food sounds relatively portable, so maybe we can serve buffet style and let people find places to sit wherever. Dana, please let the caterer know that so she doesn't expend energy with table decorations we won't need."

Amanda moved on to the next item. "Ok, next up is sleeping arrangements. We have the following people coming. She read from the list:

- Nic's mom, Anna Bianchi
- Jo's parents, Chris and Josette Martin
- Stacy's parents, Frank and Marcia Alexander
- Amanda's brother, Spencer; sister-in-law, Amy; and niece, Justine.
- Lindy and Ren from Maine
- The six of us

Ticking them all off on her fingers, Amanda pronounced, "That's a total of sixteen people."

"Maybe seventeen," Stacy said. "My friend, Maria, has volunteered to drive my parents up as far as our house a few days before the holiday. If no one objects, I would like to invite her to join us. I promise you'll like her."

"We'd better make that eighteen." Amanda laughed. "I told Jean she could join us after she closes up the office on Saturday."

"Okay, so that's it, then, eighteen, no, twenty. We forgot the caterers. What are their names, Dana?"

"Judy, and her sister's name is Brenda."

"Good." Amanda added the caterers' names to her list. "Let's figure out where we'll put everyone. We have twenty people and eleven bedrooms or sleeping areas. How about each couple figures out a sleeping plan, and then we can discuss them. We can pick the best one via majority vote.

The couples went to work. When everyone was finished, they gathered at the table. The results were interesting. Everyone agreed that all the family should stay at the neighbor's house. They all felt that it would be best if they used the house belonging to Jo's parents as a central meeting place, since it had the largest living area and the larger kitchen. The only discrepancy in the plans was how to arrange Ren and Lindy, and Jean and Maria.

Jo defended her idea. "One of the reasons for Lindy and Ren to come down, besides that we all want to see them, is because I'm consulting with Lindy on her book. Remember, she asked me if I'd advise her on police procedure. Anyway, Lindy and I want some time to meet so I can review with her the material she's written. I thought maybe it would work best if Stacy and I stay with them in the boathouse apartment. One of the bedrooms in my folks' house has twin beds. Since Jean and Maria won't know each other very well, that would be more comfortable than having them have to share a bed with someone they just met."

"Valid point," Dana observed. "But, Jo, how will your parents feel about giving up their own home and bedroom to stay next door? Won't that be awkward? We're taking over their home and evicting them, aren't we?"

"I don't think they'll mind if I explain everything to them. They're pretty 'go with the flow' people. If they object, we'll have to regroup. I'm reasonably sure it'll be acceptable to them. I'll call them tonight and confirm it's okay."

Amanda summarized their agreement, taking brief notes. "Okay then, in the neighbor's house, we have Nic's mom alone in the twin room, Jo's parents, Stacy's parents, and Spencer and his wife in the double bedrooms there." Amanda winked at Jo. "We'll give Jo's mom and dad the master suite with the queen bed to make up for evicting them from their home."

Jo added, "That'll work. The other bedrooms are about equal in size, so it doesn't matter who gets which room there. Amanda, what about your niece?"

"Oh, I forgot her," Amanda answered. "Suggestions?"

"Well, we could put her in with Nic's mom. I'd like to suggest the screened in porch for her, instead," Jo offered. "It's weather proof, like the one in my folks' house, and it's private. I'm sure both Mrs. Bianchi and Justine would appreciate not having to share with someone they don't know. If I remember correctly, there's a huge sofa out there on their porch, with removable cushions along the back, though, not daybeds. She can throw a sleeping bag on it and have her own private little sitting area when she's not sleeping. There's a television out there, too. It'll be like her own little apartment."

Continuing to write as she talked, Amanda said, "So, that leaves Dana and Nic, Mallory and me, and Jean and Maria in Jo's folks' house, with Jean and Maria in the room with two single beds, right?"

Everyone nodded in agreement.

Looking at Dana and Nic, Amanda asked, "Do you want to flip a coin for who gets the bigger bedroom?"

Dana laughed. "Nah, we'll take the smaller room." She reached over to squeeze Nic's hand, and with a twinkle in her eye, she said, "We like to be close to each other, anyway."

Jo chided them. "Maybe it's good that all the parents are in the other house. It would never do to put the two of you in a room next to Spencer."

Laughing at the good-natured teasing, Dana tossed back, "What's that saying about people in glass houses, Jo?" Everyone laughed as Nic and Jo both turned bright red.

"I know you've all made arrangements with your families individually as to who is driving whom and when. I'd appreciate it if you'd send me an email when you get your plans firmed up so we know who will be where and at what times. I'll organize it and send back a master list to you. Dana, are we buying the food, or is the caterer taking care of that?"

"No. The caterer is handling all things food related. We'll just get the bill when it's over."

Everyone groaned in unison.

* * *

A few days before the big weekend, Maria drove Stacy's parents up for a visit so they could spend extra time with Jo prior to the big weekend. They all stayed at Jo's house. Dana and Nic arrived for dinner early to help Jo and Stacy with the meal prep for Stacy's family. Mallory and Amanda had been working at the office with Jean, giving her some final pointers and last minute instructions. Just before they left, they reminded her to drive carefully on her trip up to join them for the weekend.

Jean laughed. "If you two don't get out of here, I'll beat you there. Now go!"

That evening at dinner, Stacy's parents asked a variety of questions, ranging from, "Tell us how you met each other," followed by, "Tell us about each of your family members who are coming this weekend." Each woman took a turn answering the questions.

When Dana's turn came, she revealed that since she had no siblings, and her parents and both sets of grandparents were deceased, she had to develop a different definition of family. "These women here are my family. I can guarantee that if we were related by blood, they would be no more loved than they are."

Stacy's mother, who was sitting next to Dana, reached for Dana's hand. She had tears in her eyes. "Well, I hope you'll come to think of us as your family, too. I think my daughter is lucky to have found such a wonderful group of friends."

As the evening progressed, the group continued to learn things about each other. Many questions, posed to Stacy's parents by members of the group, served to sufficiently embarrass Stacy to the point where she finally protested. "Okay, I think that's enough about me. A girl's got to have some secrets."

"If anyone wants to know more, I have a few secrets about our girl Stacy that have yet to be revealed," Stacy's mother teased.

When Stacy put her head in her hands and groaned, Jo took pity on her partner. She put a hand around her shoulder and said protectively, "Let's give my girl a break, shall we, or do I have to get out my service revolver?" To a chorus of a variety of denials mixed with laughter, Jo stood up. "Who wants coffee?"

Realizing that Jo's quick embrace was the first display of affection that her parents had witnessed between Jo and herself, Stacy quickly glanced at her parents. She was relieved to see they were chuckling right along with everyone else at the table.

Frank, Stacy's dad, who had been relatively quiet all evening, glanced at his daughter. "All right, I guess we'll have to save her baby pictures for tomorrow. I brought the eight by ten glossy of her on the bearskin rug in case anyone is interested. Jo?"

The look of shock on Jo's face, accompanied by a bright red flush, caused everyone at the table to break into uproarious laughter.

"Oh, Daddy. Behave!"

After dessert and coffee, the group adjourned to the living room.

Jean announced that she'd eaten so much she needed a short walk to help her meal settle.

"I'll come with you, if you don't mind," Maria offered.

"Great! I'd love the company."

Conversation was light and casual. Stacy's father was a consummate teller of tales, from fishing to golf stories. He told several jokes that made the group laugh. Maria and Jean returned from their walk shortly before Nic and Dana announced that they were going to head home. When they stood to leave, Jean, Amanda, and Mallory stood, taking their leave at the same time.

Hugs were exchanged all around, and Stacy overheard Jean say to Maria, "I'll give you a call in the morning and we'll make final arrangements for brunch. I have to be at work by one, so let's shoot for around ten."

Maria gave Jean a warm smile. "Thanks. I appreciate you showing me around. Brunch is on me, by the way." She gave her new friend a quick wave.

Later that evening, Stacy saw that her parents were settled in bed before she went across the hall to Maria's room.

Maria was already in bed, leaning against the headboard, a book propped on her knees. "I'm pooped," she admitted. "It's been a full day. I don't think I'll be awake for long."

Stacy sat on the edge of the bed and gave her friend a hug. "Thanks, Maria, for driving my folks up. I really appreciate it."

Maria patted Stacy's hand. "My pleasure. I mean that. I'm really enjoying myself. Your friends are great people. One is nicer than the next. I also love your partner. Jo is perfect for you. You're really happy, aren't you?"

Stacy nodded. "It's laughable how happy I am. I would never have thought this is the person I would end up with. It just feels so right." Stacy met Maria's eyes. "So, what's going on with Jean?"

"Nothing. She figured that you'd be busy with your parents tomorrow, so she offered to show me around." Maria's bland expression gave no indication of the excitement she was feeling at the prospect of spending the better part of the day with Jean, whom she found to be witty, warm and fun. "It was very considerate of her, don't you think?"

"Yes, very. I don't know her very well yet. She just started working at the office. Jo has known her for quite a while, though. She's always spoken highly of her. She helped search for Amanda last year when she took a header off the trail on her bike. Jo and a group of her friends, Jean included, participated in the search."

"She's really funny and seems like a really kind person. Jean told me that she volunteers a lot of her time. She told me some amusing stories about some of the rescues she's been on. Then she told me about searching for Amanda when she fell off her bike, and about Jo's shooting, her injury, and subsequent kidnapping."

"Yes. I met Jo while she was recovering after the shooting. The kidnapping happened when I was down home when Dad had his heart scare." Stacy leaned over and gave Maria another hug. "I'm glad you're here. I'll see you in the morning."

As Stacy stood to leave, she quickly reviewed the agenda for the next couple of days. Today was Wednesday, and they weren't leaving for the cabin for another two days. She hadn't really told Maria her plans, so she paused at the door.

"Enjoy your day with her tomorrow. Be home by five-thirty. We're going out for an early dinner. Then, if you can, I'd like you to help me pack the car. We're leaving early on Friday morning for the cabin. I'd like to get there around noon time so I can help Dana and Nic get things set up."

"Roger! I'll be home before that. Jean has to work in the afternoon, and I want to spend some time with you catching up, anyway. I'll be back after lunch."

Chapter 31

THURSDAY AFTERNOON, AFTER LUNCH, Amanda, Jo, Dana, Nic, and Jean met at the office to review the status of all the work assignments and to give Jean a final review of the protocols she should follow while they were away.

After what seemed like an endless set of unnecessary instructions, Jean finally said, "Please, ladies, you're going to be gone for a long weekend. I swear I can handle things for that long. Honest." She crossed her heart with her index finger. "If you're this nervous about leaving your business, I sincerely hope none of you ever has children, for surely it'll be an eighteen year commitment with not one day off. Really, you are all just a phone call away if I have any questions I can't answer. Now, please go and leave me in peace to do my job." She gave them a big grin to soften her criticism before pulling Jo aside to whisper, "And tell that hot house guest of yours I had fun this morning, and I'm looking forward to seeing her on Saturday."

"Moving pretty quickly, aren't you? I'm not even sure she's gay."

"No. Not really. We're just friends. Oh, and for the record, I asked. She describes herself as 'flexible.' She's really fun, and that accent. How do you manage to keep your wits about you when Stacy whispers sweet nothings in your ear? I could listen to Maria read the want ads for hours. I know what you're saying, though. She's too far away for a serious relationship, and I'm not looking to move anywhere anytime soon. So, like I said, just friends."

"Okay, have fun. We'll see you Saturday. Don't forget to put the Closed Tuesday sign on the door when you leave."

"Got it. It's on the list. I think it's item four-hundred-fifty-three."

"You know, Jean," Jo said with a grin, "nobody likes a smartass!"

Pulling Jo into a quick, firm hug, Jean replied, "Really? Could've fooled me. Have you been fibbing to me all along, then?"

"I guess so." Jo released Jean from their embrace.

"Okay, I'm out of here to go home and help entertain the in-laws. Bet you never thought you'd hear me say that, or even that I'm looking forward to it."

* * *

Her watch dial indicated Thursday, 2:37 PM. Mallory had finished cleaning the house and had prepared a snack for Amanda's brother and his family. After pacing back and forth in front of the window for over a half hour, she couldn't stand it any longer. *If I don't do something, I'll be a total nervous wreck by the time they get here.* She searched her mind for something to do. *Pool. Oh, good idea!*

Mallory selected her favorite stick from the array on the wall and racked the balls. When she struck the cue-ball, her hand slipped, causing the white ball to go flying across the room and lodge under the sofa. *Crap!* She tried to reach under to retrieve the ball but couldn't find it. *I'm going to look like an unmade bed after crawling around on the floor.* Heaving a sigh, she lay down on the floor to peer under the sofa. Using the stick, she retrieved the ball.

Just then, the doorbell rang. Leaping to her feet, she placed the ball onto the table, dusted off her clothes, and took the stairs two at a time. She didn't know what to expect when she opened the door. Forcing a big smile, she faced her fate.

Amanda and Spencer could never deny they were related. They looked enough alike to be twins. "Well, there's no doubt in my mind that you're Amanda's brother. I could have picked you out of a thousand people," Mallory said as she transferred the pool stick to her left hand to extend her right hand to Spencer in greeting. "Welcome."

"So, are you the infamous Dr. Dy..." Spencer stopped himself just in time. "Uh, Dr. Barnes?" Glancing at the pool cue in her left hand, he firmly gripped her extended hand. "I do come in peace. No need for the weapon." His grin indicated he was teasing.

Mallory was pleased with Spencer's conciliatory tone. She knew he loved to tease, though, so she thought she'd have a little fun. "Well, Spencer, someone has to keep you in line this weekend, and I drew the short straw. My stun gun is downstairs." Raising the pool cue in front of her, she said, "I must have grabbed this by mistake." Although she tried, she failed to keep a straight face and was pleased when Spencer gave a hearty laugh.

"Okay, Doc. Do you know how to use that thing for the purpose for which it's designed?"

"I seem to be having a bit of an off day. Under usual circumstances, yes, I can play." Realizing that Spencer was alone, Mallory glanced toward his car parked in the driveway. "What did you do with the others?"

He laughed. "Well, they'd been away from any source of shopping for the duration of our drive up, so they called Amanda and asked her where they could do some shopping. I dropped them off. She's going to pick them up when she finishes work and bring them home. So, you're stuck with just me."

"Then, how about we shoot a game? Can I interest you in a beer or some food?"

He gratefully accepted her offer. Following a quick snack, they headed for the basement to play. She let him break, and after a couple of shots when it was her turn, he leaned on the arm of the sofa. She was surprised when he openly stated, "You know, Doc, I'm nervous about seeing Amanda. It's been so long. I'm not sure what to say to her."

Mallory had learned long ago that sometimes silence was the best answer. She waited patiently for him to continue.

"Just to be clear, I still don't approve or accept—you know, you and her, women and women, men with men. I don't think my mind will ever change about that. I do regret that I cut her off, because I do still love her."

"Maybe the latter part of that statement is a good starting place. There's a whole weekend ahead, plenty of time to tell her the negative stuff if you feel you must. But, if you feel you have to say it, maybe leave that for the end, huh?"

"You once told me that Democrats and Republicans could be friends if they didn't talk about politics. Is that what you mean? Just don't talk 'politics' this weekend?"

"No, not exactly. I'm just saying a lot of time has passed since you've seen her. Why not get caught up first, give yourself time to re-establish your connection with her. I'm sure there will be ample time to talk 'politics' before you leave for home." Mallory took two shots and it was then Spencer's turn.

"Okay, I'll take your advice. I know you'll find this hard to believe. I actually like you."

"Thank you, Spencer. It's not hard to understand. I like you, too. We just don't agree on one specific issue. It's very likely there are a number of issues we don't agree on and many others that we will feel similarly about. Because you're hung up about my being gay, we don't get to explore the other things."

Spencer missed his next shot. "There's one thing I just don't understand."

"Really? I find it hard to believe there's only one thing. Tell me what that is."

"Okay. I just don't understand why my sister is interested in women instead of men. How can she want to, well, you know…"

"Spencer, I have two answers for you. One is serious and one I hope you'll find amusing." Mallory laid the cue on the table and leaned forward on her outstretched arms spread on the edge of the table. She looked Spencer squarely in the eyes. "The serious answer first. I can't answer for your sister. I can only explain how it is for me, and you probably won't like the answer. That's just the way it is. Plain and simple. It's not that I don't like men. I do. I enjoy their company and have some great men friends. I just don't want to have sex with them. I could kiss a man for days and feel no more excited by it than if I kissed a teddy bear. That just doesn't do anything for me. I know it is hard for you to assimilate this. The touch, the taste, the feel of a woman makes me feel normal." Mallory smiled when Spencer flinched. "Sexually, in essence, women make me feel the same way I imagine they make you feel. For me, there's more to it than just sex. To me, being in the company of women is like coming home. It's where I feel most comfortable. I don't know if that makes any sense to you. Unfortunately, it's as clear as I think I can make it."

Spencer was silent when Mallory finished speaking. He didn't say anything, just nodded.

Mallory picked up her cue and prepared to take her next shot.

"You said you had two answers for me. What's the other one?"

Mallory chuckled. "Actually, it's a joke. What do a clitoris, an anniversary, and a toilet have in common?"

Spencer immediately covered his ears and started to say, "La, la, la, la."

Spencer's behavior garnered a deep laugh from Mallory.

"Eew, Doc. The 'C' word."

"Oh, Spencer, put on your grownup hat now. Come on, what do a clitoris, an anniversary, and a toilet have in common?"

After exhaling a deep sigh, Spencer, replied, "Okay, I'll bite, what?"

"Men always miss them!"

Amanda opened the front door for her sister-in-law and niece. The sound of hearty laughter from the direction of the basement greeted them. She tiptoed down the stairs and peeked around the doorframe. "Hey, you two, what's so funny?"

"Nothing," they replied in unison. Spencer's face was still red, the result of a combination of the topic and his laughter.

Spencer hurried across the room to take his sister into a big hug. "I'm sorry it's been so long, Amanda."

"Me too, Spencer. Me too. It sounds like you and Mallory are having fun."

"No, I'm not having fun." With a smile cast in Mallory's direction, he said, "She's picking on me and all mankind."

"I learned a secret about your brother today, Amanda. I can easily keep him in line. All I have to do is say the word..."

"La, la, la, la," Spencer sang, again placing his hands over his ears.

"See," Mallory said, grinning ear to ear.

"Is it safe to come out now?" Spencer asked, uncovering his ears.

Mallory slapped him on the back. "If you want to come out, Spencer, feel free. It'll certainly make the weekend more interesting."

Rolling his eyes, Spencer asked Mallory, "Who's the smartass now?"

"No doubt about it Spencer, that would be me. Your behavior has been exemplary. For that I'm about to reward you by cooking you a nice dinner. If we play pool much longer, I'll embarrass you by beating the pants off you, so I'm going to cut you a break. Come on, I can't wait to meet your wife and daughter."

* * *

Dana and Nic picked up Nic's mother at the train station after the work meeting. They were on their way up to the cabins to get the houses ready for the arrival of their guests. Everyone else was due to arrive by late Friday afternoon. They had dinner reservations for the whole group at a local pub. Nic and Dana had volunteered to help Judy, the caterer, get all the food, and prepare the cabin for their guests. They'd hired the caterer's sister, Brenda, to help them make the beds. While they began that task, Judy worked on the shopping list. When they finished the seventh bedroom, Dana sighed. "Thank God the cleaning crew came through earlier in the week. I don't think I'm cut out for manual labor."

Nic laughed. "I know one thing we forgot. Who's going to do all this laundry?"

"You youngsters don't know what it means to work like we had to when I was young," Nic's mother replied as she tossed the pillow she had just put the cover on onto the bed.

"Come on, Mom. We can finish up and you can take a break."

"Don't treat me like an old lady, Nicolina. I can cover the pillows if you can make the beds."

"Okay, Mom, that's a deal." Knowing it had been a long day for her mother, Nic said, "I think I need a snack first. Let's see what there is to eat."

Nic took her mom downstairs where they cut up some fruit for everyone while Dana and Brenda finished up the last of the beds. Finally finished, the little group gathered for their snack. Dana turned to Nic. "Wonder how Amanda is doing with her brother?"

"What's wrong with him?" Nic's mother wondered aloud.

"Egli è un bigotto," Nic told her mother. "He disapproves of Amanda and Mallory, and the rest of us too, I suppose. I hope he doesn't ruin the weekend for Amanda."

Nic's mother nodded knowingly. "He will be fine. This I know. You are all good people. He will see this." She patted Nic's hand. "Do not worry, Cara."

* * *

Thursday evening, Mallory, Amanda, Spencer, and his family met for dinner with Jo, Stacy, and their other guests. Spencer seemed relaxed and easily fell into conversation with Stacy's father. Amanda enjoyed catching up with her sister-in-law and niece. Conversation was lighthearted, and everyone left the restaurant looking forward to the weekend.

By three-thirty the next afternoon, the entire group except for Jean had arrived, consumed a snack, settled their luggage in their respective bedrooms, and met everyone else in attendance. Drinks in hand, dividing naturally into continually rotating pairings and groupings, people socialized easily. Laughter spontaneously sprung from different locations in the room. Stacy's father proved to be popular as he related any number of jokes and stories to the appreciative audience. Jo's father was pleased to find he enjoyed fishing, and quickly organized a fishing expedition for the next morning including his daughter, her partner, Stacy's dad, and Spencer. Amanda agreed to take the rest of the group to look around the town and browse through the local shops. "We plan to leave around ten, so everybody needs to be ready by then. I think everyone will have had an opportunity to have eaten breakfast."

Ren wanted an opportunity to make some sketches of the cabin and the lake. Lindy, Justine, Maria, and Nic's mom opted to get some sun.

"It's usually too cold for me to swim this time of year in Maine," Lindy explained. "Maybe I'll give it a try here and test the waters."

"You might enjoy taking the sailboat or the canoe out, Ren," Jo suggested.

By the time they were ready to leave for dinner, everyone had plans for what they wanted to do the next day with some already talking about Sunday's activities. Jean arrived well before dinner with a report that being open that morning had been a waste of time. Amanda promised to make note of that for next year's schedule. Jean and Maria went outside to sit on the porch together. Justine and Brenda reported that everything was set for breakfast and joined them.

Although serving dinner to such a large group was difficult, the meal at the pub proved to be tasty and fun. It was interesting to Amanda, who had a tendency to want to orchestrate everything, that there was little difficulty with everyone getting ready in the morning. The men gravitated to the outside showers, while some in the group had eased the burden in the bathrooms by showering at night before bed.

Time passed quickly with loose groups banding together for different activities at different times of the day. The food was excellent and the company congenial. Dana excelled at the trivia games played in the evenings, while Nic's mother consistently beat the socks off of Amanda's brother at cards. Nic, noticing the often-serious conversations they were having during their card games, suspected her mother had made Spencer her mission for the weekend. Spencer had been on his best behavior and actually seemed to be enjoying himself.

Amanda couldn't wait to get Mallory alone in their bedroom that evening, but not for her usual reasons. She wanted to relate to her partner the worrisome conversation she'd had with her niece after dinner. Amanda was already in bed when Mallory crawled in beside her and exhaled a long breath. "This is fun, despite the fact that it's a lot of work."

When Mallory started to tell her about the fishing trip that day, Amanda interrupted. "I'm sorry to cut you off. I need to tell you this because I need your advice."

"What's wrong, Honey? Did Spencer say something?"

"No, not yet. However, I think he's going to want to kill me. Mal, Justine is gay."

"No!" Mallory's eyebrows shot up. "Tell me you're kidding me. How do you know?"

"Well, a little while ago, I noticed she wasn't around, so I went to find her. I saw Brenda leaving Justine's room. Brenda blew her a kiss as she went down the hall. If Spencer finds out, he'll have a fit."

"Did you talk to your niece?"

"Yes. She's afraid to tell Spencer. She begged me not to say anything to him."

"What did you tell her?"

"I told her it wasn't my place to say anything to him, that it was between the two of them. I also told her he would probably blame me. We both laughed when I said it, but it's probably true."

"Oh, man. Just when I thought we were making progress with him, too."

* * *

The last night of the holiday, there were fireworks over the lake planned by the town. Everyone began to migrate outside as dusk faded into darkness. Spencer asked if he could speak privately with Amanda, and they went to the kitchen to chat.

"What's the matter, Spencer? Is something wrong?"

"I don't even know how to say this, Mandy."

He hadn't called her that since they were kids, and the endearment shook her. "Just say it. Has someone or something..."

"No, Amanda, definitely not. Remember I told you I wanted to ask you something? Um, how do you know someone is like you? I mean, uh, gay."

Of course, Amanda had a strong suspicion she knew who he was referring to. "Who are you talking about, Spencer?"

"It's Justine. I think she might be, you know, uh, a lesbian." Spencer had a hard time even saying the word, let alone associating it with his daughter.

"Have you talked with her or anyone else about your suspicions?"

"Not to her. No. I talked to Mrs. Bianchi, Anna. She's a wonderful woman and I think a good mom. She has a close relationship with her daughter like I used to have with Justine. She's got a great outlook on life in general and has given me a lot to think about in regard to homosexuality." He hadn't shaved that morning, and she could hear the scratch of the stubble on his cheek as he ran his hand over it. "When I first got here, Doc and I had a good talk, too. You know, I have to admit that I really like her. She's great, as are all of your friends." He looked down, not yet able to meet her eyes. "You know," he raised one eyebrow and gave a little shrug, "there have actually been times this weekend when I've been having such a good time that I've almost forgotten you and your friends are all lesbians. You all seem like, well, just regular people. So maybe there's still hope for me?"

Amanda reached for Spencer's hand. "Oh, Spencer, I'm sorry this has been so hard for you. Change is hard work, isn't it?"

Spencer laughed. "You have no idea. Yesterday, while we were playing cards, Anna had me figure out how many hours a person lives. She said I could approximate, so I came up with a round number of eight thousand seven hundred and sixty hours per year. Then she had me multiply that by eighty five."

Frowning, Amanda asked him to explain why.

"She said that would be a good long life for an average person. Then she asked me how many hours a week I thought the average person had sex and for how long. We compromised on an hour and a half per week as an average. You know, assuming our averages are anywhere near accurate we only have sex less than eighty hours a year. Next, she said she wanted to calculate how much time that would be between the ages of age eighteen and eighty. When I argued that people often had sex before eighteen and after eighty, she made me laugh when she asked me if I really wanted to think about that considering Justine's age."

"Smart woman."

"You bet!" Spencer scratched at the stubble on his face. "Anyway, we rounded off things and used sixty years and eighty hours which, when calculated, came out to forty eight hundred hours."

"So what was your bottom line?"

"It came out to be point zero zero six, or way less than one percent. She suggested that, to allow for individual differences, for the sake of our discussion, we would use the figure of between one-half and one percent of our lives spent in sexual activity, after which she hammered home her point. I'm summarizing here. In essence, her point was that it equated to a lot of hatred and hoopla over a relatively minute portion of our lives."

"And were you convinced?"

"I'm not sure I'm quite there yet about thinking your lifestyle is something I will ever support. I will admit that it has given me a lot to think about. I mean I'm glad I came and spent some time with you. I imagine you'll find it hard to believe when I tell you I've missed you."

"I know this will sound mean, Spencer. I'm glad you missed me. It was hurtful when you and our folks banished me from your lives. It was hurtful when you cut me off from the kids." Using the information Spencer had just explained to her, Amanda pushed, slapping him with her words. "All that because you disapprove of less than one percent of my life."

"I know. Please, give me a break here. I'm trying. Really, I am."

"Let's go back to the beginning of this conversation, shall we? I'm curious, Spencer. What makes you think Justine is a lesbian?"

"It's just a feeling. She had this girlfriend about a year ago. They were really tight. What I mean is that Tina was always at our house or Justine was at her place. They were inseparable. If not together in person, they were on the phone or texting. Then, about six months ago, bang, cold turkey. No Tina, no texts, no calls. Nothing. When we asked where Tina was, she'd either say 'busy,' or just head for her room. On her best days, she sulked. On the worst she'd hole up in her room and ignore us as much as possible. My wife tried to talk to her. She told me Justine wouldn't tell her anything, either. Sometimes, we'd hear her crying in her room. It just felt like a bad break up to me. Wouldn't you agree?"

"I'm not going there, Spencer. I won't theorize about my niece's sexual preference with you. If it really matters to you, then you need to find a way to talk to her, to ask her. Otherwise, maybe it's best for you to work on being a bit more broadminded and welcoming and wait for her to come to you."

"I don't know what to do, Amanda."

"The best advice I can give you is to just love her. Just talk to her Spencer. Let her know you love her and there is nothing in this world that will change that. She'll see you're making an effort with me, with all of us. Maybe that'll help."

Amanda glanced out the window. It was nearly dark and the fireworks would be starting soon. "We need to get outside. The show should get underway shortly. I do have two more things. First, a bit of advice. You found that talking to Anna was helpful. Why don't you talk to the other men? Speak to Jo and Stacy's fathers. They might have some advice for you, especially Stacy's dad. I mean, Stacy and Jo's relationship is relatively new, and he just learned that his daughter was involved with a woman. It would give you a different perspective, a male point of view."

"That's a great suggestion, Amanda. I'm going fishing with Mallory, Jo, Stacy, and their dads first thing tomorrow morning. Maybe the Doc will help me bring up the subject. I don't know how I could just ask them out of the blue."

Amanda suddenly felt nervous about the news she was about to tell Spencer. *Okay, no time like the present.* "Maybe the information I want to share with you will make it easier for you to broach the subject. Anyway, I wanted you to hear it from me first before we announce it to the others. I know you believe that marriage is between a man and a woman. I don't know if you're aware of this or not. New York State just legalized gay marriage, and I'm planning to marry Mallory this fall. We want you to come. I'll let you think about this next statement. I'd like you to stand up with me. If you can't, I'll understand. But it would mean the world to me if you would do that for me."

"Can I think about it, Amanda?"

Amanda nodded.

A loud boom sounded overhead, causing them both to startle.

"Come on, Spencer, we're missing the fireworks."

Following the fireworks display, with their family and friends gathered around, Amanda joined hands with Mallory. Standing with Nic and Dana, she cleared her throat. "We have an announcement to make. We plan to get married in September and hope you will all be able to attend. Following the wedding, Ren and Lindy have invited all of us to spend a week at their Inn in Maine. We hope you will all join us there, as well. We'll arrange transportation, so it's our hope you'll all come." Spencer remained a bit reserved. Everyone else gathered there warmly received the news, congratulating the couples.

Everyone concurred that the Fourth of July weekend had proven to be a successful family gathering and lamented that the next day would be the last at the cabin. Those who'd spent the majority of their time on the lake fishing declared that it was Nirvana to have someone to share their favorite activity with them during their vacation.

The next afternoon, just before everyone left, Anna Bianchi joked with her daughter that if Spencer came for the next family gathering, by the time it was over, she'd have him enrolled in PFLAG. Even Spencer laughed when they explained to him that PFLAG stood for Parents, Friends, and Family of Lesbians and Gays.

* * *

On the Labor Day weekend, close friends and family gathered at Amanda and Mallory's house for the small, early, private ceremony uniting Amanda and Mallory, and Nic and Dana in marriage. Nic wore a black silk pants suit with a beautiful cream-colored fitted blouse. Dana wore a white knee-length dress with a short-sleeved lace covered jacket made from the same material as Nic's blouse. Amanda and Mallory dressed in matching suits of pale sea foam blue with cream-colored blouses. Flowers decorated the back yard and the path the couples walked up to join the minister for the ceremony.

"Family and friends, we are gathered today to unite these two couples in matrimony." Addressing the couples directly, the officiate asked, "Dana, Nic, Amanda and Mallory, you have expressed that you wish to be united by law as life partners. Will you love and respect your partner? Will you be honest with her always? Will you stand united through whatever may come?"

Each answered in turn, "I will."

"These two couples have written vows they wish to exchange with each other, and we will take each in turn. Nic and Dana, please face your partner. Nic, please repeat your vow after me. I, Nicolina Bianchi, call upon our families and friends gathered here to witness that I love you. I am committed to our marriage."

After Nic repeated the words to Dana, the minister continued. "I promise to be your lover, companion and friend, your ally in conflict, your student and teacher, your comrade in adventure, your consolation in disappointment, your accomplice in mischief, and your strength in your need."

Nic smiled at Dana and squeezed her hand as she repeated the minister's words. The minister then continued. "I seek to share with you a relationship of love, honor, and tenderness. I will always be open and honest with you. I will share my life and my worldly possessions, my thoughts and my feelings with you. I will help you fulfill your needs. I will allow you to be yourself. I will rejoice in your growth. I will stand by you through our futures together respecting you, supporting you, loving and enjoying you."

Nic finished reciting her vows and it was Dana's turn. They repeated the vows for each partner. At the conclusion of the citing of the vows, as was traditional, each couple exchanged rings and were pronounced married in the eyes of the State of New York. "You may now celebrate the conclusion of this ceremony with a kiss."

The two couples kissed each other first, then exchanged hugs all around as the friends and family surrounded the happy couples offering their congratulations.

Following the wedding was a short reception where everyone had an opportunity to eat something before boarding the bus for the trip to Sunset Island in Maine. The celebration continued for the family and friends who were traveling to the Inn on Ren and Lindy's private island.

Justine had stood with her aunt in lieu of Spencer who did attend the ceremony. However, although he was glad that she was happy, he still did not accept her marriage as a 'true marriage.'

Inspired by her friends' weddings, after the ceremony, Jo took the opportunity to quietly speak to Stacy's parents shortly after their arrival at the Inn, as they sat on the porch together admiring the view. "Lovely facility, isn't it, and what a view. What did you think of the ceremony?"

Stacy's parents nodded in unison. "Both were lovely," replied her mother.

"I want the same thing for Stacy and myself. I want to ask her to marry me. Before I do, I want to be sure that I have your blessing."

Reaching for Jo's hand, Stacy's mother looked first at her husband for his agreement then replied, "We give you our blessing and know you two will be very happy."

"While I may not be getting a son-in-law," Stacy's father replied, smiling as he shook Jo's hand, "at least I'm gaining a fishing buddy."

"I guess that'll have to do as a yes." Jo grinned happily.

"Will you ask her soon?" Stacy's mother asked.

"Yes, as soon as I can figure out how to do it. I think maybe after we get home. This time belongs to our friends."

* * *

The following weekend, Jo took Stacy out for dinner before they went dancing. When they got home, they snuggled after they made love.

"That was fun," Stacy murmured.

"Marry me, Stacy. I love you and want us to spend the rest of our lives together."

"Anything your heart desires, Jo. Anything. For now and forever."

Epilogue

THREE YEARS AFTER THE women's business opened, the leather store beneath Stacy's old apartment closed. The building was put up for sale. Amanda and Mallory, along with Dana and Nic, signed their names to the paper the lawyer slid across the table to them which transferred the property into the name of their company, *Oui, Madame*. The first floor area, formerly the leather shop, was remodeled to accommodate their business. They broke the space up into a lobby, two good-sized classrooms for group instruction, and three smaller areas suitable for tutoring.

The income from the apartment above their shop's new location, formerly Stacy's apartment, helped pay the mortgage on the property. The end-result was that, for less money than they were previously paying in rent, the business was building equity in a property they owned.

The women had all worked hard to make their business successful. When Jo became certified, they hired their friend Jean as a full-time Office Manager. This freed up more of Nic, Dana, and Jo's time to do translating and teaching.

Nic, Dana, and Jo limited both their tutoring and class instruction times to Tuesday through Thursday, which enabled them to be free to work from home or from the cabin on the remaining days.

Jo and Stacy, who ended up living in Jo's house, bought the log cabin in Edinborough from Jo's parents at a very reasonable price, since Jo's parents said they planned to leave the cabin to her, anyway. Unbeknownst to her, they put the money she insisted on paying them into a trust for her. Nic and Dana took a long-term lease on the apartment above the boathouse.

Amanda and Mallory purchased the neighbor's property next door to Jo and Stacy's cabin when it became available. This guaranteed a location for the extended family gatherings in Edinborough that they held annually on the Fourth of July holiday.

Jo and Stacy became good friends with Lindy and Ren during the time when Jo functioned as a background resource for the lesbian detective novel that Lindy wrote. When the couples visited each other, Lindy and Stacy often toyed with the idea of writing a novel together. So far, that was a project still in the talking stages and not yet realized.

Stacy did finish her novel. As it turned out, in her story, her victim did end up being a lesbian. Stacy didn't use the blackmail angle nor did she use the fact that her victim was a lesbian as the motive. Her main character, the one who died, ended up being a victim of mistaken identity, not the intended victim after all, and killed quite by accident. In the end, the fact that she was a lesbian proved inconsequential to the plot, a fact that pleased Nic immensely.

Jo never lost her limp entirely. She did, through her daily exercise regimen, build enough strength in her leg to enjoy biking again, although she was limited to shorter rides than she would have preferred. Jo and Stacy discovered a new love of kayaking that they could enjoy together, and that activity soon took the place of biking in Jo's heart.

Although Jo never saw Meg again, through Jean, she was relieved to learn that Meg ended up serving no jail time. However, she was hospitalized for the better part of a year after the incident where she held Jo captive. Jean reported that Meg had moved back with her parents in central Pennsylvania. There she'd opened her own gardening business. Meg sent word, via Jean, about how sorry she was. Although Jo felt sad about losing Meg's friendship, she was relieved at the same time, to know that Meg was at least a whole state away. Jo never gave up the habit of scanning her surroundings every time she left her home or her office. The lesson Meg taught her was that there was no such thing as being too vigilant.

Justine finally admitted her sexuality to her father, grateful for the fact that he had mellowed over the past several years of association with her aunt and her group of friends. Unfortunately, proud member of PFLAG and the term avid supporter of gay and lesbian rights would never be applied to Spencer. To his credit, his comfort level and degree of tolerance towards gays and lesbians evolved over time, and he had come a long way towards acceptance.

As for Jean and Maria, they're still trying to prove that long distance relationships can work out.

The End

About AJ Adaire

If you had told me, when I was struggling to write a one page story for my high school writing composition class, that I would one day write seven novels, I would have bet everything that would never happen. No one, especially me, ever considered it a remote possibility. Thirty years later, during a blizzard, having read all the lesbian fiction books I had in the house, I declared to my surprised partner, "I think I could write one of these." So you see, I wrote my first book just to see if I could do it. The completed novel occupied space on my bookshelf, untouched for many years. One day while in a cleaning frenzy, I considered disposing of the neatly stacked and now age-yellowed pages. As I began to read the long forgotten work, I was surprised to discover that the story was enjoyable. Editing and retyping the first book provided a new sense of accomplishment and additional tales followed.

Now retired, I live on the east coast with my partner of twenty-nine years. Because we love a challenge we provide a loving home for two spoiled cats instead of a dog. In addition to writing, any spare time is devoted to editing, reading, mastering new computer programs, and socializing with friends.

My published romance novels include books one and two of the Friends Series: Sunset Island (September 2013) and Awaiting My Assignment (November 2013). The Interim, a novelette that provides additional details about the life of Sunset Island's Ren Madison, was released in November 2013. I have four other novels in process.

Contact Information:
email: aj@ajadaire.com
Website: http://www.ajadaire.com
Facebook: https://www.facebook.com/pages/AJAdaire
Desert Palm Press: www.desertpalmpress.com

SNEAK PEEK

ONE DAY LONGER THAN FOREVER

"THE ADVERTISEMENT READ: Berkshire Mountain Retreat, Log Cabin, 1BR, Water View, Pet Friendly, Reasonable. I was wondering if it's available."

In response to the question Dr. Kate Martin asked, the rental agent responded, "Oh yes, I know that property. It's lovely—small, though."

"I can do small. It'll only be me and my dog," the woman with the soothing voice replied. "The ad said pet friendly. I hope he won't be a problem."

"Let me check the pet policy." Missy, the congested agent with a terrible cold sniffed repeatedly as she shuffled through a stack of papers. "Oh, here it is. Small dogs allowed."

Between bouts of sniffling, nose blowing, and what sounded like lung-shredding fits of coughing Missy managed to ascertain that Kate's dog fit the size limits and that the cabin was available on her specified date. Missy managed to record all the required information onto the tablet she kept next to the phone. In exchange for her credit card and other personal information the caller received the combination and instructions on how to open the lock box on the door to get the keys to the cabin.

Missy sent an email that same afternoon, minutes after she hung up, confirming the booking.

Mary Blackwell and Missy Green shared a small workspace in the real estate office that, in addition to selling properties, managed a large number of cabins. Missy Green was harried the day a woman from Pennsylvania with the soothing voice called to book their Shaw Creek cabin currently featured on their website. With Mary out for the afternoon to meet with her daughter's teacher, a number of circumstances combined to create 'the perfect storm scenario' for what would probably be the most life-altering booking error ever, just because she failed to enter the Kate's reservation into the database indicating the confirmed rental of the property. It wasn't until she was on her way home that she realized her oversight. She knew she should return to the office to fix her error. She just felt too lousy. Unable to muster the energy to drive back, a promise she made to herself that she would correct her oversight first thing in the morning the next day appeased her. It was unfortunate that her cold worsened overnight causing her to miss the next four days of work and, subsequently, to forget her failure to log in the Shaw Creek cabin reservation upon her return to the office.

The next morning, when Senior Agent Mary Blackwell checked her messages and learned that Missy was home sick, she exhaled a long breath blowing her bangs up off her forehead. It was always stressful when she was the only one staffing the office, especially during the busiest time of year when they were booking for ski season rentals.

Shortly after she sat at her desk, Lee Foster called to inquire about renting a small cabin over the holidays. "It'll just be for me. I'm driving over from Connecticut. I saw this ad on the Internet. It reads '1BR, water view'."

"Yes, I know that place." She noted the dates on her tablet she kept next to her at all times and replied, "Hang on a minute. I'll check the database to see if it's still available." A moment later, the efficient sounding agent responded, "Right, we do have that lovely little cabin on Shaw Creek available." She read the property description.

"Yes, that's the one. I saw the picture on the website. It looks lovely, and should be perfect for just me."

Another few minutes of conversation ensued. Mary entered the reservation after recording the caller's credit card information. They reviewed the lock box instructions, and when she hung up, Mary sent an email confirming the reservation.

Everything was set.

Find out what happens to Kate and Lee who are stranded during a blizzard in a vacation cabin each thought she'd rented alone.

**One Day Longer Than Forever
coming the summer of 2014.**

Other books from Desert Palm Press

The Guardian Series by Stein Willard
A Guardian's Touch – Book 1
A Guardian's Love – Book 2
A Guardian's Passion – Book 3

Scarred for Life by SL Kassidy

Friends Series by AJ Adaire
Sunset Island — Book 1
The Interim — a novelette
Awaiting My Assignment

Dark Horizons by Rae D. Magdon & Michelle Magly

Available now from Smashwords, Amazon, and CreateSpace

Coming soon
One Day Longer Than Forever by AJ Adaire
A Guardian's Salvation – Book 4 by Stein Willard
The Unbroken Warrior by Stein Willard
Phantom of the Heart by Stein Willard
Afterglow by Stein Willard

Made in the USA
Charleston, SC
13 June 2014